PRAISE FOR TR

'I was left absolutely traumati[...] Beautiful, heartbreaking, uplifting . . . Really worth a read.'

—*HELLO!*

'A pacy read . . . A great book to take to the beach!'

—*Daily Mail*

'I was entranced from the very first page and couldn't put it down until I had all the answers. Tracy weaves a seamless tale while offering brilliant descriptions and raw emotions.'

—Angela Marsons, author of *Child's Play*

'A must-read for fans of psychological suspense. Tightly plotted and intense, this novel will have you looking over your shoulder and peeking under your bed. Filled with twists and turns, it will keep you flying through the pages to the shocking end.'

—Heather Gudenkauf, author of *Before She Was Found*

Praise for Tracy's last book, *Wall of Silence*:

'*Wall of Silence* is wild, a "whodunnit" rollercoaster. The story launches with a bang with one of the most original openings I've read. Tracy Buchanan has crafted a novel where the plot literally thickens with every page turned and new secrets simmer as the reader is pulled deeper into her cast of characters' web of lies and silence. I was captivated from page one, entertained throughout, and shocked over the final reveal. Loved it!'

—Kerry Lonsdale, *Wall Street Journal* and *Washington Post* bestselling author

CIRCLE
OF
DOUBT

ALSO BY TRACY BUCHANAN:

The Atlas of Us
My Sister's Secret
No Turning Back
Her Last Breath
The Lost Sister
The Family Secret
Wall of Silence

CIRCLE
OF
DOUBT

Tracy
Buchanan

LAKE UNION
PUBLISHING

Published by Lake Union Publishing, Seattle

www.apub.com

Amazon, the Amazon logo, and Lake Union Publishing are trademarks of Amazon.com, Inc., or its affiliates.

ISBN-13: 9781542017527
ISBN-10: 1542017521

Cover design by Ghost Design

Printed in the United States of America

Dedicated to my brave mum
who continues to smile
through even the toughest of times.
And the man who helps her smile,
my wonderful stepdad Vic.

In memory of Grandad Archbold, a truly kind,
generous and thoughtful gentleman.

Chapter One

I don't like the new blinds your fake parents have got, Isla. I can barely see you through them from my hiding place at the back of your garden. Just a flash of your small perfect hand as it twirls in the air; a quick glimpse of your dark locks as you bounce around the room in your school uniform.

Now I understand why Garrett, my private investigator, has struggled to take sufficient photos and videos of you the past few weeks. I can't tell you how frustrating it's been to only be able to grasp at small pieces of you, when I ought to have you as a whole. Pain heaped upon pain. And then to be subjected to Garrett's weekly reports, too, each one confirming the mediocrity of the people who call themselves your parents.

But suddenly, there! The blinds go up briefly, and before me is an unfiltered view of you — my girl — as you sneak a look outside! The joy I feel makes it difficult to breathe for a moment.

Are you looking at me? I think you are. Maybe you sense we have the same blood running through us?

Maybe you sense we'll be together soon?

But as quickly as the blinds are opened, they are shut again. It takes every ounce of control I have to contain my rage.

I peer behind me towards the angular red crane erupting from the treetops in the distance, the digger below it poised to begin work tearing up the bed of the forest.

Not long, darling. Not long.

Chapter Two

'That's strange,' Emma said as she looked out at the red crane jutting from the top of the woods like a metal giraffe.

She was standing at her kitchen window, nursing a lukewarm cup of coffee as she waited for her daughter Isla to finish breakfast.

Emma's husband Dele grabbed a piece of burnt toast from the toaster, yelping in pain as it scorched his fingers. 'Maybe a tree's come down.'

Emma laughed. 'Do they *use* cranes for fallen trees?'

'How would I know?' Dele said as he gave her a quick peck on the cheek. 'I sell books for a living, not trees. Right, better go. See you later.'

He walked to the kitchen table where Isla was slurping up cereal as she watched her iPad. She peered up at her dad with a smile as he kissed the top of her dark hair and left the kitchen, blowing kisses at them before disappearing out of the house.

Emma smiled to herself. It was good to see him happy.

'Right,' she said, peering at her watch. 'Time to finish that or we're going to be late.'

'*Again,*' Isla said, rolling her brown eyes.

Isla was right. The first day of the new school year and it looked like they were already going to be breaking their promise to be on time every day this term. That would mean yet another sour look from the school's stern head teacher Mrs Gould and, of course, more raised brows from the mums at the school gates. It was hard enough fitting into a tight-knit community like Forest Grove as a newcomer – and yes, Emma *still* felt like a newcomer despite moving in seven months ago.

'Hurry, darling,' Emma said, clapping her hands as Isla slowly rose from her chair. 'Go get your shoes on.'

Isla backed away, one finger held up. 'Just one minute, Mum. One teensy minute. I forgot the card I made for Tegan.'

'No, get your shoes on *now!*' Emma shouted, desperately looking at the time again.

Isla paused, crossing her arms as she looked her mother up and down. 'Count to five, Mum. Come on, do it with me. One-two-three-four-five.'

Emma took a deep breath and did as her daughter asked, then realised she was allowing her ten-year-old daughter to give her anger-management therapy. She couldn't help it – she burst out laughing, and Isla did the same.

'What are you like?' Emma said to her daughter. 'Okay then, but be quick!'

Isla darted upstairs to her room, her footsteps like a herd of baby elephants on the floorboards.

As Emma was about to grab her bag from the side, the sound of shattering glass pierced the air.

She let out a gasp.

'Isla?' she called up the stairs, heart thumping.

Isla came running back down, the card she'd written for her friend in her hands. 'What?'

'Are you okay?'

4

'Yeah, why?'

'I heard glass breaking. Wait there.'

Emma walked towards the living room. Had she heard it from there? She opened the door, then gasped again.

The large window looking towards the garden was smashed, glass shattered on the carpet, the blinds covering the window tangled and broken. Lying among the glass was a boulder from the rockery outside.

Somebody must have thrown it through the window!

'What is it, Mum?' she heard Isla ask from the end of the hallway.

Emma quickly put her hand out to her to stop her walking forwards and seeing the window. 'Wait.'

She peered out at the garden. She couldn't see anyone.

'What's wrong?' Isla asked.

'The window's broken.'

Alarm registered on Isla's pretty face.

'It's okay,' Emma said with a shaky smile, trying to reassure her. 'Something will have toppled over in the garden because of the wind. Run outside, see if Dad's still there.'

Isla nodded and darted to the front door.

Alone, Emma stepped towards the window, wrapping her arms around herself. The window was the largest in the house and offered a nice view of the forest. That was why they'd been drawn to the house when they'd first viewed it the year before.

'Jesus,' she heard Dele say from behind her as he ran down the hallway.

'I chased his car down the road,' Isla said, out of breath, cheeks red, eyes sparkling with pride.

'Darling, I didn't mean for you to do *that*,' Emma said, noting her daughter's bare feet.

Dele raked his fingers through his hair as he took in the mess. Then his eyes alighted on the boulder. Emma saw confusion, then anger, registering on his face. He went to open his mouth but she quickly shook her head, eyes darting towards Isla then back again.

He looked out into the garden. 'I'll just go check there's no damage outside,' he said. 'Let me deal with this. You take Isla to school, get to work. I'll call you later.'

Emma nodded, and turned to Isla. 'Come on then, darling, shoes on!'

Isla did as she was asked, her eyes on the stone boulder in the living room. She was a clever girl; she was no doubt figuring out that someone had thrown it through the window.

As Dele walked through the kitchen and out into the garden, Emma shrugged her raincoat on, trying to puzzle over who would do this. She tried not to consider the possibility it might be a racially motivated attack. Sure, Dele and Isla might stand out a bit in a sea of white faces in the village, but there had never been a hint of racism.

Emma fixed a smile on her face. 'Right, let's go,' she said to Isla.

They walked outside. In the distance, Emma saw a long line of cars crawling down their street towards the school and rolled her eyes. No chance they'd be on time now. Not to mention the fact that she hated driving as it was, always getting the same whir of nerves whenever she stepped into her car; nerves that were compounded by any traffic or bad weather.

The village of Forest Grove was made up of several roads that wove around the woods. Their house was on the second road, so wasn't too far from the school and the forest. It wasn't ideal driving to school when they could walk there in under ten minutes through the forest. But after dropping off Isla, Emma needed to drive straight to work in Ashbridge, which was a twenty-minute drive away.

It had been a big step, taking the new job. Before moving to Forest Grove, she'd been quite happy freelancing from home in a small pretty house on the outskirts of North London. But after a schoolboy was stabbed a few streets down from them, it just rammed home to Emma that maybe it wasn't the best place to bring up Isla. Then Dele got made redundant from his editing job at a large publishing firm and it seemed like a good time to move. In an ideal world, Emma would have continued to freelance. She liked working on her own, setting her own pace, not having to endure the 'how was your weekend?' office small talk. But her freelance jobs didn't pull in enough money to cover them, even now that Dele had found a new job managing a bookshop in Ashbridge.

Emma's current job at Pink Elephant, a boutique social media agency, was one of the first she saw. She liked the idea of 'boutique'. If she *had* to endure being based in an office, then at least it would be a small one.

When she applied for the job, she just assumed she wouldn't even get an interview. Though she'd been working in digital marketing ever since she first moved to London with her sister seventeen years before, she didn't have some of the qualifications they seemed keen on. But she must have done something right, because she got an interview and they offered her the job the very next day.

She'd hesitated before accepting the offer. It would mean moving away from London, her home since she was twenty-one, their *family* home ever since Isla had come into their lives nine years before. Would it be a mistake to yank Isla out of her large city primary school and away from the friends she'd carried through from nursery? And what about Emma's friends? She'd struggled to make them, and yet she'd managed to build up a lovely circle of friends during Isla's nursery days, her usual shyness rubbed away by the sheer exhaustion of looking after a toddler.

But then, while showing Dele where Ashbridge was on Google Maps, she'd happened upon the green blooms of Forest Grove nearby. Something made her look up the village. *Welcome to Forest Grove, Utopia of the Woods,* the introductory text of the community's website had read, *Home to Strong Branches and Deep Roots.*

The more Emma read about the village, the more she felt its pull. It was just the place where she could imagine raising Isla, plus one of the two houses up for sale was perfect for them.

It felt like fate, and Emma very much believed in fate, because it was surely fate that had brought them their beautiful daughter after years of struggling with infertility. Fate that meant Isla was born at the right time in the right place to become theirs. The moment the photo of a beautiful eighteen-month-old girl had been placed before her by their social worker, Emma remembered, she had thought to herself: *This is meant to be.*

'Why do you look like you're going to cry, Mum?' Isla asked, looking half horrified, half morbidly fascinated by the sight of her mother getting emotional on a school morning.

'I love you, that's all.'

Isla's cheeks flushed pink, then she smiled. 'Love you too, Mum.'

They gave each other a hug, Emma stroking Isla's fuzz of dark hair. Then she started the engine, taking a deep breath. 'Right, Forest Grove Primary, here we come.'

Isla's school sat on the edge of the woods. Parking was minimal in a tiny gravelled area to the side of it, a physical embodiment of the head teacher's disapproval of any parents feeling the need to drive in. Forest Grove was, after all, a small village that prided itself on being eco-friendly, encouraging children to walk to school each day. But even if Emma didn't have to drop Isla off on the way to work, she wasn't sure she'd be happy about her walking to school alone along the road and through the forest like some of the other ten-year-olds in her class.

She had to confess, she could be a little overprotective of Isla. It was probably because of what she knew of Isla's first year of life, living in a tumultuous household with her young drug-addicted birth mother. If that overprotectiveness meant waiting until Isla started secondary school to let her walk to school with friends, so be it . . . even if it meant the daily struggle to find a parking space!

Surprise, surprise, when Emma arrived at the car park, she found it was full.

'Great,' she muttered under her breath.

She did an awkward seven-point turn to get back out and drove down the nearest street. Yes, she knew it wasn't the done thing to park on any of the residential streets near the school, but what choice did she have? At least she wasn't doing what the Range Rover in front of her was doing, parking up on a resident's actual drive!

Instead, Emma found a secret little spot she'd used before in a line of garages, parking in a way that would ensure any cars looking to get in and out wouldn't be blocked. She quickly bundled Isla out of the car and they jogged towards the school, Emma checking her watch as they did. Just a few more minutes and they'd be late, meaning they'd have to sign in at reception. At least if they *were* late, she'd avoid the awkwardness of standing in the playground with the other mums.

When Emma had first walked into the school playground back in February, she instantly felt out of place. She was used to a lot of the mums back in London being working mums, but here it seemed to be a rarity. Emma's spike-heeled boots and red woollen coat stood out in direct contrast to the Forest Grove mum 'uniform' of Joules or Boden raincoats and Hunter wellies over leggings. Emma understood why they wore them as she'd picked the leaves off her coat and scraped the mud off her heels that first time, all from just a walk through the car park.

Though Emma had managed to find a raincoat in the Joules summer sale, she still felt out of place. In the whole seven months she'd been in the village, she'd not made one friend. She wasn't exactly sure what she was doing wrong. It couldn't just be because she was a newbie. Lucy Cronin, the petite dark-haired mum of Poppy, one of Isla's friends, had moved to Forest Grove just three months before and she'd been embraced by all the mums. Maybe it was because her husband was the new forest ranger? Or it could just be that Lucy was supremely confident. Emma often imagined what her younger sister Harriet would say: 'Be more confident, for God's sake, Em. *Believe* in yourself. March up to them and *insist* they have coffee with you.'

Easy for her to say! Harriet had always been full of confidence. In fact, their parents often said Harriet got Emma's dose of confidence when she was born. But it was more than that. People seemed drawn to Harriet, always had done since school, leaving Emma feeling invisible next to her. Emma didn't mind that, she really didn't! She liked being invisible, burying her nose in a book, watching from the sidelines with a smile on her face as her sister caused drama after drama. That was why she'd got into social media. It was easy to hide behind 280 characters.

As Emma approached the school gates with Isla now, she saw a group of mums in a huddle. She wished she knew one of them well enough to chat through what had just happened.

'Have you seen that massive crane?' she heard one of them say. 'Whatever it is they're building better not be higher than the treetops.'

'Well, the land Melissa Byatt sold was pretty substantial,' another mum said. 'Could be a couple of houses.'

'I heard a rich architect and his glamorous wife are getting a house built there,' a third mum said.

'Where'd you hear that?' the first woman asked.

'Craig works for Ashbridge Council in the planning department, remember? He heard it there.'

'Is that van supposed to be there, Mum?' Isla said.

Emma followed her daughter's gaze towards the road they'd just come from to see a large white removals van parked behind her car. A woman of about Emma's age was standing outside it, an angry expression on her face. She was wearing smart jeans and a blue striped shirt, her long dark curly hair tied up in a neat ponytail.

'Bugger,' Emma hissed under her breath.

She looked at her watch. She could just go into school, make sure Isla got in on time and face the consequences after. But the woman had already caught her looking over.

'This your car?' she shouted at Emma.

Two mums passing by paused to watch.

Emma's face flushed red. 'Yes, sorry,' she called out with an apologetic smile. 'You can get through, right?' she added, gesturing towards the gap between her car and wall.

'Of course not!' the woman bit back.

Emma checked her watch again. 'Look, do you mind waiting just a few minutes? I don't want my daughter to be late.'

'But it's okay for my son to be late on his first day of school because you blocked us in?' the woman said, gesturing to the van. Emma peered across the road into the van to see a boy a couple of years younger than Isla sitting inside it with the same olive skin as his mother. 'We're late enough as it is. And it's not just us, what if an ambulance needs to get through?' the woman continued, her dark eyes staring so intently at Emma it made her skin prickle.

Emma sighed. She really didn't need this right now. Nearby, an older couple had stopped too and were watching with interest. She knew what some of these people were like. She saw it in the comments in the Forest Grove Facebook group. People who'd lived in the village since its creation nearly thirty years ago and acted like they did everything better in their day. They just wouldn't let it go.

She turned to Isla. 'Stay here, darling.'

She ran over to her car and jumped in. As she went to close the door, she noticed the woman was now taking photos of Emma's number plate with her phone.

'What are you doing?' Emma asked.

'I'm going to report you to the police,' the woman replied.

Emma's mouth dropped open. 'The police? That's a bit extreme, don't you think?'

'I'd say the fact I couldn't even get into my garage is extreme,' the woman snapped back, placing her hand on Emma's car door so Emma couldn't close it.

Emma shook her head. This was unbelievable! First, the broken window . . . now this, and all in the space of an hour.

'Fine, take your photos, I don't care!' she shouted back. 'But please, take your hands off my car right now and let me go so I'm not blocking your precious garage any more.'

The woman looked at her in surprise. Emma found people often did when the shy unassuming woman they thought she was showed some spirit.

But the other woman still stood her ground. 'Not until I take all the photos I need to.'

Emma's nails bit into her palms as she tried to contain her anger. But it was no use. She yanked the door shut and the woman sprang back, yelping as she snatched her fingers to her chest.

12

'You got my fingers!' she whined.

'Everything okay, Myra?' a voice called out.

Emma turned to see a brand-new sapphire-blue Jaguar pulling up. A man in his early thirties was peering out of it at the angry woman. He was handsome with neat strawberry-blond hair and sparkling green eyes. Sitting next to him was a dark-skinned woman around his age with a swanlike neck, her head twisted away as she tended to one of the two young boys in the back seat of the car.

'Oh, it's you, Lawrence!' the woman called Myra exclaimed, putting her hand to her chest as her cheeks flushed.

Emma looked between them both. They clearly knew each other.

Great, she thought. *Another person to have a go at me.*

But instead of having a go at Emma, the man – Lawrence – smiled at her. 'What's this all about then?'

'This woman has been harassing me,' Myra said. 'She slammed my fingers in the door, see?'

'I didn't mean to,' Emma said as she got out of the car again, trying to peer at Myra's hand as she clutched it under her armpit. 'I was trying to move my car like she wanted.'

'She was blocking us from our garage!' Myra shot back. 'Causing trouble right outside the school,' she added, peering at the two mothers and the elderly couple who were all still watching with interest.

Emma felt like crying. How had it escalated so quickly?

'There's a decent enough gap for you to get through, Myra,' Lawrence said. 'Would you like me to have a go, so you mums can get the kids to school on time? Just needs some careful manoeuvring.'

'Oh, you really don't have to,' Myra replied, flustered.

'It's fine, really,' Lawrence said.

Emma gave him a grateful smile.

'My wife can walk with you both. Tatjana?' he called over to his wife.

His wife turned around and smiled.

Emma stepped back in surprise.

She looked just like Isla's birth mother, Jade!

Chapter Three

*I can hardly breathe as I look at you, Isla. Of course I've seen photos of
you up close thanks to Garrett, countless photos tracking your growth
over the past few years. But to see you in the flesh before me, more beautiful than I could ever have dreamed of . . . I can see the similarities,
too. Not just the obvious ones, but little things, like the way you tilt
your head or that slight lopsided smile of yours.*

It's like looking in the mirror.

Do you notice it, too?

*I force myself to look away from you and take in again the woman
who calls herself your mother. She has changed since the last video I
received of her a few months ago. Her hair is shorter – to her shoulders now, and dyed a tacky dark red to cover the previous dull brown.
She's put on weight, too – not a good look when she's as short as she is.
Probably all those corporate dinners she goes on now she's working for
that awful agency in Ashbridge.*

*Boutique, honestly, what does that even mean? And what kind of
company name is Pink Elephant?*

*The contrast between you and her is astounding, like a diamond
against dirt.*

The urgency I feel to get you away from her rushes at me again. If I didn't have more restraint, I would just take you now and march you away from this awful woman.

But no, I must be patient. Just to be here in the same vicinity as you is enough for now. In fact, it just goes to prove how fateful this all is. Of course, I counted on seeing you in the school playground. I was looking forward to it, and also to seeing your fake mother rattled after discovering those precious blinds of hers all ruined. I confess, that was a bit of a risk, throwing that rock through the window. It could have easily backfired. One of you might have seen me hiding behind the tree. But luckily, I managed to get away and back home in time to see you in the playground.

I hadn't planned on happening upon you like this with your fake mother causing trouble right outside your school, a confirmation of all my concerns about her fitness to look after you.

As Emma looks at me, I see what a mess she truly is. Eyeliner not quite in line with her eyelid, blusher over-applied. She clearly got ready in a hurry and what does that say about her aptitude as a mother? Disorganised, rushed, loose . . . and loose means gaps, gaps you could fall through.

Thank God I'll be there to catch you.

Chapter Four

Emma watched the woman – Tatjana, the man had called her – as she slipped out of the car. She was tall with short black hair, wearing a long olive cotton dress over expensive-looking brown boots, chunky wooden bracelets tangled around her slim brown arms. She held herself with confidence and ease.

Tatjana turned her feline gaze to Isla and Isla returned it, staring up at her in fascination.

Emma looked between the two of them, a faint feeling of discomfort swirling around her tummy. They looked so *alike*. Sure, Tatjana's skin was darker, but they had the same long limbs, the same brown eyes.

All the same features Isla's birth mother had, too.

Of course, this woman couldn't *be* Isla's birth mother. Other than the way she looked, the woman Emma had met nearly nine years ago at their one and only contact meeting couldn't be more different from the sophisticated, assured mother standing before her right now.

This woman looked Emma right in the eye, whereas Jade Dixon could barely meet her gaze as she'd sat in that cold meeting room all those years ago, her back hunched. She was tall like Dele – Emma knew that from the details shared about her – but sitting there that day, she had looked short, diminished. Emma saw the hints of why that might be in the needle marks she glimpsed when Jade had pulled up the sleeve of her grubby jumper to scratch herself, and the bruise on her neck, no doubt caused by one of the string of violent men she'd been associated with . . . one of whom was Isla's father, though nobody knew which one he was. She never named him on the birth certificate.

Emma had felt sorry for her. She'd read Jade's case history: a childhood spent with an alcoholic mother and an absent father in one of the roughest estates in London. She'd expected her to be more vocal. Jade had requested this meeting with Emma and Dele, after all. But sitting opposite her that day, Emma couldn't help but wonder why Jade wanted to meet if she wasn't even going to engage with them. Maybe it was just to see the couple who'd soon be taking her child. It certainly helped Dele. He wanted to be able to see Isla's birth mother with his own eyes.

But it was difficult for Emma.

There were moments during that meeting when she'd seen a hint of what Jade could have been with a better start in life, all the qualities she'd passed on to her daughter. Not just her beautiful oval-shaped brown eyes and her gorgeous black Afro hair. But also her fierce stare when she eventually looked at the couple who were going to adopt her child, a hint of the intelligence that was buried in there somewhere, judging by Jade's early school reports.

And now, as Emma looked at Tatjana, she realised she resembled everything that Jade Dixon *could* have been.

'Tat, this is Myra,' Lawrence said, introducing his wife to the angry woman who was still glaring at Emma as she held her hand under her armpit.

'Oh, your new PA!' Tatjana exclaimed. 'How lovely to meet you, Myra.'

Myra gave her a shaky smile. 'You too, Tatjana. I'm sorry we had to meet in these circumstances,' she added, giving Emma a look.

'House moves never go very smoothly, do they?' Tatjana said. 'Shall we all head to school then?' she asked Emma as she smiled down at Isla.

'I'll follow you,' Myra said as she jutted her chin at her son to get out of the van.

'Just us then!' Tatjana said.

Emma allowed herself to be swept along by her, jogging after Tatjana as she strode towards the school with her little boy, feeling Myra's eyes on them. The boy looked like Isla, too, with his dark-brown hair and distinctively shaped eyes . . . could almost be her little brother.

'Gosh, she's a bit intense, isn't she?' Tatjana said, peering over her shoulder as Myra fussed over her son's hair, her eyes narrowing as she watched Emma. 'But then the intense ones often make the best PAs, don't they?'

'Hmmmm,' Emma said non-committally. She wasn't sure she could deal with a PA like that!

'We haven't properly said hello,' Tatjana said. 'I don't think I got your name?'

'It's Emma. I haven't seen you around before?'

'We're moving here,' Tatjana replied, looking out at the forest with a contented smile.

Emma followed her gaze. 'The crane. That's yours?'

Tatjana laughed. 'Well, the *crane's* not ours! But yes, it's part of our building site. We're living in a static home on site at the moment – honestly, it's a nightmare. But hopefully we'll be in in a few weeks.'

Emma looked at her in surprise. 'A few weeks? But . . . the building's only just started. Don't houses take ages to build?'

'It's a pre-fab house. It's been put together in Germany. My husband Lawrence is an architect so he designed it. Once the foundations are done this week, the house will be delivered pretty much intact. You'll know it's coming when you see a big lorry drive through the village with a house on board!' She laughed a deep warm laugh as she looked down at Isla again. 'Zeke's *so* excited.'

The little boy nodded enthusiastically as Isla smiled at him.

'You look smart,' Isla said. 'Is this your first time at Forest Grove Primary?'

She was so good with younger children; they always seemed drawn to her. Emma often felt sad that Isla wouldn't have a little brother or sister, but Dele had been adamant they just needed the one.

'Yes,' Zeke replied, whacking a branch as he passed it. 'I'm five now and super strong!'

'Looks like it!' Isla said, laughing.

'You two are getting on!' Tatjana said. 'We'll be having a party when the house is all done. You must come, Isla – and your parents too, of course,' she added to Emma, as if an afterthought.

'Yay!' Isla said, clapping her hands.

Tatjana laughed with her. 'Aren't you just delightful? And look at that hair! Just gorgeous.'

'Nightmare to control,' Emma said.

Tatjana smoothed her hands over her short haircut. 'That's why I cut mine. Hair like ours can be a challenge, Isla. I can give you some tips, though?' she suggested as Isla nodded enthusiastically. 'I had years getting to grips with it when I was young. It's difficult for other people to understand unless you have hair like ours, right, Isla?'

Emma frowned. Was that a little dig?

'In fact,' Tatjana said, reaching into her bag and handing Isla a small tube of hair oil, 'this oil is *fantastic* for hair like ours. I have lots of samples like this. If you do a search for Whitney White on YouTube, you'll find lots of tutorials to help you.'

'Wow,' Isla said, taking the oil as if it were an elixir. Emma tried to ignore the feeling of jealousy swirling inside as she took in the way her daughter was staring at this woman like she was some kind of goddess.

'So what do you do, Emma?' Tatjana asked as they entered the school gates.

'I work in social media. You?'

'I used to be a fashion designer.' She stroked her son's hair. 'But the boys are my number one priority now. I wouldn't want work getting in the way.'

Emma raised an eyebrow. Another dig?

'You were a *fashion* designer?' Isla asked, a look of awe on her face.

'I used to design clothes. Have I got a budding designer before me?'

'Yes,' Isla said. 'I love design!'

'I had a feeling you might be part of the creative tribe when I first saw you,' Tatjana said to Isla. 'I can always tell a kindred spirit when I see one.'

Isla beamed with pride, throwing her shoulders back and jutting her chin out. 'I am *very* creative.'

'Isla definitely is,' Emma said, putting her hand on her daughter's arm. 'We're very proud of her. In fact, we were doing some designs this weekend, weren't we?'

'Oh really?' Tatjana asked curiously.

'She has books where you can design outfits. TOPModel books – the spiral-bound things kids like nowadays,' Emma said as Tatjana just looked more confused. 'We spent ages on them this weekend.'

Isla scowled. 'We didn't spend *ages* on it – you said you were bored when I got you to colour in one of the dresses.'

Emma's face flushed. 'I had to make the dinner!'

'Oh, I adore colouring in,' Tatjana said. 'I can spend hours and hours doing it, can't I, Zeke?'

Her son nodded enthusiastically and Emma tried to conceal her annoyance. There was a slight hint of smugness in this woman's voice that grated on her a bit. Tatjana would fit in well at Forest Grove – there seemed to be more than the usual average of smug mums in the village.

'Isn't this a lovely little school?' Tatjana said as they stepped into the playground. The school was a brick and wooden structure. Beyond the building, in the forest, were a selection of desks and blackboards among the trees. Parents were gathered in huddles as children darted off to play with each other. Some peered over, their attention caught by the glamorous newcomer.

Lucy Cronin, the mother of Poppy, strode over and gave Tatjana a quick hug, completely ignoring Emma, as she seemed to do most days.

'You're finally here, Tatjana!' Lucy gushed. 'Come meet the others!'

How could Lucy know Tatjana already?

She pulled Tatjana away towards a group of mums, leaving Emma standing alone. Emma resorted to her usual ploy: pretending to be incredibly busy looking at her phone. She ought to be used to it by now, standing alone in the playground. She'd had months of this, after all. It still stung, though. In fact, it reminded her of the way it had been at her own school. Before her sister arrived, Emma had endured three years of loneliness, watching as other children formed friendship groups, her own painful shyness making it difficult for others to be drawn towards her. And then her sister Harriet had started school when Emma was eight, a vivacious five-year-old who seemed to naturally draw close to her every child within her vicinity. Maybe it was her golden locks and dimpled cheeks. More likely it was Harriet's personality, already shining through. Even at that young age, she had tried to draw Emma into her little circle of friends, sensing her sister's loneliness. But it just made Emma feel even more of an outsider. Shouldn't it have been the other way around, the older sister trying to help the younger sister fit in?

As Emma looked towards Tatjana and the other mums now, she felt the same burning sensation of embarrassment and inadequacy again. She imagined Harriet pushing her towards the group. 'Go on, just join in.'

Instead, she stayed where she was, all her old insecurities bubbling up inside. She knew Dele didn't have this problem on the occasions when he dropped Isla off. He'd come back talking about something one of the mums had told him. But then he'd always been popular, his laid-back vibes seeming to draw people to him just like Harriet's spirited ways had, *especially* kids. In fact, the first time they met Isla at their short introduction session at her foster parents' house, she'd crawled straight towards Dele. The social worker had been surprised. Isla was usually shy around men, as she was used to just being with her mother and grandmother. Emma remembered feeling a pinch of jealousy. Silly, really. But she'd been so desperate for Isla to adore her as much as she knew she'd adore Isla. What colours would Isla like? What smells? Would she want her future mother to wear her hair up or down?

As she'd watched Isla climb on to Dele's lap, she'd started to regret her choice of a soft blue jumper and jeans. Should she have gone for brighter colours? Dele was wearing a white shirt. She'd read that babies liked black and white. Maybe she'd put too much perfume on?

But then Isla had looked over at her and put her chubby arms out towards Emma.

'She wants you to hold her,' said the foster mother who Isla had been staying with the past six months.

When Emma had lifted Isla into her arms, Isla leaned her cheek against the soft wool of her jumper, peering up at her with her big brown eyes.

That was it: love at first sight. Emma had never felt more accepted, more needed, more *loved* than in that moment.

She looked at Isla now as she played with her friend, Tegan. As though sensing her mother's eyes on her, Isla stopped playing and turned to look at Emma, giving her a big smile. Emma smiled back, her heart swelling. None of it mattered really, all this school playground popularity. All that mattered was the way Isla was looking at her right then and there.

Then she felt someone else's eyes on her.

It was Tatjana. Was it Emma's imagination or did her eyes narrow as she watched Emma and Isla hug each other?

The school bell rang out and when Emma looked back at Tatjana, she was smiling.

Yes, it must have been her imagination.

Chapter Five

Welcome to the Mums of Forest Grove Facebook Group

Home to Mums and Grandmothers Dedicated to Making Their Children's Lives in Our Beautiful Village as Natural, Carefree and Creative as Possible

(Set up by Kitty Fletcher, the world-famous Natural Nanny ©)

Closed group. 500 members

Monday 14th September
9.30 a.m.

Malorie Cane
Can I take the chance to say a big thank you to the mother who parked right across the entrance to the garages on Birch Road, blocking a removals van from entering? Not exactly the best welcome to the new residents who have moved in next to me and Graham.

Rebecca Feine
Nothing like a bit of passive aggressiveness to kick the week off, Malorie!

Belinda Bell

Let me guess, another school mum thinking she rules the road. I am sick to the back teeth of seeing the number of cars parked on grass verges and paths around here. What is wrong with these people? Disrespectful, ignorant and utterly selfish!

Lucy Cronin

I agree, Belinda. I just don't understand why parents can't just walk their kids to school like I do. Every day is a nightmare around the streets closest to the school. God forbid any emergency services ever need to get through. The number of times I've raised it with the council since I moved here, to no avail!

Kitty Fletcher

Quite right, Lucy! A brisk walk through the forest is just the thing to start a child's day! Regular exposure to the outdoors has been proven to enhance a child's cognitive functioning and improve their mood. There are too many children battling Nature Deficit Disorder.

Lucy Cronin

Hear hear, Kitty! I have absolutely no doubt this particular mother doesn't care a jot for all that. Her poor child is probably stuck indoors all day on her iPad.

Rebecca Feine

Hold your horses! You have to remember many of these parents have no choice but to drop their kids off on the way to work, like my daughter used to when she had little ones.

Belinda Bell

Rubbish! When I had a brief stint working at one of the banks in Ashbridge when mine were young, we still walked to school. All it took was setting our alarm thirty minutes earlier. Honestly, the pure laziness of people today! When I was five, I trekked through snow blizzards and across major roads to get to school.

Vanessa Shillingford

Five? Are you sure about that, Belinda?! And Rebecca's right. Some parents have no choice but to drop kids off on the way to work. It's not like they can just plonk their kids on the side of the road thirty minutes before school time, is it?

Belinda Bell

What would your mum think of you saying that, Vanessa? Jackie thinks herself a bit of an eco-warrior, doesn't she? You better tell her it's going to get even worse when those new houses are built in the forest.

Rebecca Feine

New houses? Where'd you get that information?

Belinda Bell

Don't you see the size of the crane that's suddenly appeared in the forest overnight?

Pauline Sharpe

Oh no! Surely they're not building houses in the forest! What about falling trees? Remember what happened during the storms back in 2014?

Lucy Cronin

Well, my husband is the ranger now and he's putting plans in place to ensure that doesn't happen again. As for the trees, it's just the one house being built, actually. It's owned by the Belafontes, a lovely young family. I met them all while walking the dogs at the weekend. They showed me the plans and mock-ups of how it will look. Absolutely gorgeous, honestly.

Vanessa Shillingford

Yes, my mum and I met Lawrence Belafonte at the cafe the other day. He's an architect, and his wife runs a fashion business, I think. Rather big house for one family though, I have to say.

Kitty Fletcher

I've seen the plans too through my contact in the council. It looks like it's going to be a monstrosity, like a black industrial unit tainting the beauty of its surroundings. As the current plans stand, the roof of the house will be viewable by anyone looking at the forest from the village and sad to say, from what I've seen of the designs, that roof is a big black blip on the horizon. This will not be good for those who gain from the psychological restorative benefits of seeing natural colours outside their windows.

Rebecca Feine

Well that's certainly one way to describe a nice view, Kitty!

Vanessa Shillingford

It can't be that bad, they must have got planning permission after all?

Belinda Bell

You'd hope so! But they clearly have money and money gets you everywhere nowadays.

Rebecca Feine

I personally don't mind, about time something was done with that land.

Belinda Bell

But it's our forest! And who are these people anyway? Just turning up out of nowhere?

Ellie Mileham

I've met them. Lucy's right, they're a lovely family.

Belinda Bell

Always makes me suspicious when people describe someone as 'lovely'.

Rebecca Feine

Are you being serious, Belinda?

Malorie Cane

Well as long as they don't block the way to our garages, they can do what they wish!

Chapter Six

Emma stood outside the school's reception, waiting for Isla to be let out from her after-school club that evening. She was in the club three nights a week – Mondays, Tuesdays and Wednesdays. On Thursdays, Dele left work early so he could pick her up, and on Fridays, Emma did. It worked out well. Isla actually enjoyed the clubs, though sometimes moaned that there was only a handful of other kids in with her, a testament to how skewed the community was towards stay-at-home mums in Forest Grove.

Stay-at-home mums like Tatjana Belafonte.

Emma hadn't been able to resist googling her when she'd got into work that morning. It was a good way of taking her mind off the smashed window while she waited for Dele to call her. She bet a lot of the other mums had done some googling about Tatjana, too; some of the dads as well, judging by the way their mouths had dropped open when they saw this new model-esque woman appear in the school playground. There wasn't much about her online, just a website showcasing her fashion business and an Instagram account, too, its feed mostly dominated by gorgeous models wearing Tatjana's designs. There were also some family photos showing

Tatjana with her husband Lawrence and their two boys in some exotic holiday location or other, as well as solo photos of Tatjana looking wistfully out of the window with a cup of tea in her hands. Emma noticed many of the village's residents were already following her, including Lucy Cronin (of course!) and Kitty Fletcher.

Kitty was a bit of a local celebrity in the village. She'd written a book on parenting and had appeared on some daytime TV shows, calling herself the Natural Nanny. She held weekend sessions to 'help balance a parent's nurturing core' so as to ensure they 'set a good example' for their children. When Emma had first seen the leaflet that had been conveniently posted through their letterbox the day they moved in, she'd laughed out loud at some of the things Kitty promised to help with: digital detox, connecting with nature, the benefits of organic sugar-free food. She wasn't surprised when she discovered Kitty had never had a child herself.

Even funnier, when Emma did a search for Kitty's name and dug down several pages, it delivered a hilarious MySpace page from back in 2005 showing a purple-haired Kitty in her early thirties, complete with a photo of her smoking a joint against the backdrop of a room filled to the brim with everything she now railed against: fast food, a TV, a computer. Emma wouldn't mind. Sometimes the best 'gurus' were people who had turned their lives around and seen the light. But in this case, Kitty made no mention of her rock-girl past. In fact, according to the profile on her website, her life from a young age had revolved around a model of 'natural, nurturing' living.

The hypocrisy of it all!

The doors to reception opened and Emma smiled as she spotted Isla among the group of kids. A little knot formed in her stomach as she thought of the smashed window again and the awful run-in with Lawrence Belafonte's PA after. At least Emma hadn't had a call from the police, something she'd been worried about, considering Myra had threatened to send the pictures to them. She was now more worried about the smashed window. Dele had called her from the bookshop where he worked just before lunch and told her he'd called the police, who'd explained that some teenage boys from Ashbridge had been prowling around the area, so it may well have been them. But Emma wasn't convinced. It seemed so random. No other neighbours' houses had been targeted, from what she could gather.

Maybe that was the problem. Maybe it *wasn't* so random.

Anyway, Dele had managed to board the windows up. He'd even ordered a new window pane . . . a window pane that was going to wipe out what little they had left of their savings.

Isla's eyes lit up when she saw her mum and she ran over. Emma wrapped her daughter in her arms, leaning down to press her nose into her thick hair, taking in the smell of her apple shampoo.

'Hello, darling, how was your day?' she asked.

'Cool. Look,' Isla said, digging around in her bag. 'There's a new after-school club. I *have* to sign up. It's on the day Dad leaves early to pick me up, so he can take me.'

Emma took the flyer.

DESIGN DIVAS
EVERY THURSDAY
FOREST GROVE COMMUNITY CENTRE
4–4.45 P.M.
YEARS 3–6
A GREAT AFTER-SCHOOL CLASS FOR BUDDING FASHION DESIGNERS.
SIGN UP FOR THIS 10-WEEK COURSE WITH FASHION DESIGNER TATJANA BELAFONTE.
£100 FOR 10 WEEKLY SESSIONS.
LIMITED PLACES AVAILABLE, APPLY SOON TO AVOID DISAPPOINTMENT

Emma frowned. Why hadn't Tatjana mentioned it that morning when they were talking about Isla's love of fashion?

'I'm sorry, darling,' Emma said, shoving the flyer in her bag. 'Thursday is your time with Dad. Plus you're already signed up to this kids' club three afternoons a week. It's too expensive to add yet another thing.'

'But we've just got a new kitchen and those blinds!'

'Exactly! And now we're needing to replace those new blinds, not to mention the window, too.'

Isla's face dropped as she remembered the smashed window.

'I'm sorry, darling,' Emma said. 'We just can't spare the money.'

Isla crossed her arms. 'But how come you get to do those yoga classes, and Dad does tennis? What about me?'

'Oh, let me think. Kids' club? Guitar lessons?'

Isla gave her a look. 'Kids' club? Like *that's* any fun. I only have to go to kids' club because *you're* always working.'

Other parents peered over, raising eyebrows.

Emma looked at her daughter in surprise. Isla rarely gave her a guilt trip about working!

'You go to kids' club three afternoons a week, that's all,' Emma said quietly, steering Isla away. 'And why do you think I work? I do it to pay for the clothes on your back and the house *and* the bills.'

'Exactly! So you *can* pay for the art class,' Isla retorted.

'Pay for what?' a voice asked.

They turned to see Tatjana standing behind them with her two boys.

'Mum won't let me do your arts club,' Isla sulked. 'She said it's too expensive.'

Emma's face reddened. 'Isla, don't be silly.'

Tatjana frowned. 'I thought ten pounds a session was reasonable. Several of the other mums have already signed up,' she said, waving at some of the parents nearby. 'That's why I'm here with the boys, we're going to grab a coffee with one of the mums to chat about it.'

Emma felt a touch of annoyance. 'I didn't quite rule it out,' she said. 'I just need to chat to Isla's dad about it.'

'Look,' Tatjana said, leaning close to Isla and lowering her voice. 'How about I give you a discount? How does eight pounds a session sound?'

Isla's face lit up. 'Thank you *so* much.'

'That's very sweet of you,' Emma said, 'but it wouldn't be fair on the other mums.'

'They don't need to know,' Tatjana replied, touching Emma's arm lightly. 'Just our little secret.'

Emma gave her a tight smile. 'I don't feel right about it. Of course we'd pay the full price.'

Tatjana clapped her slim hands together. 'Oh, wonderful news. I'll add your name to the list then, Isla.'

Isla started squealing in excitement as Tatjana and her boys laughed.

'Aren't you a delight?' Tatjana said.

'Sorry to give the wrong impression,' Emma said firmly, determined to stick to her guns. 'But I really do need to talk to my husband about this, so please don't add Isla's name quite yet.'

'Oh well,' Tatjana said with a shrug. 'You can't say I didn't try, Isla.'

Isla's face dropped, her dark eyes filling with tears. Emma felt bad, but she wasn't going to let this woman steamroller her into something she hadn't discussed with Dele yet.

'Right, we better go. Have a lovely evening!' She shot Tatjana a quick smile then walked away, aware of the woman's eyes on her back.

Isla was quiet as they walked to the car, jumping into the back seat and turning her face away when Emma turned to look at her.

She continued with her strop when they arrived home, jumping out of the car and storming to the front door, not even glancing at the large board now covering their shattered living-room window. Emma noticed it, though; she'd spotted it the moment they'd turned into their road.

As Isla crossed her arms and tapped her toe while Emma searched her bag for her keys, Emma couldn't help but smile. Truth was, Isla was uber cute when she was angry.

During the adoption process, Emma and Dele were encouraged to talk about the kind of child they would like. Back then, Emma had naively imagined a ten-year-old as being obsessed with princesses and fairy wings. She would never have envisaged a mini teenager, already obsessed with make-up and having strops. But really, she wouldn't have it any other way. She *preferred* this version to the Disney version, even if it was very different from the way Emma had been as a child. She used to love all the Disney stuff, and would watch *The Little Mermaid* over and over again, snuggled up with her mother who was also a Disney fan, a contrast to her sister Harriet who'd prefer to watch the Grand Prix and old Westerns with her dad.

Sometimes, though, Emma worried that Isla was growing up too fast. But despite her grumpy moments, in the main Isla was a charming, polite and lovely little girl . . . to other people anyway, and that was what counted, wasn't it?

Emma let them in and Isla ran straight upstairs, slamming her bedroom door behind her. As she did, Emma paused at the living-room door. Dele had cleared up all the mess; the carpet was newly hoovered. But the large board looked ugly and so out of place and made the room so dark.

A few moments later, Dele walked in the front door looking as dishevelled as ever after a day of working in the bookshop. Or in this case, an afternoon after a morning sorting the mess.

She liked him that way, though, black hair all messy, his dark skin smelling of books. It still made her tummy tilt, just as it had when they'd met at her sister's engagement party in a cramped pub events room in Islington fifteen years ago. Emma had moved to London with Harriet two years before then and was an assistant at a small PR company, while her sister worked for a government think tank. Dele was a friend of Alba, Harriet's new fiancé. Alba was the latest in a string of whirlwind lovers that Harriet had met in their two years in London, a fiery Italian whose family owned a string of restaurants in West London. This wasn't Harriet's first proposal of marriage; she'd had a couple already. But it *was* the first one she'd accepted, which had made Emma wonder if this time it really was serious. It helped that Emma liked Alba, too. Yes, he was a bit overdramatic and passionate, but he really seemed to love Harriet . . . plus he had a gorgeous friend.

Dele had been to university with Alba and was an editorial assistant at a publishing firm at the time. He was tall – almost six foot three – and was wearing a George Orwell *1984* T-shirt when Emma first met him at the engagement party. It helped that he was easy on the eye, too, which seemed at odds with how *badly* he was dancing. When they were introduced later by a very drunk Alba, Emma surprised herself by saying: 'Oh yes, you're the one with the dad-dance moves.' Usually she wouldn't be as bold as that, but there was something about Dele's manner that made her feel at ease.

Despite the fact that she'd insulted his dancing, they somehow ended up talking for two hours straight, finding a quiet corner in the bar. As people got even more drunk and raucous around them, Dele asked her if she wanted to go somewhere quieter and Emma surprised herself by saying 'yes' without hesitating.

Thing was, she wasn't like Harriet, who dated someone new every month. She was waiting for the right one, something her sister blamed on Emma's Disney film obsession.

'Honestly, hon,' Harriet would say, 'there are no Prince Erics in Battersea.'

Emma had only had a couple of boyfriends, one a quiet maths student she'd met while studying marketing at the University of York. But that soon disintegrated after she caught him cheating on her with her roommate. Then there was one of her sister's clients, a German marketing director. On paper, he was ideal for Emma: fascinated by marketing, especially digital marketing; handsome and quiet, like her. But after a year, she ended it. She just didn't feel enough of a connection with him . . . which may have had something to do with the fact that he was clearly in love with her sister.

And now here was this vivacious, gorgeous, passionate man who was as obsessed with books as she was and actually seemed to find her fascinating. And not *once* did his eyes slide over to Harriet as she launched into her sexy Señorita dance when a Shakira song came on later in the night. It sealed the deal, and three years later they got married in a small ceremony at Islington Town Hall.

Dele walked in now, giving her a peck on the cheek as he slung his leather satchel bag on the side cabinet. 'You okay?' he asked.

'Yep. Thanks for sorting the window.' She glanced at the board again and Dele followed her gaze.

'Eyesore, isn't it?' he said.

'You could say that.'

He followed her into the kitchen and she handed him the cheese grater. 'Can you grate some cheese?'

He nodded and went to the sink, pulling the sleeves of his plaid shirt up and washing his hands.

'Do you really think a bunch of teenage kids did it?' she asked.

'Who else would do it? It happens, Emma, even in nice little villages like this.'

Emma pursed her lips, then nodded. He was right; no point making a big deal out of it . . . unless it happened again.

She inwardly shuddered at the thought. It *wouldn't* happen again, would it?

'You okay?' Dele asked, tilting his head as he examined her face.

She smiled. 'Yep. Just had a rubbish day to be honest.' She told him about the run-in with Myra, and Dele shook his head.

'Wow, she sounds delightful,' Dele said sarcastically.

'At least her boss seems like a decent bloke.'

'Boss?'

'Mr Belafonte,' she said in a faux-posh voice. 'You know that crane in the forest? He's building a house there.'

They both looked out of the window towards the treetops at the side of the house. It was dark outside now, the forest a silhouette against the night sky, a crescent moon peering down at it, its light just catching the edge of the crane.

'Fancy,' Dele said. 'Where's Isla?'

Emma rolled her eyes. 'She's in a strop.'

'What is it now?' Dele asked as he started grating the cheese. 'You didn't let her have a Wham bar just before dinner?'

Emma laughed. 'Not this time. She wants to do this.' She pointed at Tatjana's flyer, which was lying on the kitchen worktop.

'Belafonte?' Dele said, reading it. 'This the wife of the knight in shining armour from this morning?'

Emma nodded.

'Why can't Isla do this?' he asked as he read it.

'Look at the price. Anyway, Thursday's your day. Actually,' Emma said as casually as she could, 'I'll be interested to hear what you think when you see Tatjana.'

'Why?' Dele asked.

'She looks a bit like Jade Dixon,' she whispered.

Dele rolled his eyes. 'Let me guess, she's black.'

'Not just because of that!'

Emma knew it did Dele's head in, the way people would tell him he looked like any random black actor they could pluck out of the air – Idris Elba, Will Smith, even Morgan Freeman, despite being half his age. He clearly thought Emma was doing the same with Tatjana, comparing her to another black woman she knew, Isla's birth mother.

He laughed. 'Emma, do you seriously think Jade Dixon is now married to a rich architect and is building a massive house in the middle of the woods?'

'I didn't say it *is* her,' Emma said, reaching for some more salt and sprinkling it into the mince she was frying. 'Just that she *looks* like her. You'll see what I mean when you meet her.'

'Okay, I get it now,' Dele said as he looked at the flyer.

'Get what?'

'Why you don't want Isla doing this.'

'No, no, it has nothing to do with that! It's a cost we could do without right now, that's all.'

Dele raised an eyebrow. 'Really, that's all? You don't mind a glamorous young black mother teaching your child her favourite subject? Do I detect the green-eyed monster?'

Emma flicked a tea towel at him and he ducked, laughing.

'What's all the laughing about?' Isla said as she strolled in. She went straight to her dad, giving him a hug as she glowered at Emma. Emma shook her head and got the rice out of the microwave.

'So Mum tells me you want to do this fashion design thing?' Dele asked Isla.

'She won't let me,' Isla said, grabbing some of the grated cheese and stuffing it in her mouth.

'Maybe it's less about not letting you,' Dele said, 'and more about the fact you assume we'll just say yes to everything.'

Isla looked confused. She often did when Dele tried to explain things to her in his philosophical way.

'By assumed,' Dele said, 'I mean you just think we'll say yes without even considering we might say no.'

'I *really* need to do it though, Dad.'

'You mean you really *want* to do it,' Emma said as she divided the rice between three plates. 'Want isn't the same as need, Isla.'

Isla's shoulders dropped, and Dele caught Emma's eye over her head with a look she knew well: the 'my daughter is wrapping me around her finger right this very moment' look. 'I don't mind it being my evening,' he said with a shrug. 'It's only forty-five minutes. Plus I got that overtime money.'

Emma rolled her eyes. Great, now if she said no, she'd look like the big bad witch.

Thanks, Dele.

'Okay,' Emma said. 'If this was in my office and one of the team wanted to attend a training event, our boss would ask us to do a quick presentation on why it's worth it.'

'A presentation?' Isla asked, her confused expression deepening.

Dele's mouth twitched into a smile. 'Don't worry, Isla, Mum got me to do the same when I proposed to her.'

Emma flicked a tea towel at him again. 'I did not!' She sighed and walked over to Isla, putting her hands gently on her daughter's shoulders. 'You don't need to do a presentation, darling. Just tell me why it's so important to you.'

Isla thought about it for a moment. 'I like fashion, I have all my life.'

'Yes, all the ten looooooong years of your life,' Dele said.

Emma resisted the urge to smile. Isla looked so earnest!

Isla gave her dad a look, then turned back to her mother. 'I'm always doing those fashion books,' she continued, '*and* art is my best subject at school. Miss Morgan says I'm awesome at it.'

'That's right, you are,' Emma admitted.

'And I – I want to . . .' Isla paused, thinking about it. 'I want to take it up the stairs. I want to be *serious* about it.'

It was now Emma and Dele's turn to look confused. 'Up the stairs?' Emma asked.

'You know what I mean,' Isla said. 'Like when you told me why you were going to take that new job and move here.'

'Oh, you mean take it up a level,' Emma said, smiling. 'Oh darling.' She pulled Isla into her arms and stroked her hair. 'You are *such* a clever thing.'

Isla peered up at her, her long black eyelashes batting away. 'Does that mean yes, I can do it?'

Dele and Emma looked at each other over their daughter's head, and Emma sighed. 'Fine. You can do it.'

Isla whooped and ran around the kitchen, shouting, 'Victory lap, victory lap!' as Emma and Dele laughed. How *could* they say no to her when she reacted like this?

◆ ◆ ◆

That evening in bed, Dele put his book down and turned towards Emma. 'I think we did good parenting this evening,' he said.

'Yes, I think we're approaching this adulting business rather well.'

He smiled. 'Seriously. We did the right thing. Isla really is great at all this design stuff – we should encourage it.'

'I know,' Emma agreed.

'And don't worry, this glamorous black beauty of a fashion designer will never match up to you,' he said, leaning over and taking her reading glasses off.

'Oh yes, I am the epitome of glamour,' Emma replied, gesturing to her old Harry Potter Hufflepuff nightdress.

'I actually find nine-year-old nightdresses with ripped sleeves *very* sexy,' he said, tracing his lips up her arm.

She laughed as she stroked his hair. 'Nine years, that's very specific. How on earth do you remember that?'

He peered up at her. 'You were wearing it the night we decided to adopt, remember?'

'Now *this* is why I find you so sexy,' she said, wriggling down the bed so she was face to face with him. 'Your mind for detail.'

'Oh yeah, detail is exactly what my mind's made for, like this detail,' he said as he lowered his head, lifting her nightdress and pressing his lips against the birthmark on her hip. 'And this,' he said, voice going muffled as he gently parted her legs.

Later, after they'd made love, Emma stared out of the window towards the treetops. They always kept the curtains open a touch so she could see the forest at night. She liked watching the swaying outlines of the trees in the distance, and the moon above. It helped her go to sleep.

She thought of that night when they decided to adopt. She always knew she might have problems conceiving because of the polycystic ovary syndrome she'd been battling since she was a teenager, but when she still didn't fall pregnant after a year of trying, Emma went for some tests and discovered that she now wasn't ovulating at all. The chances of her ever having a child were close to zero. When their first round of IVF didn't work, Emma was devastated and considered just giving up on the idea of children altogether. But then one freezing cold evening over Christmas, while lying in bed with the new Harry Potter nightdress Dele had bought her, he broached the idea of adopting.

She wasn't sure at first. It wasn't the usual obstacles: bonding with the child, worries about what 'baggage' that child might bring with them. Emma knew in her heart she could love and bond with a child no matter what.

No, it was doubts about *herself.* Was she worthy of being a mother to a child who would need the very *best* kind of mother? There were things in her past that made her wonder if she was really capable of helping a child with a troubled background.

But as she'd looked into Dele's eyes, she knew with his help she could.

'Okay,' she'd said. 'Let's do it.'

Emma looked towards the wall that separated their room from Isla's. It *was* the best decision they'd ever made. It made her shiver to wonder what would have been if she hadn't agreed to adopt that day.

How could she contemplate a life without her darling Isla?

She smiled and closed her eyes. She didn't have to worry. She was safe here now.

◆ ◆ ◆

When Emma arrived in the school playground with Isla the next morning, Tatjana Belafonte was the first person they saw. She was surrounded by other mums and had already adopted the village 'uniform', effortlessly combining the exotic with the homely in her uber-expensive wellies and raincoat over a chic patterned jumpsuit.

How did she do it, just a day in?

'Bit of a glamourpuss, isn't she?' a deep voice said from beside Emma as Isla ran off to play with her friends.

She turned to see it was Shawn Fenton. He played football with Dele and had been to the house a few times over the summer with his two children to chat to Dele over a beer or two. Emma always enjoyed his company – he was a good laugh. She hadn't properly met his wife yet. She was a busy solicitor, so was often straight in and out of the playground. On the odd occasion when Shawn did pick the kids up, he created a bit of a buzz around the school mums because of his good looks. He wasn't Emma's type, but she could see the appeal with his blond hair and muscular form.

'What are you doing here?' Emma asked him, relieved to have someone to talk to.

'Faye has a meeting. So who *is* that?' he asked, gesturing towards Tatjana.

'She's moving into that house in the woods. Have you seen the crane?'

'Oh yeah, Dele mentioned that on the footie WhatsApp group last night. They must be loaded.'

'Yes, judging from her Burberry wellies.'

Myra rushed through the school gates then, her son dragging his heels after her. She looked smart in trendy black check trousers and a black raincoat, black-rimmed glasses over her perfectly made-up face. Clearly it was her first day at work. She glanced at Emma as she passed, her face clouding over.

'Uh-oh, here she comes,' Shawn said.

Emma followed his gaze to see Tatjana making a beeline for them.

'Hello, you,' Tatjana said, kissing Emma on each cheek. Behind her back, Shawn raised an eyebrow.

Emma moved away, flustered. 'Oh. Hi.'

'So will we be graced with your beautiful talented daughter every Thursday?'

For a moment, Emma didn't understand what she meant. Was she inviting Isla somewhere? Then she remembered about the fashion design class. 'Actually, yes. Dele and I had a chat and—'

'Fab!' Tatjana said, interrupting her. She looked over at Isla. 'Did you hear, Isla?' she shouted across the playground. 'Good news. Your mum said yes to doing Design Divas.'

Isla ran over, face flushed with excitement. 'I know, isn't Mum the coolest!' She squeezed her cheek into Emma's arm as she looked up at her.

Tatjana's smile faltered.

'Have you got lots of kids signed up?' Emma asked her.

'Well,' Tatjana said, her long fingers flicking up to her chest as it flushed. 'A few.'

Emma could tell she wasn't happy with the numbers. 'You should pop it on the school's Facebook page.'

'Or that God-awful mums' group Kitty Fletcher runs,' Shawn suggested.

'Shawn!' Emma said, unable to stop the smile appearing on her lips.

'I didn't know there was one,' Tatjana said. 'How interesting. Are you a member, Emma?'

'I was, but I left,' Emma admitted. 'It all got a bit much for me. It *is* popular, though, if you want to get word out about Design Divas.'

'Thank you, I'll look into it.' Tatjana turned to Isla, a big smile on her face. 'Your hair looks fab, Isla! You've been using the oil I gave you, haven't you? And you watched those YouTube videos, I can tell!'

'Did I do it right?' Isla asked, shyly patting the top of the sleek bun she'd spent ages on that morning.

'Perfect. Absolutely perfect.' Tatjana placed her palm on top of Isla's hair, the large diamond on her engagement ring shining in the morning light. 'Unbelievable, how she was able to do her hair like that from a YouTube tutorial . . . all at the age of ten! Must be those clever genes of hers.'

Emma gave her an uncertain look. What a strange thing to say!

The school bell went and Tatjana waved goodbye, taking her son to his queue.

'Right, you,' Emma said, giving Isla a kiss on the cheek. 'Have a good day!'

When she was out of earshot, Shawn turned to Emma. 'Funny one, isn't she?' he said as he looked at Tatjana. 'She definitely seems to think Isla's the best thing since sliced bread.'

Emma followed his gaze, watching as Tatjana's dark eyes tracked Isla as she walked into class.

She *did* seem a bit obsessed with her.

Chapter Seven

Welcome to the Mums of Forest Grove Facebook Group

Wednesday 16th September
6 p.m.

Tatjana Belafonte

Hello everyone! The fabulous Kitty Fletcher and lovely Lucy Cronin recommended this group to me. I've just moved to Forest Grove and am already in awe of what a wonderful community this is. Thank you to everyone who has helped me so far. I thought I'd remind all the primary school mummies in the group of the Design Divas after-school club I'm running every Thursday at the Forest Grove Community Centre from 4 to 4.45 p.m. You should have received a leaflet in your children's school bags. Just PM me if you're interested in your child joining us. We start tomorrow!

Kitty Fletcher

What a wonderful initiative! And can I be the first to welcome you, Tatjana, and say what a delight it was chatting to you at the cafe at lunchtime, clearly a woman after my own heart.

Tatjana Belafonte

Thank you, Kitty! I've already ordered your book and can't wait to get stuck in.

Lucy Cronin

Kitty's book is wonderful. We all follow the Kitty Fletcher way around here . . . well, some of us do.

Myra Young

This is my first time posting too and I want to say I devoured your book in one day, Kitty! It really is wonderful.

Kitty Fletcher

How kind of you, Myra!

Malorie Cane

I thought this post was about Tatjana's little fashion club, not the Kitty Fletcher appreciation club.

Rebecca Feine

Oh Malorie! What are you like?

Ellie Mileham

My daughter Zoe would absolutely love this club, Tatjana. Will you be considering running some at the weekend? I pick Zoe up from her after-school club at 5.30 p.m.

Tatjana Belafonte

I'm so sorry but I wouldn't want to take time away from the kids at the weekend, especially now my oldest is at school. I miss him sooooo much. We plan to have lots of outdoor fun at the weekend, no work for me!

Kitty Fletcher
What a marvellous attitude!

Samantha Perks
It's a shame this isn't open to older kids. My daughter would absolutely love this. She's planning to study fashion at uni.

Tatjana Belafonte
It's on the cards, Samantha, I just need to find the time.

Malorie Cane
Isn't fashion design a bit of a narrow subject? My grandson likes cars, what about car design?

Samantha Perks
Boys are into fashion design too, you know, Malorie.

Tatjana Belafonte
Quite right! Myra has already signed her son up for it, haven't you, Myra?

Myra Young
Absolutely! There are plenty of male fashion designers around.

Malorie Cane
Oh really? Name one boy you know who's into fashion design!

Tatjana Belafonte
Alexander McQueen?

Lucy Cronin
Karl Lagerfeld?

Vanessa Shillingford
Ralph Lauren?

Kitty Fletcher
Wonderful examples, ladies! Right, I'm off to London to deliver a seminar. Once again, welcome to the community Tatjana, I'm sure you'll be a wonderful asset and role model for the young children of Forest Grove!

Chapter Eight

Thursday 17th September
4.45 p.m.

Look at him, standing there in his hipster clothes with that ridiculous leather bag over his shoulder like he's one of the mums. I thought Emma was bad, but now I see Dele Okoro the way he is now, I realise you really are living in hipster-snowflake hell, my poor love.

What did the report say he did? Editor, that's it! Now a bookshop manager after he couldn't even hold down his job. Average man on an average wage doing an average thing. It pains me to know you have to endure this mediocrity. That you have no idea of the spirit that runs through your blood, a spirit that's had me dragging myself up by my fingernails the past few years to get where I am now.

Would the people who claim to be your parents have achieved all I have if they'd been born in a tower block like me? I doubt it. I very much doubt they know what it's like to fight for what you want. Emma, for example, has been given everything on a plate, judging from the look of her mother. As for her father, he wasn't always a pathetic drunk. There was a time when he was a so-called upstanding member of the community, a police detective!

What happened to him? What made him turn to drink and allow his marriage to collapse? Was it a weakness that Emma inherited? A weakness she will try to instil in you too, Isla.

At least my parents had some fire in them, even if they used it in the worst possible way. It's all about how you use that fire.

What chance do you have of doing something exciting *with your life? Who will teach you how to strive?*

Dele doesn't look anything like you, either! I know what those use- less social workers would have thought: Oh, look, he's black, he'll do! *But it's clear to anyone that the two of you look nothing alike. And it isn't just about how you look. I can tell you're a creative like me. My girl will most certainly* not *be selling books or doing PR when she grows up.*

Won't be long now, Isla, not with what I've got planned . . .

And luckily, thanks to you attending Design Divas tonight, that plan has just officially begun.

Chapter Nine

When Emma walked into the kitchen after work on Thursday evening, the first thing she heard was Isla's gushing voice.

'. . . so cool, she's even cooler than Miss Morgan.'

'Who's cooler than Miss Morgan?' Emma asked as she walked into the room. 'Is that even *possible*?'

'Tatjana Belafonte,' Dele said with a wry smile.

Emma ignored him.

'You're early,' he remarked.

'Yep, I finally got the proposal off.' She'd been working on a new business proposal to run the social media for a chain of coffee shops all week and she'd finally got it into a state she was happy with.

'So Design Divas was good, was it?' she asked Isla.

'It was awesome!' Isla enthused. 'We're designing costumes for the Halloween party.'

'What Halloween party?' Emma asked.

'Apparently the Belafontes are holding a big Halloween party when their house is ready,' Dele said with a raised eyebrow.

'It's going to be for the *whole* village,' Isla said. 'How cool is that?'

'Don't we have a community centre for that type of thing?' Emma asked. She kissed Isla on the head. 'Guess what I got for dinner?'

'Pizza?' Isla asked hopefully. Pizza was her most favourite meal in the world.

'Yep.'

'Yay!' Isla declared as Emma revealed the large pepperoni pizza box she'd been hiding behind her back. The local pub, Neck of the Woods, did lovely wood-fired pizzas to take away.

'Let's eat it outside,' Emma said. 'Make the most of the sunshine before it leaves us for autumn and it starts getting dark early.'

'But it's cold!' Isla said.

'Not really. Wear your coat if you have to.'

Truth was, it wasn't just the sunshine that appealed. The house seemed so gloomy now the window was boarded up. It made Emma feel uncomfortable.

They went out into the garden, sitting at the wooden table as Emma laid plates out. It *was* a little chilly, but the sun was shining bright above and Emma felt fine in her cardigan.

She liked being outside, hearing the rustle of the forest leaves in the distance, watching the birds and squirrels root around the various bird feeders she'd hung in their trees at the back of the garden. It was especially gorgeous at this time of the day as the sun began to set. Leaves were turning copper, so it created a stunning orange halo in the distance and gave the light in the garden a strange quality.

'So what costume are you designing then?' Emma asked Isla as she handed her a slice of pizza.

'It's a secret,' Isla said, tapping her nose. 'Honestly, Mum, Tat is *so* talented,' she continued, brown eyes sparkling.

Tat? Emma mouthed to Dele as he smiled.

'She showed us how to sew super quick,' Isla continued, 'and literally, in like five minutes, she'd sewn a whole sleeve on to a top.'

'Talent indeed,' Emma said, unable to keep the sarcasm out of her voice. Dele's smile widened as he looked down at his plate.

'She's super creative,' Isla said. 'She told me after I was her *best* student.'

'She shouldn't be choosing favourites,' Emma said.

'She probably couldn't help herself,' Dele said. 'I mean, this is *Isla* we're talking about.'

Emma nodded. 'Very true.'

'Aw shucks, thanks!' Isla said. She took a bite of pizza and carried on talking, mouth full. 'And oh my God, she is so pretty! Her make-up is flawless,' she said, flicking her hand up dramatically.

'Don't eat with your mouth full!' Emma said, catching sight of her reflection in the glass of the French doors as she spoke. She was anything *but* flawless, strands of her red shoulder-length hair escaping the clip she'd pulled it up in, smudged eyeliner and a poorly concealed spot developing on her chin.

Dele squeezed her hand. 'Hey, beautiful.'

She smiled at him, squeezing his hand back. He knew her so well.

'Anyway,' Isla continued, 'Tatjana said if I want, I can go to her house and have extra lessons!'

Emma put down her slice of pizza. 'Whoa whoa whoa! I think *not*.'

'But why?' Isla whined.

'Your mum's right, Isla,' Dele said. 'It's just a bit . . .'

Weird, Emma mouthed to him.

Dele nodded slightly.

'Fine,' Isla said. 'I can just be *bored* all weekend like normal.'

Emma looked at her daughter in surprise. 'Bored? So the cinema is boring, is it?'

'I want to do *creative* stuff.'

'You have tons of creative stuff,' Dele said, gesturing to the room that was to the side of the kitchen, full to the brim with Isla's kits. 'Bracelet sets, paints, even that weird glow-in-the-dark sand thing your grandparents got you for Christmas last year, which you *still* haven't touched.'

Isla scowled. 'It's not the same as fashion design.'

Emma bit her lip. She could do fashion! All she needed was some material, a few gems . . . surely it couldn't be that hard?

In fact, didn't she have that old sewing machine her mother had given her in the loft?

After they finished eating, Emma headed up to the loft and searched in the semi-darkness, eventually finding the sewing machine in the corner. As she walked towards it, she noticed the other box next to it, which was labelled 'Isla's old stuff'.

She paused, going to that box instead and opening it. Inside was everything they'd collected during the adoption process, including the small items Isla had come with when she'd moved in: a soft yellow duck toy and a pastel-green blanket. Emma reached in, pulling out the huge folder she'd put together during the process. It hadn't taken as long as she'd been warned it would. When she made the initial nerve-wracking call to register their interest, an event was taking place for prospective adoptees that very weekend. Though the social workers there had been careful to paint a realistic picture of how things happened and how challenging it could be to adopt a child, for Dele and Emma the positives outweighed the negatives.

They came away with an initial application form, and a few weeks later a social worker was visiting their house to chat to them. The next few months passed in a blur of various events and interviews. By the end, Emma felt their assigned social worker knew more about her and Dele than anyone.

Well, she knew about *most* of Emma's life, anyway. There were some things best left unsaid.

Nearly six months after first applying, they went to an adoption panel and were approved. Three months after that, their social worker got in touch to tell them about an eighteen-month-old girl who'd been living with foster parents the past six months after being taken from her seventeen-year-old birth mother.

They were not shown a photo of Isla then, just some brief details, but Emma knew, she just knew, this little girl was *their* daughter!

As soon as they said yes, they got more details. Insights into Isla's first year with her mother and grandmother. Some of it good – you could see Jade tried her best; some of it bad. They learnt that when Jade had discovered she was pregnant with Isla, she'd taken real steps to kick her addiction to heroin, getting a place on a well-regarded programme where expectant mothers got the chance to live together in a house with specialists who helped them wean themselves off the drug.

From what Emma read of her records, Jade had remained drug-free for the first six months of Isla's life. It wasn't an ideal environment for a baby to be brought up in. Jade's mother Evie struggled with mental health issues and had a fierce temper, too, the two women often coming to blows. But compared to the way Jade's life had been before Isla came along, it was certainly calmer, safer. It *must* have been for social services to think it was fine for Isla to remain with her mother.

But after six months, it became clear that Jade had fallen into her old ways. Isla would be left alone with her grandmother, who struggled to cope, and Isla was once left completely alone in the house when her grandmother went out shopping. The final straw came when a social worker visited to find Isla playing next to a used hypodermic needle – one of Jade's new boyfriends sitting nearby, smoking a joint. By then, even Jade knew in her drug-addled mind that Isla would be better off away from that environment. It must have been heartrending for her, though. She'd tried so hard to be a mother.

When Emma and Dele decided they wanted to adopt Isla, they met her several times over at her foster parents' in the coming months, just so she could get used to them and they to her. When the day came to bring her home and Emma fed Isla her bottle, sitting by the cot she would now be sleeping in – the same cot she'd watched Dele put together – she felt a strange mixture of contentment and nerves.

Up in the loft, Emma ran her fingers over the soft blanket that Jade had given to her baby. Isla had slept with it each night after she came home. Then, when she turned three, she decided she didn't like it any more and instead wanted to sleep with the little pink blanket that Emma had got her. It had felt bittersweet for Emma, putting Isla's old green blanket away. Sweet because it meant Isla had fully embraced Emma as her new mother after a rocky few months of tears and attachment issues. Bitter because Emma couldn't help but imagine how Jade would feel if she'd known that the blanket she'd sent with her child was now being packed away. But as Dele had reminded Emma, Jade *had* had the opportunity to maintain letterbox contact with them, so she could watch Isla develop over the years through photos and letters, and yet she'd never once picked up the letters they had sent via the social worker's office.

Emma sighed and turned away, picking up the old sewing machine. A few moments later, she came down armed with the ancient machine, some needles and thread and some old scarves.

She laid it on the kitchen table, and called Isla and Dele in.

'Who said we can't do fashion design here?' Emma said.

Isla's eyes lit up at the sight of the sewing machine. 'Why didn't you tell me we had this?'

'It's your Nanny Blake's old one.'

'Oh my God, Mum, it is *so* cool!' Isla skipped over and ran her hand over the smooth black metal as Dele and Emma exchanged smiles.

'It's a proper old-school sewing machine,' Emma said proudly, 'so we need to be careful. If you like it, we can look at getting you a new one for Christmas.'

'Yes!' Isla said, jumping and clapping her hands together. 'What shall we make first? I know, I know! Let's make a purple dress from this scarf,' she said, grabbing an old silk scarf, 'with, like, a jagged skirt and long sleeves which turn up at the bottom and—'

'Whoa,' Emma said, laughing. 'Calm down. Let's start small, okay? Maybe a skirt?'

Isla thought about it, then shrugged. 'Sure, a skirt.'

'I think I'll leave you two to it,' Dele said, giving them both a kiss on the forehead. 'If it's okay with you, I might go for a run. I'm hoping to see an epic costume made by the time I come back.'

The costume, however, was anything but epic by the time Dele returned home an hour later. In fact, Isla was upstairs in her room watching her iPad as Emma shoved their attempts at a skirt in the bin.

'Oh,' Dele said when he walked into the kitchen. 'That bad, was it?'

'Terrible,' Emma said. 'I don't know why I bothered.'

'Ah, the life of a high-end fashion designer. What happened?'

Emma sat down at the kitchen table, shoving the old sewing machine away. 'I thought I knew what I was doing, but the machine kept jamming. Isla got a needle in her finger, then when we did manage to create something that looked vaguely like a skirt, the scarf material was so thin it just tore apart. Isla lost interest after about half an hour.'

Dele sat next to her, smelling of mud and sweat. She leaned her head on his shoulder. 'I'm no Tatjana bloody Belafonte, that's for sure,' she said.

'Thank God for that,' Dele said. 'Shawn was telling me she thinks a bit too much of herself, that one.'

'Yeah, well, you would if you had over a hundred thousand Instagram followers.'

'Really?'

Emma nodded, digging her phone out and finding Tatjana's Instagram account. 'Look.'

'All looks a bit fake to me,' Dele said as he scrolled through her feed. 'I prefer yours with its wistful videos of squirrels falling from trees and selfies of you dressed as an elf from Christmas.'

Emma shoved her shoulder into his. Why did he always have to take the mick?

'She's really getting to you, isn't she?' he asked seriously.

'Not really.'

Dele gave her a cynical look. 'Oh yeah?'

'Fine, I admit it, I'm jealous. My daughter thinks the sun shines out of the arse of some gorgeous perfect woman.'

He laughed. 'Don't take it personally, babe.'

'Really? You heard the way Isla was gushing about her earlier.'

'Yeah, but you have to see it from Isla's point of view. What does she see when she looks in the mirror? She sees something *different* from the other girls here in Forest Grove.'

Emma moved her head away from his shoulder and examined his face. 'You mean from me, too? What if she was blonde, we'd still be different!'

Dele smiled, sweeping a strand of Emma's hair from her eyes. 'You know it goes deeper than that. Look at this place,' he said, gesturing to the forest in the distance. 'How many black women lived here before Tatjana came along?'

Emma tensed her jaw. 'It shouldn't be about colour.'

'But it is,' Dele said softly. 'It's just the way it is.'

'So what? Tatjana comes along and is like a piece of the missing jigsaw puzzle?'

Dele sighed. 'Not *quite* like that.'

Emma sighed. Maybe he was right. And from Tatjana's point of view, it was probably refreshing to see people like Dele and Isla in the village. Maybe she was worried for her boys, that there would be no other kids with the same skin colour as them? So to see Isla looking happy probably gave her comfort.

Emma thought of the broken window again. Had someone who felt the opposite of comfort at the sight of Isla and Dele done that?

Dele put his hand over hers. 'When you think about it, it's no coincidence that you thought Tatjana looked like Jade when you first met her. You're just transferring your insecurities to this woman. She's a manifestation of what you wish you were: Isla's birth mother.'

Emma felt tears fill her eyes. How did he always hit the nail on the head? 'Maybe you're right.'

'I am. But you have to remember, our girl loves her mum, her *real* mum, more than anything. *Nothing* will break that bond.'

As he said that, they heard Isla's footsteps in the hallway. When she appeared at the doorway, she was already in her pyjamas, a soft white set with polar bears on them that always seemed to make her look like a toddler again.

'Mum, can we snuggle on the sofa before I go to bed?' she asked.

Emma smiled, putting her hand out to her daughter. 'Come here, snuggle buggle.'

Dele was right. He was completely right. Nothing could break their bond.

◆ ◆ ◆

The next morning was the usual stressful affair. They'd stayed up a little longer the night before because Emma just couldn't stop herself snuggling up with Isla. But that had consequences the next day with Isla struggling to wake and being even more fussy than usual. Hair not right. Porridge too hot. Tights too bumpy. A regular little Goldilocks. By the time they finally got out of the house, Isla was in a sulk because Emma had refused to let her wear her new black trainers to school instead of her school shoes.

Miraculously, though, despite leaving later than usual, Emma managed to find a parking space on the street in front of the school and for a moment, she thought the day might go okay after all. But as they walked through the school car park, she realised Isla was the only one wearing her school uniform. All the other kids seemed to be wearing blue jeans or skirts.

'Shit,' she hissed under her breath.

'Mum, you swore!' Isla said.

'Sorry, I'll wash my mouth out with soap. Is there a chance it could be non-uniform day today?'

Isla frowned. 'There *is* one this week, I think. You have to wear blue for a charity that helps sick kids . . .' Her voice trailed off as she looked around her, her cheeks reddening when she realised she was the only one wearing a uniform.

'Mum!' she shouted. 'Why didn't you tell me?'

'I didn't know!' Emma said.

Lucy passed by with her daughter Poppy.

'Oh my gosh,' Poppy said as she looked Isla up and down. 'Isla's in her *uniform*!' She started giggling and Isla looked like she was about to burst into tears.

'Is it non-uniform day?' Emma asked Lucy. 'I didn't get a message?'

'Yes,' Lucy replied, 'there was a letter in the kids' bags on Tuesday about it. Bit short notice, but isn't it always? One has to be on the ball around here!'

Emma ignored that dig and explored her memory. She was *sure* there hadn't been a letter. She'd got a letter about a school trip to Warwick Castle that Isla was excited about, but definitely nothing about a dress-down day. Having said that, she didn't check Isla's bag as regularly as she should. She wasn't sure she'd even looked in it since Tuesday.

Bugger. She checked the time. There was only a minute or so until the school bell. Maybe she could go home, grab something and bring it in? But then she'd be late for work . . . and damn it, she had a meeting at nine-thirty; it would be too tight. She peered at Isla who was blinking back tears, clutching her book bag to her chest.

'I'm so sorry, darling,' she said. 'Look, why don't you take your cardigan off and we can tie up your blouse, like from *Grease*?'

She started unbuttoning Isla's shirt but Isla shoved her away. 'No, I'll look stupid, and anyway, what's *Grease* and what's it got to do with the colour blue?'

'It's a really cool film, trust me,' Emma said, continuing to try to unbutton Isla's shirt.

'I said no!' Isla shouted, shoving her away again as Lucy raised a disapproving eyebrow.

'Isla! There is no need to be so rude,' Emma said.

'Why can't you just remember things, Mum?'

'Because there was nothing to remember,' Emma said quietly, aware of other parents' eyes on her. 'I didn't get a letter about this.'

'You must have done, everyone else did,' Isla said, gesturing to the sea of blue heading into the playground.

Emma blinked. 'They must have missed yours out, darling.'

'They didn't, admit it! You just forgot!'

'I swear, I didn't.' Or at least she thought she hadn't. Life was so busy lately and she *did* sometimes let things slip.

Didn't all parents?

'It's because you're too busy,' Isla said with a sigh.

'Everything okay here?' Emma turned to see Tatjana striding over, clutching Zeke's hand. Of course he was dressed in blue – even Tatjana was, a long blue tunic over mustard tights.

'Mum forgot it was dress-down day,' Isla grumbled.

'Oh, easily done!' Tatjana said, giving Emma a sympathetic smile. 'You're in luck. I was just about to drop these off with Myra to post,' she said, giving Myra who was standing nearby a little wave. 'Just some samples for a new children's range venture I'm considering, and lucky you, there happens to be a very cool blue T-shirt among them all.'

'Honestly, don't worry,' Emma said. 'I can rush home and get something.'

Screw the meeting. She'd just have to rearrange it. This was more important. She went to get her phone out to call her client.

'It's no bother, really,' Tatjana said. She dug around in the cloth bag that was slung over her shoulder and pulled out a parcel, ripping it open to reveal a blue T-shirt with reversible sequins on the front spelling out 'I'm totes blue'. She held it up to show Isla, smoothing her hand over the sequins so they changed into a pink heart saying 'I'm totes happy'.

It was Isla's dream top. Reversible sequins *and* a sassy logo.

'See,' Tatjana said, 'you can change it depending what mood you're in.'

'It's *perfect*!' Isla gushed.

Emma was about to protest again but Isla was already pulling the top on over her blouse. And anyway, how bad would it look if yet again she refused Isla something in front of Tatjana?

'It looks *fabulous* on you,' Tatjana said.

'It does,' Emma grudgingly admitted. 'Perfect size and everything.'

Isla looked down at herself proudly. 'I was like this,' she said, changing the sequins so they returned to the original 'I'm totes blue', 'but now I'm this, thanks to you,' she said to Tatjana, changing them to 'I'm totes happy' as Zeke giggled.

'How wonderful to see you smile,' Tatjana said as she stroked Isla's cheek.

Emma bristled. She didn't like how tactile Tatjana was being with Isla. 'That's very kind of you,' she forced out. 'I'll get it cleaned and returned to you asap. Right, better get you into school.' She took Isla's hand and started walking towards the playground.

'Oh no, she can keep it,' Tatjana said as she jogged to keep up with Emma. 'I wanted to catch up with you actually, and say Isla is *such* a talent. Just one session and I can see how creative she is, and funny too. What a sense of humour!'

That'll be ten pounds fifty for your membership of the Isla fan club, Emma felt like saying.

But instead, she smiled. 'I know, she has me and Dele in stitches all the time.'

'I bumped into your husband this morning at the shop,' Tatjana continued. 'He was telling me about the fashion disaster you guys had last night.'

Emma felt her cheeks flush. Dele told Tatjana about that?

Isla rolled her eyes. 'The sewing machine Mum used was *ancient*,' she said.

'Yep,' Emma said, 'we just need a better sewing machine.'

'I'll make the topic at next Thursday's Design Divas about how to make skirts the *proper* way,' Tatjana said with a laugh.

She held Emma's gaze, and Emma knew she wasn't imagining it: there was a challenge in Tatjana's eyes.

'Ah, but where's the fun in that?' Emma said, crossing her arms. 'We both had *such* a giggle about it, didn't we, Isla? I think it makes it more fun, don't you? Perfection can be boring, that's what I always tell Isla. It's good to make mistakes. It helps us *grow*.' She looked Tatjana in the eye, surprising herself with her own confidence.

Tatjana clenched her jaw, then nodded. 'Absolutely. Right, must go! Have to give this package to Myra!'

Then she strolled off, hauling her son behind her.

Emma watched her through narrowed eyes.

She hadn't imagined it, had she? That little dig? There had been too many from this Tatjana woman for her liking. What was her problem?

'Mum, the bell's going.'

Emma dragged her eyes away from Tatjana, then smiled down at her daughter. 'Love you, darling, have a good day.'

'Love you too!' Isla said, rushing off.

Emma walked to her car and got in, sitting in it as she watched Tatjana in the distance, chatting to Myra and some other mums.

She pulled her phone from her bag. She needed to talk to her sister. Harriet always helped when she was feeling a bit out of sorts.

'Hey, to what do I owe this pleasure?' Harriet asked in her sing-song voice as she answered.

'Just wanted to say hi.'

'I call *bullshit*. You sound rattled. Spill.'

Emma sighed. Her sister really did know her so well. She used to do the same when they lived in their poky little flat together in Battersea. Any little hint of anxiety in Emma – work related, Dele related – Harriet would home in on it and always make things better.

Yet again, it reminded Emma that it really should have been the other way around considering Emma was born first. But Harriet had always acted more like the older sister. While Emma would need to be constantly attached to their mother as a baby, Harriet was a content baby, able to sleep alone. Their father in particular liked to remind Emma of that on a regular basis.

'Be more independent like your sister Harriet,' she remembered him saying whenever she was upset or shy. 'Your little sister was sleeping in her own nursery from two months!'

As they grew older, the comparisons grew more intense from their father.

'Be more like Harriet, for God's sake, Emma,' he'd say as they walked away from yet another parents' evening where the teachers told them Emma just needed to come out of her shell a bit more.

'Look at Harriet talking to those kids,' was what she'd hear during their regular summer camping holidays in the south of France. 'She doesn't let language differences bother her.'

Their mother would rarely say anything, instead casting occasional sympathetic glances towards Emma. But when they were alone, she'd hold Emma close and tell her she loved her just as she was. She just couldn't bring herself to say that in front of her domineering husband.

At least she'd found her own voice now they were divorced and she was with her new husband, the quiet, kind Ray.

'So . . . ?' Harriet asked now. 'What's up?'

'There's this woman that has moved into the village and when I first met her, I thought she was Isla's birth mother. Of course, it isn't her,' Emma quickly added. 'How can a drug-addicted girl from an impoverished background become a well-off sophisticated fashion guru in the space of eight years?'

'People can turn things around. It happens all the time,' Harriet said.

She would know. The reason she'd moved to London was to work in politics, specifically for a think tank used by the Labour Party. She had a strong belief that people could pull themselves up from difficult circumstances if only they had the help.

Emma peered towards the crane poking out from the middle of the forest. 'Maybe. Anyway, it's not her, *obviously*. It's just that Isla thinks the sun shines out of her perfect butt.'

'So you're jealous of her?' Harriet said with a laugh.

'Oh, shut up,' Emma said. 'You totally know I am!'

'Oh sis, you are such an insecure little petal. How many times do I need to tell you: you are an *awesome* mother. Isla is so, so lucky to have you.'

'I know,' Emma whispered.

'But that's the problem, Em, you don't know that. All these years later, you still think you haven't got the chops to be an awesome mum but you are *living* it, hon, Isla is proof of that.'

Emma picked at a loose bit of nail. She really needed to stop biting them. 'I guess I'm just always scared one day someone's going to turn up and say, "Hey, you, the one who thinks she can parent? We caught you out, we know you're a fraud. Now give that child back to us!"'

'For a start, they can't do that. Isla is yours now. Unless you do something terrible, social services have no reason to check up on you.'

'But I *did* do something terrible,' Emma said in a low whisper.

'I'll pretend I didn't hear that,' Harriet snapped. 'Remember what Dad said. *Never* mention it out loud, never even *think* about it. Anyway, it was way before you met Isla.'

Emma looked out at the forest, blinking away tears.

'Now repeat after me,' Harriet said. 'I am a fabulous mother, Isla is lucky to have me and no sassy little newcomer is going to take her away from me.'

'I am a fabulous mother,' Emma said as she looked at herself in the wing mirror, 'and she *is* lucky to have me.'

But as she said it, she couldn't help wondering if she really was.

Chapter Ten

Emma sat in the bakery opposite Isla, watching her as she sipped at her hot chocolate. Dele was at football, so Emma had encouraged Isla to get her wellies on and head out into the forest. Isla had never been the outdoorsy type, preferring to stay in making stuff or curled up watching a film. It was the one thing that could calm her when she first arrived at Emma and Dele's house, a good film on TV and the sofa. Emma had felt guilty at first. In her naivety, she thought she could get away with restricting Isla's TV watching. But after a day trying to comfort a sad child who was missing her birth mother and the foster parents who'd been looking after her, Emma realised anything was better than having to endure Isla crying.

After a few months, Isla settled in and of course, they enjoyed walks in the park near their house in London and visits to local attractions. But still Isla would prefer to sit in and 'snuggle', as she referred to it. It was hard getting her out, especially when it was cold.

They'd had a nice time walking through the forest that day, though. They'd even visited the hedgehog park, a little hidden gem they'd discovered when they'd first moved to Forest Grove. Emma liked it as it wasn't always busy like the large wooden playground near the forest centre . . . and it didn't have Kitty Fletcher's stamp all over it. Kitty had helped design the larger park, the idea being that it had enough natural sensory stimulation to keep children entertained and away from electronic screens. Problem was, it was just too busy at the weekend, meaning the main sensory stimulation came in the form of screaming, excitable children or parents from the 'Kitty Cult', as Dele had taken to calling the mums and dads who attended Kitty's weekly parenting sessions at the centre.

After their walk, Emma took Isla to the little bakery in the village's courtyard. The courtyard was made up of several units including a Forest Foods organic store, a beauty salon, the Neck of the Woods pub and the Into the Woods bakery as well as a doctors' surgery, library and chemist, all forming a square around a large tree in the middle. Work was taking place in one of the empty units where a charity shop had once been, with rumours of a new restaurant appearing. That would be good; they usually had to travel out of Forest Grove if they wanted more than pub grub or pizza.

'How's school, darling?' Emma asked Isla as they sat at a small table looking out at the courtyard. 'Is it fun?'

Isla shrugged. 'Yeah, it's okay.'

'You're still liking it though, right?' Emma had been worried Isla would struggle joining a brand-new school, but she seemed to have fitted right in.

'It's just school, Mum. It's fine. Oh!' Isla added, her face lighting up. 'Have we got tickets for the disco yet?'

The school held a family disco each term to raise funds. Emma had been pleased they had an excuse not to go to the first one, as they were visiting her mum in Dartmouth. She just didn't fancy the idea of sitting drinking watered-down fruit juice and not really having anyone to talk to as Dele chatted to the multitude of friends he'd made since moving to the village.

'I don't know, sweetie,' she said to Isla now.

'Pleeeeeeeeeease!' Isla begged, putting her palms together.

Emma sighed. 'I'll see if there are any tickets left.'

'Cool. Can I play on your phone?'

'No, Isla. Let's talk like humans are supposed to.'

Isla gave her a pointed look. 'Talking is *boring*.'

'You seem to do plenty of it in the playground with your friends.'

'Yeah, but they're not old, like you.'

'Charming!'

Isla laughed. 'Oh mother, you know I love you. I just know what you're going to say. "How's school, dahhhhhling?" "Did you do any tests this week, sweeeeetie?"'

Emma couldn't help but laugh. 'I do *not* sound like that.'

'You *so* do.' Isla put her hand out. 'Phone, pleaaaaaase?'

Emma sighed, digging her phone out of her bag. 'Okay, but as long as you let me play too.'

'Fine. But please remember I lose points if the outfits you choose are lame, so take my advice.'

'I will, style goddess.' She shuffled her chair over and leaned in close to Isla as she opened up the online stylist game she liked to play. After a while, Emma decided to leave her to it and leaned back in her chair, sipping her chai latte as she peered outside.

This is nice, she thought. She didn't come out here enough, her weekends usually taken up with sorting stuff in the house or cinema trips.

As she thought that, the door to the bakery swung open and Kitty Fletcher walked in with Lawrence Belafonte's PA Myra. Kitty was wearing a trademark scarf over her short white hair, shiny red wellies and a yellow raincoat. She must have just come from her parenting workshop. Though they were held in the forest centre a few minutes' walk away, Kitty liked to get everyone out in nature

72

when it was dry. Emma would often see them if she went for a walk at the weekend, traipsing through the forest as Kitty spouted off about something. In fact, she'd seen them during their walk, and among them was Myra, who was enthusiastically striding alongside Kitty and chatting away to her as her son looked thoroughly bored.

Emma watched as Kitty walked to the counter now with Myra.

'That's a record for me,' Emma heard her say. 'Over fifty parents attended! Best session yet.'

'Well done, Kitty,' Myra said. 'It's really quite something to see what you have achieved here. I'll be sure to report back very favourably to that MP I know from my time working in London, he takes child development very seriously. He really does have the ear of the prime minister. Who knows, maybe we'll one day see a Kitty Fletcher School? You must be *so* proud.'

Emma arched an eyebrow. It was amazing how someone as sour as Myra could be so gushing when the time was right.

Kitty puffed her chest out, clearly pleased with what Myra was saying. 'Yes, it's lovely to see my teachings being put into place,' she said as she looked out at a group of teenagers strolling by in the forest. 'Teenagers taking walks in the forest instead of sitting indoors on their phones taking selfies.'

Myra nodded in agreement. 'Good, it gives them a bit of grit. All this staying indoors nowadays makes them soft.'

Emma smiled into her drink. Those very same teenagers had been huddled around a tree earlier, smoking a spliff while one of the girls took a selfie of her exposed breasts. Emma had had to cover Isla's eyes and rush her away as she tried to look through the gap in her mother's fingers.

'If parents knew just what mobile phone use can do to a child's brain,' Kitty said, shaking her head in dismay as she pointed out a loaf of bread to the baker. 'You might as well shoot heroin in their arm.'

'Quite,' Myra said.

Emma's face flushed as she looked at Isla, who was completely engrossed in her game. She thought about quietly telling her to hand over the phone, but then she realised she had no reason to do that. They'd just spent nearly two hours outside, and would be going back that afternoon to do some crafty stuff! Ten minutes playing a game on Emma's phone wasn't going to rot Isla's brain, for God's sake.

No, she refused to let Kitty Fletcher's presence guilt her into depriving Isla of a few minutes of digital fun.

Kitty paid for her bread, then started to leave. But Emma saw Myra jog her in the arm, nodding towards Isla. Kitty paused, then raised an eyebrow before reaching into her bag and walking over to their table.

Emma felt like shrinking into her coat. Instead, she gave Kitty a shaky smile.

'Hello, I believe you're new here,' Kitty said to her.

'Actually, I've been here seven months.'

'New in Forest Grove terms!' Kitty said. She handed a leaflet over, the same one Emma had received about Kitty's workshop the first day she'd moved in. 'All parents are welcome,' Kitty said, her eyes gliding over to Isla, who was still wrapped up in her game. 'The number of parents who have told me what wonders it's done for their children, not least their academic life.'

'Oh yes, thanks, we've got one of these already,' Emma said, doing her best to keep calm under the patronising gaze of Kitty and her new best friend, Myra.

'We do a marvellous digital detox for children,' Kitty continued, looking pointedly at the phone in Isla's hand. 'Screen addiction has been proven to create lasting damage, you know.'

Emma's mouth dropped open. She quickly recovered herself. 'Well, y-y-yes,' she stammered. 'I can imagine if a child is stuck in front of a screen most of the time, it wouldn't be good for them. Luckily, we don't have that problem with Isla.'

Isla looked up at the mention of her name. 'Huh?'

'Looks like she has a problem to me,' Emma heard Myra whisper to Kitty.

'What did you say?' Emma asked, pulse pounding in her ears. Myra could say what she wanted about her, but she wouldn't get away with being rude about her daughter!

'Oh, she's just saying, when you have such beautiful scenery around you,' Kitty said, gesturing to the forest outside, 'why would one need to stare at a phone?'

'We've just spent the morning walking through the forest!' Emma said. 'Jesus, you need to dial it down – it's all about a happy medium, you know? We parents feel guilt-tripped enough as it is.'

Isla looked at her mother in surprise, then her mouth twisted into a smile. 'Go, Mum!'

'Goodness me!' Kitty said. She turned to Myra. 'I can assure you, this isn't how the wonderful mums here *usually* act.' Then the two women stalked out.

Emma felt the tears start to come. She quickly took in a deep breath.

Don't cry here, not here.

Isla put her hand on Emma's. 'Are you okay, Mum? What a cow.'

'Wasn't she just?' a voice said from above them. They looked up to see Tatjana standing over the table with a loaf of bread in her hands. 'I can't believe what Kitty just said to you! Oh Emma, is everything okay? You look like you're going to cry.'

Heat rose in Emma's cheeks.

'I'm fine,' Emma said, quickly blinking the tears away.

Tatjana smiled sadly as she crouched down, her elbows on the table. 'You don't have to pretend,' she whispered as Isla watched them. 'Kitty was out of order. It's the worst, when someone makes a mother feel guilty, am I right?'

Emma nodded, aware of people's eyes on them. 'It is.'

Tatjana leaned back and gestured to her top, which was stained with what looked like yoghurt. 'Do you know, I've had to change *twice* today – in the end I just gave up! It's so hard keeping on top of things, don't you think? I struggle and I'm not even holding down a job like you are.' She looked out of the cafe window towards Kitty, who was striding away towards the forest. 'Ignore that old busybody,' she said. 'You're doing great. I mean, seriously, everyone here likes to pretend they're so *perfect,* don't they?'

Emma smiled in surprise. Maybe she'd got Tatjana all wrong? 'Tell me about it,' she whispered back. 'I bet they're all seething messes under the surface.'

Tatjana leaned towards her, brown eyes sparkling mischievously. 'Oh, I reallllllllly hope so.'

They both laughed.

'We should do coffee sometime,' Tatjana said. 'In fact, what about lunch on Monday? You can come watch the house be delivered. Honestly, I am desperate for someone like you to talk to, I'm going mad stuck in Stepford Grove.'

Emma frowned. Wasn't that moment something they'd want to share as a family, not with some random like her hanging around?

'It's difficult to get out,' Emma said. 'I'm super busy at work.'

'Consider it work. Lawrence *really* needs to sort his social media accounts out,' Tatjana said, gesturing to her husband who was standing outside with their sons. 'Maybe you two could have a quick chat about doing some work for him?'

'Go, Mum!' Isla said. 'It'll be so cool!'

Emma peered towards the forest and the top of the bright-red crane. It *would* be interesting to see the house all come together. More importantly, it would be good to win some new business, too.

What she hadn't realised when she took on the job at the consultancy was that they were in desperate need of new business after one of their major clients dropped them. The last thing Emma needed was the company collapsing.

And yes, she could do with an ally in Stepford Grove too, as Tatjana had referred to it.

She examined Tatjana's face. Her sister always said that there was more to people than met the eye. Maybe she'd been too quick to judge Tatjana? Dele was right, the fact that she looked so much like Jade had clouded Emma's assessment of her.

'Sure,' Emma said, shrugging. 'I usually have lunch at one, so shall we say I'll be at yours by quarter past?'

'Perfect,' Tatjana said. 'I'll make us some nibbles. Can't wait! Enjoy the rest of your weekend, especially you little fashionista,' she added, looking at Isla. '*Loving* the necklace.'

Isla put her fingers to the heart choker she was wearing and smiled.

Tatjana waved at Emma and headed outside.

'You've made a friend, Mum,' Isla said. 'A friend who happens to be the *coolest* person in the village.'

Emma laughed. Yes, she *had* just made a friend.

Chapter Eleven

Saturday 19th September
11.40 a.m.

I need to talk to you about grit, Isla. By now, you may have heard of the term 'snowflake' to describe someone who is over-emotional and easily offended. You will know it intimately yourself, having lived with two snowflakes for the past nine years. What happened in the bakery just now is an example of this. Though I rather enjoyed your fake mother nearly bursting into tears getting told off by Kitty Fletcher, it also made my heart sink.

It just proved to me that Emma Okoro has absolutely no grit about her. Now, 'grit' might sound like a negative term to you, Isla. It might make you think of those little bits of stone that dig into the soft palms of your hands or the thin skin of your knees when you fall over. But think of it like this. Those tiny little bits of stone must be pretty strong to cause such damage, right? Especially when they're all put together.

You need to think of yourself as being made up of all those stones; it's just a case of getting them all together in the right place to get some grit about you. You need to be strong. You need to be focused. And yes, sometimes you need to bruise a few knees, even cut them, to get what you want.

I can easily handle a snowflake like Kitty Fletcher. But your pretend mother fell apart in her presence. Not just today's incident, but yesterday too, when she clocked that she'd 'forgotten' dress-down day. Honestly! Talk about overreaction. But then that's what I hoped for when I had a quick rifle through your bag before the Design Divas session. Something to throw her off guard, make her doubt herself.

To be honest, I wasn't hugely confident that it would be enough just to dispose of the letter. Parents talk about such things with each other. But then I underestimated just how unpopular Emma is.

Now, of course, she thinks she's found a friend. How wrong she is . . .

Chapter Twelve

Emma drove down the main road that linked Ashbridge with Forest Grove until she got to a small turning into the forest, taking the dirt track that led to the huge clearing where the Belafontes' home was to be built. As she approached, she saw a massive area had been filled with concrete to create the house's foundations. Overlooking it all was the famous red crane and behind the foundations, among some trees, was a long, rather luxurious-looking static home.

It was a beautiful day, the sky bright blue. *How lovely it would be to live right in the middle of the forest*, Emma thought as she got out of her car. She often eyed the houses that had gardens backing on to the forest with envy. But they were over £100k more expensive.

'The price people pay for a view,' Dele had said as they compared the two properties online.

As Emma took in the size of the concrete slab before her, she wondered what price the Belafontes were paying for all this.

Emma checked her reflection in the car window and smoothed down her red hair, quickly reapplying her nude lipstick. Then she headed towards the static home, passing three cars – the Jaguar she'd seen, a large Range Rover and a small red Mini Convertible – on the way. Before she could reach the door of the static home, it swung open, Lawrence appearing in the doorway. He was wearing gold-rimmed glasses, his strawberry-blond hair slightly tousled.

'Emma!' he said. 'Tatjana's just waking Phoenix from his nap. Come in, let me get you a drink. The lorry is just thirty minutes away.'

'Thanks.' She stepped in, looking around her. The static home was massive. One end was dominated by a modern-looking kitchen, the other by a dividing wall from behind which Emma could hear Tatjana's voice as her youngest son Phoenix giggled. In the middle was the living space with one large grey sofa across from two mustard armchairs with a low clear coffee table between them, a variety of different foods laid on its surface. On the wall was a blue-and-white painting of a proud-looking African woman.

'What do you fancy drinking? We have everything,' Lawrence said, gesturing towards the large fridge.

'Orange juice would be great. You must be excited about the house being delivered. I heard you're an architect – did you design it?'

'I was involved in the design, yes. Come, sit,' he said. He handed her the orange juice and then gestured to the sofa. He took one of the armchairs across from her and crossed his legs. 'Let's have a quick chat before Tatjana comes in – she mentioned you work in social media?'

Emma nodded. 'I do. I actually took the liberty of doing some research into Belafonte Designs. You have a Twitter account?'

He grimaced. 'Yes, a Twitter account that hasn't been updated for a year. My old PA set it up, but he's left and Myra doesn't have that kind of experience.'

Emma thought of the way Myra had just watched with a smug grin on her face as Kitty talked down to Emma on Saturday. She could get revenge right now, say it was unusual for a PA not to have social media experience nowadays.

But instead, she smiled. 'Don't worry, it happens a lot. I actually think it's Instagram where you need to be. Twitter is fine for connecting with influencers, those high-end clients you might want to engage with. But to really showcase your beautiful work, you should definitely be on Instagram.'

Lawrence leaned forward, regarding her with his sparkling green eyes. 'So is that something you can do, set us up on there?'

'Absolutely,' Emma said enthusiastically. 'We can set up a content schedule, make sure your channel is fresh with regular content, drive up those followers with some tricks of the trade we've learnt. Come up with campaign ideas. There's a whole roster of services we can offer.'

'Would you recommend we wind down our Twitter then?'

She shook her head. 'Nope, you should keep it, but change the focus to be more about engaging with clients rather than showcasing your work. Look, why don't I put a proposal together for you? Then maybe we can have a chat on the phone?'

'That sounds excellent.'

'A proposal featuring all the social media recommendations I've made over the years,' a voice said. They both looked up to see Tatjana walking into the living room, her youngest son in her arms. She was barefoot and was wearing a long olive maxi dress that swished around her smooth dark ankles.

'Yes, my wife has been on at me for a while to sort my social media out.' Lawrence got up and took his son from Tatjana. 'Right, I'll leave you two to it. Phoenix and I need to do a site inspection.' The little boy giggled as Lawrence walked out with him.

'Welcome to our mansion,' Tatjana said sarcastically.

'Well, it is for a static home!' Emma said as Tatjana sat next to her.

'It's not bad, is it? Still, I'm desperate to be out of it and into our new home.' She picked up two wooden plates and handed one to Emma. 'So, lunch. I've gone for a Spanish tapas vibe, I hope that's okay?'

'It's perfect, thanks. You really didn't have to go to all this trouble.'

'It's a pleasure! Drinks!' Tatjana exclaimed. 'I forgot drinks. Wine?'

'Don't worry, Lawrence got me an orange juice.'

'Oh come on, one teensy wine.'

'I don't drink, actually.'

Tatjana paused. 'Really? Why's that?' Emma's face flushed. 'Sorry, I shouldn't pry. I hope you don't mind if I drink though?'

'Of course not.'

Tatjana padded through to the kitchen and pulled a bottle of wine from the fridge, pouring herself a glass. She sat down beside Emma, even closer to her now, and draped her long arm across the back of the sofa.

'It's so nice to have someone to chat to,' she said as she sipped her wine. 'Honestly, the other mums are lovely enough, but a little dull.' She bit her lip. 'Am I allowed to say that?'

'You can say what you want,' Emma said, reaching for her orange juice. 'I thought you were getting on quite well with them all, though.'

'One has to play the school-run game, doesn't one?' Tatjana replied in a faux-posh accent.

'My mum always tells me that,' Emma said. 'She reckons it's the only way a child gets invites to playdates and parties. But Isla's never had any problem with that despite me . . .' Emma paused. Despite her what . . . not being popular?

'*This* is why you're so refreshing!' Tatjana said. 'Someone who knows their own mind. Someone who doesn't feel the need to fit in. It's great!'

Emma took a sip of her juice to hide her embarrassment at the compliment. 'That's very kind of you, but I don't think I'm quite the maverick you make me out to be.' She leaned forward and started piling food on to her plate, just to drive the attention away from her. 'This looks delicious.'

Tatjana filled her plate, too. 'Yes, I made it all last night. I really think the flavour improves when you leave it overnight.'

'You *made* all this?'

'Of course.'

'Wow, impressive. I'm afraid it's M&S all the way for me.'

'Well, you're too busy doing your working-mum thang,' Tatjana said, popping an olive into her mouth.

'Actually, I'm not *that* busy,' Emma said quickly, not wanting Tatjana to think she was obsessed with work. 'I get to leave on time most days, I don't take much work home with me, we have a monitoring rota so that—'

'Oh God, I wasn't criticising, no!' Tatjana said. 'I miss my working days and plan to get right back on it when the little one goes to school.'

Emma laughed nervously. 'Sorry, I can get a bit defensive about being a working mum. It seems like the worst thing you can be around here!'

'That will be Kitty bloody Fletcher's fault. She was so rude to you on Saturday!'

Emma looked down at her plate. She was still reeling from that. When she'd told Dele, he'd wanted to march right over to Kitty's house and have a go at her.

'In fact,' Tatjana said with a mischievous smile, 'I bumped into her during a walk with the boys yesterday and I *had* to get my own back on your behalf.'

Emma peered up at her, curious. 'What did you do?'

84

'I took great delight in telling her I would be returning to work as *soon* as I could. I know how obsessed she is with mums being at home as long as they can. Then I told her how I'd read a study on how beneficial moderate screen time can be for children's creativity. She didn't know what to say!'

Emma laughed. 'I would love to have seen that!' She leaned back against the sofa, feeling relaxed. 'You must be excited about going back to work – is someone else looking after your company while you're off?'

'Oh no, I just let clients know I'm taking a break. I've been doing the occasional piece, though. I finished a stunning wedding dress in the summer.'

'I was checking out your Instagram account, consider me impressed.'

Tatjana put her hand to her chest. 'Why, that *is* a compliment coming from the queen of social media.'

Emma laughed again. 'Hardly. So how long have you been in fashion?'

'It feels like forever.' Tatjana sank back into the chair, too, the light that was coming in from the ceiling window above highlighting just how perfect her skin was. She really was beautiful.

Just like Jade was . . .

Emma pushed the voice away.

'I used to design clothes in my bedroom when I was, I don't know, seven or eight?' Tatjana continued. 'By the time I was in my teens, it was a side hustle, making dresses for my friends and smuggling them into school, getting a fiver a dress. It snowballed from there really.'

'When did it go beyond school friends?' Emma asked.

'When I went to university to study fashion, I knew I needed to take it to the next level or it'd come to nothing. So I signed up for a university course, then opened a market stall during my weekends. That old chestnut, hey?'

'It clearly worked. Where did you grow up?'

'Sussex.' Tatjana stabbed her fork into a cube of cheese. 'Anyway, the stall became a shop, then the shop became a website run from my flat. I mean, honestly, the rent on high-street stores, no wonder the high street is going bust. The website had minimal overheads and the money just flooded in.' The tops of Tatjana's cheeks went red. 'Sorry, that sounds crass, talking about money.'

'No, you should be proud! Is that how you met Lawrence, through the business?'

'No, actually, we literally bumped into each other outside my university digs.' A dreamy expression appeared on her face. 'One look and that was it, love at first sight. Do I sound naive saying that?'

'Not at all. Same with me and Dele.'

Tatjana leaned over and gently clutched Emma's arm. 'How brilliant. See, I *knew* we'd get on. Are you sure you can't stay all afternoon? It would be so lovely to have some female company.'

'Sorry, I'd love to, but I have work, Tatjana.'

'Tat,' she said. 'Call me Tat. All my friends do.'

Emma felt a warmth clutch at her heart. *Friends.* Was that what was happening – they were becoming friends?

Emma realised then just how lonely she'd been since arriving in Forest Grove. It hadn't been an obvious kind of loneliness. She was busy, always doing things. But that was with Dele and Isla. She didn't have any girlfriends to talk to about stuff like this. Sure, she had her sister and her best friend from uni, Jo. But Jo had moved to Australia three years ago. They'd talk over Messenger or WhatsApp, sometimes call too. But it wasn't the same. Not like this, sitting across from another woman, talking about the kinds of things she felt Dele simply couldn't *get* as a man.

'Let me go talk to Lawrence,' Tatjana said, jumping up.

'Honestly, I must get back, I—'

But it was too late, Tatjana was already opening the front door and leaning her head out. 'Lawrence, darling, come here, will you?' she shouted.

A few moments later, he appeared at the door, his son still in his arms. 'Everything okay?'

'Convince Emma to stay all afternoon, won't you? Call her boss, tell her it's business?'

Emma stood up. 'You really don't have to, Lawrence.'

'It's not a problem,' Lawrence said with a beaming smile. 'I've just been checking out your website and your LinkedIn profile on my phone. I'm impressed. We need to sort our social media out and I'm all for working with people we know. I'd love to take you on to help us.'

Emma blinked in surprise. 'But I need to do a proposal. Let you know our fees. I—'

'Oh, he'll pay anything,' Tatjana said, waving her hand about.

'I don't know, I feel like I ought to send the proposal at *least*,' Emma said, feeling a bit overwhelmed by how fast this was going.

Lawrence laughed, his son giggling in response. 'Am I going to have to convince *you* to say yes to new business?'

'Of course not,' Emma quickly said. 'We'd love to work with you!'

'Then it's settled. Send me your proposal tomorrow and we'll get it all signed off,' Lawrence said. 'Now you get to celebrate with my wife.'

'But . . . I have other work to do.'

'I'll call your boss,' Lawrence said with the air of a man who was used to telling people in senior positions what to do. 'I'm sure he'll be very happy to hear his business has just won a new client *and* that I want to buy your time for the next . . .' He looked at his expensive watch. 'Four and a half hours if you finish at six? I'll pop out to pick Zeke up so you can stay here, Tatjana.'

A loud rumble sounded out in the distance and Lawrence turned, a huge smile spreading over his face. 'And just on time, here comes our house.'

'Champagne!' Tatjana said. She darted to the fridge and got out a large bottle of champagne along with some fizzy juice. 'Don't worry, you can have this.'

Emma watched them both, her head spinning. 'I feel bad, being here for your special moment as a family.'

'Don't be silly,' Tatjana said. 'Lawrence will be fawning all over the windows and fittings, won't you, darling? I'll need the company.'

'Absolutely,' Lawrence said.

Emma took a deep breath, looking between these two glamorous, gorgeous, rich and successful people. She thought of the looks stay-at-home mums like Lucy Cronin gave her at the school gates. At the way Dele would say before going out for dinner with his football friends: 'You know you can go out too sometime, don't you?' Or her sister the last time they spoke: 'So anything planned this weekend, other than hanging out with your husband and daughter?'

Emma smiled. 'Go on then!'

What harm could it do?

◆ ◆ ◆

Emma walked towards the school gates the next day, smiling as she thought of the afternoon before. Tatjana was a riot! They'd talked and talked and talked. Lawrence had joined them in-between dealing with Phoenix and picking up Zeke, and he was as charming as his wife.

Even more amazing, Emma got to see the Belafontes' house arrive on board a massive lorry. For some reason, she'd imagined it coming in one piece, balanced atop a trailer. But it actually came delivered like a giant Ikea cupboard with sections piled on top of each other.

Tatjana and Emma had sat watching it being offloaded from the trailer, Tatjana sipping champagne. It really had been quite something to see the German builders put the windows and walls together piece by piece. The whole house would be up and waterproof within seven days, and ready to be occupied by the middle of October. It blew Emma's mind, but then as she spoke more to Tatjana and Lawrence, she realised they were the kind of people who simply got things done.

Their drive and ambition made her think of Harriet. When she declared she wanted to get a job helping others when she was seventeen, she did it, defying their parents' wishes for her to go to university and instead starting work at a housing charity. When she said she wanted to move to London without having a job, she did that too, dragging Emma (who *did* find a job) along with her. It helped that their dad had inherited his parents' old flat so they could live there. No surprise, Harriet found a job herself very quickly and a great one at that. But her methods weren't conventional: after reading an article about a think tank set up by a go-getting twenty-five-year-old, Harriet had waited outside their offices until she saw the woman in question. She followed her to a bar and managed to start up a conversation with her, getting a job offer by the end of the night.

'How very Harriet of you,' Emma had said when her sister had told her, so proud of her brave sister and wishing she had a bit of her chutzpah, too.

Emma felt that same warmth and buzz of being on the edge of something thrilling with the Belafontes that she felt with her sister. Maybe that was why she had decided to stay into the evening, calling Dele to see if he could pick Isla up from her after-school club? She wanted to keep talking to Tatjana. She wanted to keep watching this miracle of a house being assembled before her eyes. When she came home at eight, Dele was happy. 'Good on you,' he'd said.

Emma walked into the playground now and spotted Tatjana straight away, standing with Lucy and Myra. Emma's heart sank when she saw them. She didn't really want to go over with Lucy and Myra there.

But then Tatjana waved to her so Emma joined them anyway, her tummy doing circles.

Jesus, Emma, it's just the school playground!

'How's the head?' Emma asked Tatjana.

'Not good,' Tatjana confessed.

They both burst out laughing.

'What's this all about then?' Myra asked, looking between the two women with a fake smile.

Tatjana linked arms with Emma. 'I drank a little too much champagne in this young lady's company yesterday. She didn't drink a jot and yet still managed to be *such* a laugh!'

Lucy and Myra exchanged surprised looks.

'Then you'll have to come out for coffee with us in a minute,' Lucy said to Emma. 'You can tell us all about it.'

Emma regarded Lucy with surprise. Was that all it took, the nod of approval from a woman like Tatjana? How shallow. But then if it meant the school run might be less awkward, Emma could deal with shallow.

'I'd love to, but I have to go to work,' she replied, giving Lucy an extra-warm smile. She looked at her watch. She needed to somehow write an entire proposal for Lawrence by the afternoon.

'Next time,' Lucy said as the school bell rang.

Now Emma was truly astonished. 'Absolutely,' she said with another smile.

Was she finally fitting in at Forest Grove?

Chapter Thirteen

Welcome to the Mums of Forest Grove Facebook Group

Tuesday 22nd September
12 p.m.

Kitty Fletcher

Can I just say to the person who clearly took a large chunk out of their day to fake a MySpace profile of me that you're fooling nobody. Anyone who isn't blind can see it's a completely doctored image of me. I am speaking to MySpace right now to get it taken down.

Ellie Mileham

MySpace? Wow, been a long time since I saw that site mentioned in a sentence.

Kitty Fletcher

This is serious, Ellie! The page is just awful!

Vanessa Shillingford

You know everyone's going to go searching for the page now, don't you Kitty?

Kitty Fletcher

No skin off my nose. You get used to stuff like this when you're as high profile as me, but this has taken it to the next level.

Rebecca Feine

Do you mean this one, Kitty? Myspace.com/PurpleLoveKitty. I must say, the purple hair really does suit you! ☺ And what IS that you're smoking . . . ?!

Kitty Fletcher

It is NOT me, Rebecca!

Belinda Bell

Are you sure? It looks a lot like you. And that painting on the wall in the background is up in your office, isn't it?

Myra Young

Oh come on, anyone with decent eyesight can see it's not Kitty, and as for the painting, there are several photos of Kitty's office online, it could easily have been taken from that. Whoever has created this page needs to take a long hard look in the mirror considering all Kitty has done for this community.

Vanessa Shillingford

Could it be kids having a bit of fun?

Myra Young

The kids love Kitty here!

Belinda Bell

Says the woman who's lived here less than a month!

Rebecca Feine

'Love' is a bit of a strong word for how people feel about Kitty, Myra . . . weren't some of Kitty's posters which were hung in Forest Grove High defaced a few years back?

Kitty Fletcher

Thank you for bringing that up, Rebecca. May I remind you they found the culprit, one silly little boy.

Tatjana Belafonte

So sorry to hear about this, Kitty. Something similar happened to me after Vogue online ran a piece about one of my designs.

Kitty Fletcher

Ah, you understand what it's like, Tatjana. We had this discussion when we bumped into you at the woods on Sunday, didn't we? I understand even more why you've decided not to return to work if things like this happen. A mother does not need such negativity around them. So what happened to you?

Tatjana Belafonte

A photo was doing the rounds on Facebook suggesting I had my clothes designed in a sweatshop. I found out it was a former university friend who I'd had a falling out with. She had a lot of experience with social media so it was no surprise really, when I look back. Might you have a disgruntled former client, Kitty?

Kitty Fletcher

Oh no, none of my wonderful clients would do this!

Tatjana Belafonte

Then someone you've had a run-in with lately?

Kitty Fletcher

Ah. I did have a bit of an altercation with someone at the weekend, now you mention it. Myra was with me at the time.

Myra Young

I was.

Pauline Sharpe

What happened?

Rebecca Feine

Don't mention names here please!

Kitty Fletcher

I wouldn't dream of it, Rebecca. Certainly food for thought though . . . especially when you mention the fact they'd need to know social media, Tatjana. This person would fit the bill perfectly.

Lucy Cronin

Hmmmm, I think I know who you're talking about. I've heard some other things about this woman that's rung alarm bells for me today.

Ellie Mileham

I think this discussion needs to end before it gets out of hand.

Kitty Fletcher

Fine, comments closed.

Chapter Fourteen

Wednesday 23rd September
8.40 a.m.

Emma walked towards the playground with Isla, checking her phone as she did. She'd sent Lawrence's proposal for her boss to check over the night before and he'd already sent his feedback – it was going to be a busy morning! There was also an email from the school saying the deadline for payment for Isla's trip to Warwick Castle had been extended until the week after next, which was *great* as it meant one less task for her to deal with. She quickly moved the payment reminder to the new date and popped her phone back in her pocket.

She wouldn't be needing her phone now she had other mums to chat to!

She was actually looking forward to going into the school playground that morning. She'd even got tickets for the school disco, which was taking place the next week. In fact, she was going to suggest they all sit at the same table.

In the distance, she saw Tatjana, Lucy and Myra chatting in a circle. She walked over as Isla was pulled away by one of her friends. It felt so good to finally feel part of the 'in crowd'.

But when she approached, all three women fell silent, Lucy and Myra exchanging dark looks.

Emma hesitated. Had she done something wrong?

'Oh look, there's Ellie,' Lucy said. 'I really must chat to her about the harvest assembly. Have a good day!' She hurried off, peering over her shoulder at Emma and frowning.

What was *that* all about?

'I'd better head off, too,' Myra said. She rubbed Tatjana's arm, giving her a smile, then wandered off.

'Do I smell or something?' Emma said, pretending to sniff her armpits.

Tatjana laughed, a light tinkle. 'You smell divine! They're just busy doing mum stuff. Speaking of which, I *must* grab Zeke's teacher, I'm worried he has a bit of a temperature so want to warn them.'

She gave Emma a wave then skipped off, leaving her alone.

Emma bit her lip. Was it her imagination, or were other mums around the playground giving her funny looks?

It was the same the next few mornings and the whole week after that, too. While Tatjana was fine with her, chatting away about how her house was coming along and the big Halloween party they were planning for when it was finished, the other parents seemed to blank her. Emma felt like she was back to being that lonely kid in the playground again.

No, actually, it was *worse* than that. At least she was invisible then. Now she felt *seen* and reproached, too.

What on earth had she done wrong?

She was starting to regret getting tickets for the school disco now. If things continued like this, it was going to be awful!

When the time came for the disco the next Friday, Emma stared at herself in the mirror. Was she a bit overdressed for it? She was wearing a pair of shiny black trousers and a bright-red off-the-shoulder top. Sort of rock goddess/casual-smart. She pushed a stray lock of her red hair behind her ear, peering at her face. Maybe she'd put too much eyeliner on? She grabbed a tissue and rubbed at it.

God, she was just so nervous about it! It wasn't just the fact it was the first school disco they'd be going to in Forest Grove: back in London, the stale sandwiches and awful music didn't really justify much more than a rub of lip gloss and a clean pair of jeans. But everything was so well thought out in Forest Grove. There would probably be a bloody champagne fountain with performances from some trendy local band!

No, it wasn't just that. Emma still had the sense that the other mums were talking about her. It had been the same the past few days, even at the weekend when she'd popped into the courtyard to get some bread and noticed a couple of the school mums giving her what appeared to be filthy looks. She couldn't put her finger on it, but something felt off kilter. Could it be that little to-do she'd had with Kitty Fletcher in the bakery? Or something else?

'Wow. I feel a bit underdressed now,' Dele said as he took in her outfit. He was in his usual uniform of skinny jeans and a checked shirt.

'It's a bit much, isn't it?' Emma said, going to pull her top off. 'I'll wear something else.'

'No, don't!'

'So I look good?'

He paused for a few seconds. 'You look great. Really great,' he said, giving her a quick kiss on the cheek.

'You hesitated!'

He laughed. 'You always say that. Don't read into it, it's just my inability to decipher women's fashion. Remember when I referred to that jumpsuit you wore at Isla's celebration gathering as a boiler suit?'

Emma laughed, too, remembering that day. It had been so special. Isla had been living with them for a few months and had been officially adopted. A few weeks after the court hearing to confirm the adoption, there was a celebration day which gave them the chance to welcome Isla into their family. It had been particularly special for Emma as she just hadn't been able to relax until everything had been made official, thinking any moment that the rug would be pulled out from under their feet and Isla would be snatched away from them. Her nerves had been even worse on the court day itself. Emma and Dele were not allowed to attend, but Jade was – and Emma had spent the day wondering if something would go wrong. But in the end Jade hadn't even turned up and no nasty skeletons had reared their heads.

It all went perfectly.

So when the celebration day arrived, Emma felt relaxed. Emma's mother and Ray had come; Harriet had been there too, along with Dele's parents and two sisters. The only blip was that Emma's father hadn't been there. Though her mother and Harriet had pleaded with Emma not to invite him – the last time he'd attended one of his niece's weddings, he'd got so drunk he'd had to be carried out by his brothers – she felt she needed to. She pitied him. Since her parents' divorce, while her mum flourished, her dad was struggling. He was now living in his parents' old flat – the same flat Emma had once lived in with her sister in London – drinking his life away and refusing any help from anyone. They rarely saw him now, not that they didn't try. He hadn't even met Isla yet, despite Emma offering to bring her to meet him. He simply hadn't replied to Emma's texts or letters about the celebration, though he had sent a small gift of books and a card when Isla came to live with her new parents, and he had once written back to one of Emma's letters that she had filled with photos of his new granddaughter.

Surely he would come to the celebration day, too? This was such an important milestone in Emma's life . . . in his granddaughter's life! But her dad hadn't turned up.

Still, she didn't allow his absence to ruin the day. Isla was wearing a gorgeous white dress; there were balloons and cake. It was wonderful to officially welcome her into their family and after all the ups and downs of the adoption process – and those first few whirlwind months of having this beautiful, energetic and yes, confused and clingy two-year-old in their lives – things were finally beginning to feel normal.

As Emma recalled all this, Isla walked in. She was wearing a plain beige jumpsuit, which Emma was planning to pack away to go up in the loft with the other summer stuff.

'Won't you be a bit cold in that, darling?' she asked her daughter.

'I'm wearing a throw,' Isla declared, lifting a small green blanket up and draping it around her shoulders.

Emma looked at it in surprise. It was the baby blanket Jade had given her! How had it got downstairs? Emma looked through to the spare room to where the sewing machine was waiting to go back up in the loft. It must have accidentally snagged on there when she brought it down the other day.

'That's your baby blanket, darling,' Emma said gently, as Dele frowned.

'I know,' Isla said with a shrug.

'Be careful with it,' Emma continued, searching her daughter's face to see if she understood why it was so important. 'It's the one you came to us in, darling.'

Isla was quiet for a few moments, then she smiled. 'Oh. It goes with my outfit, doesn't it?'

'It does,' Emma agreed. She always felt she was treading so carefully around Isla whenever anything cropped up to remind her she was adopted. They'd been transparent with her from the start and she had her life book to look through, too. But Isla preferred to avoid the subject and rarely mentioned it.

'We ready to go?' Dele asked.

Emma took one last look in the mirror, then nodded.

They all set off, heading towards the forest. As they walked along their road, the air smelt of bonfires and dying leaves.

Isla leaned in close to her. 'It's so dark, Mum!' she said in an excited whisper.

'Not long until Halloween and bonfire night!' Emma said.

She squeezed Isla's hand as they entered the forest. Around them, the trees seemed to press in, the crunch of twigs nearby making Emma jump.

'You're jumpy,' Dele said with a laugh.

'Mum's scaaaaaared!' Isla added.

She *was* jumpy.

When they got to the school, Emma saw the doors to the school hall were wide open, the scent of burgers and frying onions filling the air.

'Loving the look, Isla!' Isla's teacher Miss Morgan said as they passed her. She was so popular with the kids, despite only moving to the village a year ago, and stood out in Forest Grove with her blue hair and pierced nose.

'Shawls are *all* the rage, don't you know?' Dele said as Miss Morgan laughed.

'Daddy,' Isla said in a low hiss. 'You're being sarcy-astic.'

'Yeah, stop being sarcy-astic, Dele,' Emma said as Dele smiled.

Walking into the hall, Emma could see it was already pretty busy. The lights were low and the wooden tables the school used for lunchtimes were set out for parents and children.

'That iPad would've been nicked within five minutes where we used to live,' Dele remarked as he eyed the iPad that was providing music through some speakers.

'Oh, not here in Utopia,' Emma replied, looking around her, pleased the lights were low so people couldn't see her.

'Let's hope they have better beer than Isla's old school too then. Look, Shawn and his wife are there,' Dele said, gesturing towards Shawn and Faye who were sitting with their son at a table in the corner, their twelve-year-old daughter Charlotte chatting to a friend nearby. 'Why don't you go join them and I'll get the drinks,' he suggested to Emma.

Emma looked at Faye. Would she be funny with her, too? Emma had never really talked to Faye – hopefully she was nice. She took Isla's hand and they made their way over to the table.

'I see you've got Dele to work,' Shawn said, gesturing to Dele who was ordering drinks at the bar.

'Isn't that what husbands are for?' Faye retorted, giving Emma a wicked grin as she twirled a lock of her blonde hair around her finger. She usually wore her hair up on the rare occasions Emma saw her in the school playground. Having it down and around her shoulders made Faye look less severe, more approachable.

'Sexist!' Shawn declared.

Faye threw a napkin at him as Emma laughed.

Maybe this disco wouldn't be so bad after all. She took a seat across from Faye, smiling a hello to Shawn.

'You must be Dele's wife,' Faye said. 'I'm Faye.'

She put her hand out and Emma noticed her nails were bitten like her own.

Emma nodded shyly, taking her hand as Isla leaned against her, eyeing the crowds for her friends. 'Nice to meet you, Faye.'

'Please tell me you're drinking wine too?'

Emma pulled a face. 'Sorry, I don't drink, but I make a very good companion to wine drinkers.'

'Good, I'll need a companion tonight. How else am I meant to get through a school disco?' Faye said.

Two of Isla's friends, Poppy and Tegan, ran up to her, pausing as they looked her up and down. They were wearing the standard school-disco outfits for girls of Isla's age: denim shorts over thick tights topped by sparkly jumpers.

'What *are* you wearing, Isla?' Poppy asked.

Isla jutted her chin up. 'It's fashion,' she declared.

'I like it,' Tegan said.

'I agree, Tegan,' Emma said. She liked Tegan. In fact, she imagined she'd get on well with her mum, too, on the occasions she saw her. But she was usually in a rush to get her youngest son to pre-school so they never really had a chance to chat.

'Thanks, Tegan,' Isla said, giving Poppy a glowering look as they headed off to the dance floor.

'I come bearing gifts!' Dele said, weaving through the dancing kids to bring their drinks over. As he passed Emma her lemonade, Tatjana appeared with her husband and kids. She was wearing a jumpsuit *just* like Isla's, a mustard-coloured shawl draped around her shoulders.

Had they consulted or something?

Emma looked down at what she was wearing. She suddenly felt very nineties rock compared to Tatjana's effortless chic.

She watched as Lawrence slung his arm around Tatjana's shoulders, their two boys holding their hands. The whole family looked like they'd stepped out of a Boden catalogue.

Emma saw Isla wave shyly at Tatjana. Tatjana waved back, then gently pushed the boys in Isla's direction. They ran on to the dance floor and Isla took both their little hands as Tegan and Poppy fussed over them too.

Isla looked so much like the boys!

Like siblings.

Emma shifted in her seat.

'There's your buddy,' Dele said as he noticed Tatjana for the first time.

'Buddy?' Faye asked with a raised eyebrow.

'Oh, I had lunch with Tatjana the other week,' Emma said. 'It was in their static home, it's like a bloody mansion!'

'What's she like?' Shawn asked. 'Faye's convinced she's a fake.'

Emma tilted her head. 'A fake?'

'Shawn, honestly, I didn't *quite* say it like that,' Faye said. 'Emma is her friend, remember?'

'Oh, I don't know her *that* well,' Emma said. 'It was more a business meeting. I've done a social media proposal for her husband.'

'Is that how they do business meetings in the world of social media?' Shawn said. 'Having lunch with your client in a static home?'

They all laughed.

'So why do you think she's fake?' Emma asked Faye, intrigued.

'Okay,' Dele said, standing up, his beer in his hand, 'I think this is our cue to find some of the other football lads.'

'Agreed,' Shawn said, standing with him.

When they walked off, Faye shuffled her chair to be closer to Emma's. 'For a start, don't you find her accent weird?'

'How do you mean?'

'Like she's faking it. I swear I heard her slip into a Cockney London accent the other day.'

London? . . . Like Jade.

'I hadn't really noticed it,' Emma said, looking over at Tatjana, who was laughing at something Lucy Cronin was saying.

'You will now I've mentioned it. Another thing. When I asked her about her qualifications to run the Design Divas session . . .' Faye gave her a meaningful look. 'Look, if someone's going to be spending an hour with my daughter, I want to be reassured. Anyway, Tatjana told me she studied fashion at Edinburgh University, but they don't even *offer* fashion there. I just don't trust her,' Faye concluded, watching Tatjana through narrowed eyes as she took another sip of wine.

'I hear you're a solicitor?' Emma asked, feeling uncomfortable talking about Tatjana like that.

'That's right, family law. I hear *you* work in social media. Do you deal with crisis management?'

'Absolutely. In fact, I spent most of today fielding tweets from students at Ashbridge University after their servers broke down.'

'Ouch, poor them. You know, it's the one thing I can't quite wrap my head around,' Faye confessed, 'but I'm finding it increasingly comes up in my job. We deal with a lot of adoption cases and honestly, the number of birth parents managing to track their kids down on social media is ridiculous.'

Emma paused with her drink halfway to her mouth. 'That is interesting. I don't know if you know, but Isla is adopted?'

'I had no idea!' Faye said as she watched Isla on the dance floor. 'How interesting. I always thought how much she looks like you and Dele.'

'You think so?'

'Sure. How old was she when you adopted her?'

'Two. She'd been living with a foster family for a year.'

'And before that?'

'Birth mother.'

'Ah yes, that's when it becomes difficult for us, as the birth parent *does* tend to have more rights if their child has lived with them over a year.'

Emma frowned, and Faye bit her lip. 'Oh God, how insensitive!' Faye said. 'Shawn says I always get too carried away when talking shop. Don't worry, you have nothing to worry about, it's very rare, birth parents coming to look for their kids. How about we change the subject?'

Emma smiled in relief. 'Yes, please.'

'So, how long have you been with Dele?' Faye asked as she watched their husbands talk to some of the other dads.

'Fifteen years. What about you and Shawn?'

'Twenty! Do you know what?' Faye said as she looked at Shawn. 'I didn't fancy him when I first met him.'

'Really?'

'Yeah! I know he's gorgeous, but I never really went for the obvious hot-guy look. *He* had to pursue *me*, can you believe it!'

'I *can* believe it, you're gorgeous!'

'Not with this thing,' she said, referring to her long, slightly crooked nose, which Emma thought actually added to her attractiveness. 'Anyway, it's all different now, of course,' Faye said as she laughed. 'I can't keep my hands off him. Funny, isn't it, how it turns around? He used to be the one that was pursuing me but now I swear to God, I'd go crazy if anyone tried to take my man off me! It's the one thing that just turns me into a monster.'

'*Is* anyone trying to take him off you?'

'Oh, come on, you must see the way the other mums look at him?'

As she said that, Emma noticed Myra making a beeline for him. As far as she knew, Myra was single. She'd heard other mums talking about the fact that she'd split up with her son's father just a year after he was born. Did she have Shawn in her sights? Maybe she didn't realise he was married?

'I'm more into the hot-geek look,' Emma said as she caught Dele's eye and he blew her a kiss.

'Aren't you two cute? So,' Faye said, 'tell me more about the Belafontes.'

Over the thirty minutes while Dele and Shawn talked to various football buddies and checked on the kids, Faye and Emma chatted. Emma found Faye refreshing: outspoken, passionate about her work and confident.

'More wine?' Emma asked her after a while.

'Sure.'

Emma got up and walked to the bar, ordering herself another lemonade and Faye a glass of wine before weaving her way back to the table, not caring when Lucy and Myra watched her. At least Faye was being nice; that was all she needed.

'Emma!'

She looked up to see Dele beckoning her over. He was standing with Tatjana and Lawrence. Emma strolled towards them.

'Thirsty?' Tatjana asked with a laugh when Emma got to them.

'Oh, they're not both for me,' Emma replied, laughing with her. 'The wine's for Faye.'

'We were just talking about the new restaurant that's opened at the courtyard,' Dele said. 'Lawrence and Tatjana have been.'

Tatjana nodded enthusiastically. 'It's fabulous. We really enjoyed our meal, didn't we, darling?'

Lawrence nodded. 'Maybe we can all go there together some time?'

'That'd be great,' Dele said.

'How about tomorrow night?' Lawrence asked. 'We can see if Shawn and his wife want to come, too. I was chatting to Shawn about joining the football team.'

'Nice one! We can do tomorrow, can't we babe?' Dele asked Emma.

Emma hesitated. Two nights in a row being out? She'd much rather be snuggled up with Dele watching Netflix. It had been a busy week.

'If you're too busy with work . . .' Tatjana said, letting her voice trail off.

'I don't work at the weekends,' Emma said, frowning. Why would she say that? 'Of course we'll come, it'll be great.'

As they walked back to the table, Dele examined her face. 'You okay?'

'Oh I'm fine, just hyperventilating at the idea of two nights out in a row, you know me!'

Dele rolled his eyes as he laughed. 'It's called making friends, Emma. I know that's an alien concept to you, my love.'

Emma's mouth dropped open. She shoved the drinks she'd just got at him. 'Do me a favour, will you? Take this to my *friend*, I'm going to the loo.'

Dele flinched. 'Shit. Sorry, Emma, I didn't mean it like that.'

But she didn't listen. She just glared at him, then marched to the toilet. When she got into her cubicle, she sat down on the toilet seat. How dare Dele imply she couldn't make friends – hadn't she just spent half an hour talking non-stop to Faye? Just because she wasn't some exuberant glamorous woman like Tatjana with a zillion friends didn't mean she couldn't *make* friends.

The door to the toilets opened and there was the sound of chatter.

'. . . deserve a night off, for Christ's sake!' a woman with a gravelly voice said. It was Lucy! 'Sammy was up half the night and guess who was up with him?'

'You, of course,' her friend said. Emma recognised that voice too: it was Myra, Lawrence's PA.

'Exactly,' Lucy said. 'The one time I mention to Fraser how unfair it is that I'm always the one getting up, I get told he has to be fully rested for work. Like what I do *isn't* work. I'm on my feet *all bloody* day. The day men think being a stay-at-home mum is work is the day hell freezes over.'

'I have *complete* respect for what you do, even though I work,' Myra said.

'Only part-time!' Lucy said. 'And you were a stay-at-home mum before your divorce.'

'Quite. If my useless ex provided more maintenance, I would still be a stay-at-home mum. Anyway, it's not just *men* who don't get what hard work it is,' Myra said. 'Some women think the same too.'

'Really?' Lucy said.

'Yep.' Myra lowered her voice. 'Women like Emma Okoro.'

Emma put her hand to her mouth in shock. She leaned close to the door, half wanting to hear what was said next, half not.

'I heard she *really* looks down her nose at stay-at-home mums,' Myra continued. 'Apparently, she thinks they're a lazy bunch with too much time on their hands.'

Emma's face flushed. She'd never said anything *like* that!

'She's always been a bit cold though, don't you think?' Lucy commented, the anger evident in her voice. 'The way she stands there glued to her phone.'

'Pretending she's looking at work emails but I bet it's just the *Daily Mail*,' Myra said.

They laughed.

'Not just that.' Myra lowered her voice. 'You know that post on Kitty's Facebook group about someone doctoring her MySpace page? We all said it would need to be someone with social media experience, and guess who has it?'

'Emma Okoro,' Lucy whispered.

Emma's eyes flooded with tears. Bloody Myra! Why was she trying to accuse Emma?

A small thought occurred to her then. Myra worked for the Belafontes . . . and she'd told Tatjana about Kitty's MySpace page when she had lunch with her the week before. They'd also talked about the struggle between staying at home and working, but Emma hadn't said she thought stay-at-home mums were *lazy*.

Had Tatjana twisted their conversation so it sounded like Emma had insulted working mums? But why?

To discredit you, a small voice said.

She saw Isla's birth mother in her mind again, Jade's face overlapping with Tatjana's.

She thought of what Faye had said: *The number of birth parents managing to track their kids down is ridiculous.*

She shook her head. No, no, Tatjana was not Jade!

She waited until the two women left, then opened her cubicle door. If she were her sister, she'd have gone out to confront them. But what good would that do? Lucy was the mother of one of Isla's best friends; she couldn't jeopardise that friendship. She'd find another time to talk to her.

She leaned her hands on the sink, looking at herself in the mirror. Then she took a deep breath and applied more lipstick before walking back out into the hall, her mind still churning over what she'd overheard. As she walked towards Dele and Isla, the music seemed to be louder, the room darker. Eyes turned towards her, and to Emma they seemed accusing, angry.

She saw Tatjana chatting to Lucy and Myra nearby. They were all laughing about something.

Was it Emma they were laughing about?

Emma suddenly felt like all the breath had been sucked out of her. She needed air!

She ran out of the school hall, stepping into the darkness.

Chapter Fifteen

I follow Emma as she runs outside and I hide in the shadows to the side of the hall, watching her.

She's standing under a nearby tree, her face lit up by the light from her phone as she talks into it.

Who's she talking to?

Whoever it is, that phone seems to always be in her hand. It's all she can look at! It gets more attention than you, Isla! No wonder she's getting so pally with that Faye woman . . . she's the same, head in her work and nothing else. How awful for you, my darling Isla, to be so low on her priority list.

I want to grab the phone from her hands right now and smash it against a nearby tree.

Emma pauses, looking around as though sensing my eyes on her.

She's a little more astute than I thought. Certainly more astute than her new friend Faye was a moment ago, stumbling across the dance floor. Reminds me of my mother after returning from my parents' daily evenings out at the pub, stumbling into the living room, not even asking how me, an eight-year-old, had coped the whole evening looking

after my little brother alone. Or the time they turned up at parents'
evening so out of it, the teachers had to call the police.

I know this might not be pleasant to hear about your grandparents,
Isla, but it's important you know exactly how far I've come . . . and
how a difficult upbringing can give you the grit required to navigate
your future.

Like the way I'm navigating this now, my little strategy to get you
back. Just a little tweak here, a small push there, and soon your fake
mother will be exposed for what she is: a useless parent.

But is it really enough to hide school letters and spread a few
rumours?

In fact, what if I strode over to her right now and picked that log
up by her feet, smashed her head in? Dragged her by the legs into the
forest, then left her there?

I look around. There's nobody else out here. It would be easy
enough.

But no, I have to be patient.

I have something in the pipeline, after all. Something that may
upset you, Isla, but it'll be worth it.

I slip back inside.

Chapter Sixteen

Emma peered around her in the darkness, her skin prickling.

'You okay?' her sister's voice said on the phone.

'Yeah, just thought I heard something.' Emma wrapped her arms around herself.

'Look, just rise above it. The school gate can be vicious. They really are a bunch of bored school mums, clearly. As for Tatjana, she must have been gossiping about you. Can't be a coincidence it's the exact same things you talked about over lunch.'

Emma peered towards the disco. 'But Tatjana seemed so nice! I can't believe she'd spread rumours about me.'

'Ask her!'

'I can't face going back in there.'

Dele appeared at the doorway to the hall then.

'Gotta go,' Emma whispered. She quickly tucked her phone back into her pocket as he strolled over.

'Where's Isla?' she asked him coldly.

'Shawn and Faye are keeping an eye on her.' He sighed. 'I'm sorry, babe, I shouldn't have said what I said. It was wrong of me, a really naff attempt at a joke.'

Emma flexed her jaw. 'You were right, though, I do struggle to make friends. It's always been so easy for you. You don't know what it's like standing in that school playground with no one to talk to. It's not like I don't try.'

Dele took her hand. 'I didn't realise it was like that for you.'

'Well, it is. It was the same at school, Harriet was always the popular one.'

Dele frowned, looking down at his feet. 'I wish you talked to me more about stuff like this.'

'Why would I when you say things like making friends is an alien concept for me?'

He flinched. 'That was out of order, I see that now. Come here,' he said, pulling her close. At first, she resisted. But then she found herself sinking into him. 'I like the fact you're shy,' he whispered in her ear.

'Maybe it's not good for Isla, though. For her sake, I should be making more of an effort.'

'Isla seems perfectly happy to me. But it doesn't harm, does it? That's why it'll be good for us to go out for dinner with Lawrence and Tatjana tomorrow.'

Emma stiffened in his arms. Should she tell him about what she'd overheard and her worries that Tatjana might be behind the rumours?

No, not until she'd spoken to Tatjana. It might have nothing to do with her!

'Shall we go get Isla and head home?' he suggested.

Emma thought about it. 'No, she's having a good time. Let's stay for a bit longer.'

When they walked back inside, Isla was still dancing with her friends. Emma went over to her and picked her up, swirling her around as Isla giggled. Tonight was about Isla. Harriet was right, she shouldn't let the other mums get to her.

Then she looked over at Tatjana, who was watching them intently. Emma caught her eye and smiled.

Tatjana frowned, then turned away.

◆ ◆ ◆

Emma walked towards the village courtyard the next night, Isla's hand clutched in hers, Dele's arm around her shoulders. Capadocia was a smart Turkish mezzo restaurant with a wooden interior. They passed the courtyard tree, which was draped with fairy lights. It was very pretty at night, all the other buildings displaying solar lights in their windows, creating an almost festive feel.

As they approached the restaurant, Emma could already see Tatjana in there. No surprise, she looked stunning in a long mustard silk dress that on anyone else would look OTT for dinner at a small restaurant like this, but somehow it worked on her.

Emma took in a deep breath. Could she really be behind those rumours?

Dele rubbed her back, sensing her unease, even though she hadn't told him what she'd overheard.

As they walked inside, Tatjana gave them all a hug. 'Welcome!' she gushed as though she were welcoming them to her own home. 'Come on,' she said, taking Isla's hand. 'The others are waiting for you.'

They followed Tatjana to the back of the restaurant towards a large table. To Emma's surprise, sitting at the table with Shawn and Faye . . . were Lucy and Myra, too!

'I didn't realise they were coming,' Emma said, that conversation she'd overheard in the toilets still at the forefront of her mind.

'We thought we'd make it a bit of a party,' Tatjana said. 'The more the merrier,' she added with a smile.

Emma examined her face. Was that smile genuine?

'All right mate,' Dele said as he shook Shawn's hand.

'You can't get rid of me,' Shawn said as Faye waved at Emma.

Emma waved back, then looked around the table. The only place she could sit was right next to Lucy and across from a prim-looking Myra.

'There's only room for two here,' Emma said.

'Oh, the little fashion superstar will be with me and the other children at the fun end,' Tatjana said, gesturing to the other end of the table where her two boys were sitting along with Lucy's daughter Poppy, Myra's son Justin and Faye's two children.

Isla looked delighted at the idea.

Emma was about to protest, but Dele put a calming hand on her back, so she nodded and sat by Lucy who gave her a cold smile.

'Hello, we met when you moved in,' Lucy's husband Fraser said as he leaned over his wife to greet Emma. He was short with a receding hairline and ruddy cheeks. He'd visited them on their first week to go through the challenges of living so close to a forest. It was clear he took his new job as forest ranger very seriously. Emma wondered what he thought about the Belafontes living right in the forest, vulnerable to any storms.

He gave Dele a salute. 'Hello, football buddy.'

Dele saluted back. 'All right mate. Where's the little one?' he asked, referring to Lucy and Fraser's two-year-old son.

'With his grandparents . . . might get a decent night's sleep,' Fraser added with a wink.

A waiter came over. 'Drinks?'

'I hear you work in social media, Emma?' Fraser asked as everyone ordered their drinks. Lucy stared frostily ahead, sipping at her water.

'That's right,' Emma replied.

'I don't think I've ever met anyone who actually *works* in social media,' Fraser said.

'That's because you work with trees, darling,' Lucy said, putting her hand on her husband's knee.

'Must be nice, working amongst nature,' Emma said.

'Actually, Fraser is very busy,' Lucy said. 'Just like you, Emma. Except *unlike* you, he doesn't always have his head in his phone. More iTree than iPhone,' she said with a high-pitched laugh, as Myra suppressed a smile.

Emma felt a flush creep across her cheeks.

Silly cows.

'Actually, work's not the reason I look at my phone, I'm usually looking at the *Daily Mail*,' Emma snapped back, repeating what she'd overheard Myra say about her.

Myra blinked rapidly and Emma could see she was wondering if Emma had indeed overheard her. At the other end of the table, Tatjana was clearly listening too, her head tilted slightly.

'I hope it doesn't give the impression I'm too *cold*,' Emma added for good measure. 'But one has to keep up with all the Kardashian gossip.'

Myra laughed nervously, then waved for the waiter. 'Actually, can I have wine?'

Emma smiled to herself. She was rattling Myra. Great! She was clearly channelling her sister today! Harriet would be proud.

Over the next twenty minutes, Emma shared some social media stories with a surprisingly interested Fraser: like the time the MD of one of her big household name clients accidentally posted a link to a porn site from the company Twitter account. By the end of the conversation, Lawrence was joining in too, sharing hilarious stories about other architects he knew. The group were all getting on brilliantly . . . apart from Lucy and Myra, who both seemed strangely quiet, and Tatjana, who was more preoccupied with the children, *especially* Isla.

'I'd recommend the sea bass,' Tatjana said as they all looked at the menus. 'They call it *levrek*, it's simply delicious. The boys in particular like it, don't you, boys?'

Her sons nodded enthusiastically as Isla wrinkled her nose. She was so fussy, even though Emma and Dele had tried hard to make her try different foods.

'Oh, don't you like fish, darling?' Tatjana asked Isla.

Darling?

'It's okay,' Isla said with a shrug, but it was obvious from her tone it was anything but okay. 'I prefer pizza though.'

'Yep, my two as well,' Faye said. 'Actually, have they got a kids' menu?'

'Oh, I hope not!' Myra said. 'I just don't get children's menus, full of absolute crap like pizza and nuggets. Why not just do mini versions of the adult meals?' Emma noticed Myra's voice had gone up an octave and had a slightly hysterical tone to it.

'Totally agree!' Lucy said.

'You sound like Kitty Fletcher,' Faye said, and Emma couldn't help but smile.

'I'd take that as a compliment if I were you, Myra,' Lucy said, jutting her chin out. 'All Myra is saying is that if you fill your children with crap, their brains will turn to crap.'

Isla's shoulders sank, and Emma felt like getting up and taking her in her arms.

'I'm a huge fan of pizza actually,' Lawrence said to Isla. 'Hasn't done me any harm, has it?'

Isla's eyes lit up, and Emma wanted to reach right over and hug Lawrence for that.

Everyone around the table laughed except for Lucy and Myra.

When their food was brought over, Emma watched with amusement as Poppy looked at her seabass with utter disgust.

'Well, *bon appétit!*' Lawrence said, lifting his glass.

Everyone echoed him, then tucked into their food, apart from Myra's son Justin who, despite Myra's constant nagging, refused to touch his sea bass and instead stole one of Isla's chicken nuggets.

'He's got a bit of a funny tummy,' Myra said, trying to make excuses for her son.

Lawrence caught Emma's eye and they both smiled.

'So, I was impressed with your proposal,' he said. 'I'll get Myra to send the letter of agreement to you as soon as she can, then we can get to work.'

'Can't wait!' Emma said. And she really couldn't. She'd never worked with an architect before and was looking forward to the challenge. Though she wasn't sure how she felt about having to liaise with Myra.

Lawrence examined her face. 'You clearly enjoy your job.'

'I love it.'

'I keep telling Tatjana she ought to return to her business. She just has this thing about wanting to be there *every* second for the boys.'

'I thought she was returning? That's what she told me.'

Lawrence looked surprised. 'Really?'

'Maybe I misheard.'

He looked down the table at his wife, a worried expression on his face. 'You know, I thought I'd see more of you after you came over for lunch the other week. I'm sure Tatjana mentioned something about going to the Neck of the Woods or getting takeaway in one night?'

Emma laughed nervously. 'Really? I can't remember.'

He paused for a moment. 'I know Tatjana can be . . . challenging sometimes,' he said quietly.

Emma looked at him in surprise. 'Really? How do you mean?'

'She's a bit fragile, you know. Beneath that confident exterior, she's quite an insecure soul.'

Emma looked at Tatjana, who was now curling her finger around Isla's hair and showing her how to pin it behind her ear.

'She was worried about moving here,' Lawrence continued. 'You know, being the only black person in a village like Forest Grove. So it was a relief when she met you guys.'

Emma felt bad for suspecting Tatjana of spreading rumours then. What reason would she have? Maybe Tatjana had just mentioned something in passing to Myra and it had spiralled out of all proportion.

'Mum,' Isla shouted down the table, excited, 'Tat just said I can go to the London Fashion Show next year!'

'I was just telling Isla about how *fab* London Fashion Week is,' Tatjana said. 'I'm planning on taking the boys next year, and it'll be easy to get an extra ticket – my friend Flavia helps with the show's PR.'

'Ah yes, Flavia,' Lawrence said to Emma with an eye roll. 'Honestly, you should meet this guy. Last time I saw him, I swear he was wearing a peacock for a hat.'

Everyone laughed.

'You love him really,' Tatjana said.

'Can I go, Mum, please?' Isla begged.

'We wouldn't let you go without one of us, darling,' Emma said firmly.

'Dad?' Isla asked, turning to her father.

Dele shook his head. 'No, maybe when you're older though.'

Isla crossed her arms. 'That is so unfair, you're both so basic.'

All the adults exchanged confused looks.

'What do you mean, basic?' Dele asked.

'It's slang for boring,' Myra said, her eyes on Emma. Emma wasn't misreading the look in them; they were full of spite.

'Boring?' Emma said, putting her hand to her chest in mock shock. 'How could you call me *boring*? I have a purple phone case, for God's sake.'

'Stop being so sarcy-astic,' Isla huffed.

That was it, the whole table fell about laughing; even Lucy couldn't help it. But Myra stayed stoic.

'Well, the ticket's hers if you change your mind!' Tatjana said. 'I wouldn't be surprised if a modelling scout made a beeline for her while she's there, she's such a beauty!'

Emma couldn't help but feel a bit uncomfortable. She really *did* fawn over Isla, but then maybe it was like Lawrence and Dele had said: it was refreshing for Tatjana to see Isla so happy in a small, mainly white village like Forest Grove.

'She's not beautiful when she's dribbling in her sleep,' Dele said jovially.

'Dad!' Isla said, cheeks flushing.

'I've been wondering since I met you actually, Dele,' Tatjana said. 'Are you of Nigerian heritage?'

'Yes, spot on,' Dele said. 'And yours is . . . Jamaican?'

Tatjana shook her head. 'Nice try. No, Bahamas.'

'Isla is of Bahaman heritage!' Dele said.

Tatjana frowned. 'But if *you're* of Nigerian heritage . . .'

'Isla's adopted,' Emma explained.

Lucy and Fraser exchanged a look. She presumed they might know, but then Isla didn't really mention it.

'Well, that makes you extra special,' Lawrence said to Isla.

They all continued eating, chatting about work, the weather, how drunk one of the dads had got at the disco the night before.

'So, did you get the list of items the kids need to take on the Warwick Castle trip?' Fraser asked Emma as their pudding was brought over.

'I didn't get a list,' Emma said. 'Anyway, isn't the payment deadline next week?'

Lucy shook her head. 'No, it was last week.'

'But it was extended, right?' Emma asked. 'That's what it said in the email.'

Lucy's brow wrinkled. 'What email?'

Emma dug around in her bag for her phone. 'There was an email that went out from the school saying the deadline was extended.'

Lucy shook her head. 'I didn't get an email. All the places have been allocated. We got the letters yesterday to confirm. Any children's parents who missed the deadline don't have a space,' she added primly. 'I'm afraid if you haven't paid, Isla isn't going.'

'What?' Isla said overhearing the conversation. 'But I'll be the only one in class not going!'

'Emma?' Dele asked.

Emma's heart started pounding in her ears. 'If you just give me a second.' She found her phone and went into her work email, scrolling through it with a trembling finger. 'Bugger,' she said, unable to find the email. 'I must've deleted it after I added the new payment deadline to my Google calendar.'

'Are you sure you didn't just miss the deadline?' Myra asked.

'I bloody didn't!'

The table went quiet and Emma's cheeks flushed.

'This is the worst day of my life,' Isla said, slumping back down in her chair as Tatjana pouted and rubbed her back. 'You *always* forget stuff, Mum. It's so unfair!'

'I do not!' Emma said, feeling tears prick at her eyes. As she said that, she was sure she saw Tatjana's lips quirk into a little smile.

'Isla, don't be rude,' Dele said. 'I'm sure we'll get this all cleared up.'

Emma bit at her nails. She did *not* imagine that email!

She couldn't relax for the rest of the evening. All she could think about was the Warwick Castle trip. She was *so* sure she'd got an email!

When they were back home, Emma composed an email to the IT person at work, Suzie. She was an absolute whizz-kid when it came to things like that; maybe she could retrieve the email? She wouldn't mind doing Emma a favour – she was desperate to get a pay rise and knew how well Emma got on with their manager, Saul. Emma clicked send, then buried her phone back in her pocket.

When she went to the school's reception on Monday and explained the issue, she was told by the head teacher Mrs Gould that there was no way Isla could go on the trip now. 'You must have misread one of our emails,' Mrs Gould said, clearly sceptical because Emma couldn't even show her what she'd received.

When Emma got into work, she opened her messages to see that Suzie had managed to retrieve the deleted email.

'Yes!' she said as she opened it.

It looked *just* like the usual school email, with the logo and everything. But when she clicked on the 'from' field, she had to double take. While the name was what she was used to – simply 'Forest Grove Primary' – the actual email address it was cloaking was a strange one she didn't recognise: info@67584912.co.

She looked at past emails from the school and clicked the 'from' fields. They were all the same, not this weird address.

Her breath quickened. Did this mean the email was *faked*?

She quickly wrote back to Suzie, who wasn't in yet, asking if the email could be faked and if so, whether she could find out who sent it.

Suzie replied quickly:

> *Yep, looks like someone has faked this email to you, sorry hon. As for tracing: that's the interesting thing about this (and what made me think it's faked). Usually it's pretty easy to trace an email back to its source IP. But whoever sent this has used some pretty sophisticated kit to stop me doing that. They mean business! You want me to try to track it? On a train at the mo but can look when I'm at my desk in 20 mins?*

Emma wrote back an instant 'yes'.

After a meeting that afternoon, Suzie was waiting for her at her desk.

'You traced it?' Emma asked her.

'Yep.' Suzie handed over a printout. It all just looked like nonsense to Emma. 'See this?' Suzie said, pointing at an address she'd highlighted. 'That's the person's host address. It's located in the Bahamas.'

Emma's heartbeat trebled. Tatjana came from the Bahamas! Surely she couldn't be behind this?

'Can you track down exactly who sent it?' Emma asked.

Suzie shook her head. 'Sorry, babe, no. But you can contact the host to try to get them to hand over details. It's unlikely though.'

'You really are a genius.'

Suzie smiled. 'It's a pleasure. I *live* for this kind of stuff.'

Emma looked at the time. Nearly two thirty. If she left now, she might be able to have a quick word with the head teacher and show her the email before picking Isla up.

She turned off her computer and grabbed her bag. 'I'm going to leave early,' she called out to everyone. 'Have a bit of a headache.'

She darted out of her offices and drove to the school. When she got there, she marched into the main reception area, instantly catching sight of the head teacher at a copier machine.

'Mrs Gould!' she called. 'May I talk to you about something?'

She looked up. 'Of course, Mrs Okoro.' Mrs Gould led Emma into her small office, which had a view of the forest beyond.

'Remember I told you I got an email saying payment for the Warwick Castle trip was delayed?' Emma said.

'Yes.'

Emma got her work iPad out and opened the message Suzie had forwarded. 'My IT person managed to track it down. Looks like a normal email from the school, right?'

The head teacher leaned forward to look. 'It does,' she admitted. 'But we certainly didn't send this, there was no extension.'

Emma zoomed in on the 'from' field, flicking on it. 'Recognise this domain?'

The head teacher blinked as she looked at it. 'That's strange. The email address is wrong.'

'Precisely,' Emma said.

'It's not just that,' the head teacher added, zooming in even more. 'That's our old logo. All emails sent out this term would have the new logo.'

'Then it *is* a fake?' Emma said, feeling vindicated.

'Let's not be hasty, we'd have to look into it,' the head teacher said carefully. 'Is there any reason you think someone might fake something like this, Mrs Okoro?'

Emma thought about it. *Was* there a reason? She couldn't help but think of Tatjana, especially with the Bahamas link. But that really could just be a coincidence. Maybe it was Myra – she worked for the Belafontes, after all, and could be using their host in the Bahamas.

But why? What would her motivation be?

Emma shook her head. 'No.'

'Rest assured, Mrs Okoro, we will do all we can to find out who faked this email. We take racism very seriously here.'

'Racism?' Emma said. 'I didn't say anything about racism.'

'No, no, of course, it's just one of the possibilities,' the head teacher replied. 'Could you forward the email to me, Mrs Okoro?'

'Sure,' Emma said, forwarding the message as she spoke, her mind still on the idea that this might be something to do with racism. 'I hope Isla is allowed on the trip now in light of this? I can pay today.'

'Absolutely.' The head teacher stood up and surprised Emma by putting her hand on her arm. 'I appreciate you letting me know about this. I'll keep you posted.'

'I really appreciate that, thanks.'

That night, Emma took the chance to mention it all to Dele, not just the faked email but what she'd overheard Myra and Lucy saying at the disco.

'The weird thing is,' she said carefully, 'Suzie traced the host back to the Bahamas. Guess who else comes from the Bahamas?'

'You're saying Tatjana is behind all this?'

'Well, she could be the source of the rumours, we did talk about all that stuff the other week.'

'Nope,' Dele said, shaking his head. 'Just doesn't ring true to me.'

'Then who the hell is behind all this? I did wonder about Myra with her having access to their server, if it is based in the Bahamas. What if she's trying to get revenge for the parking incident?'

'Come on, that's ridiculous!'

Emma nodded. It did seem far-fetched.

Dele was quiet for a few moments, then sighed. 'How many black kids are there in Forest Grove, Emma?'

'I know what you're saying. Mrs Gould seemed to think the same thing. But I don't think it's that. Sure, there are a lot of pale faces around the village, but we've *never* encountered any racism.'

'Really?' Dele asked. 'What about the smashed window?'

Emma frowned. He was right.

'Look, I didn't want to worry you about the window, but I *did* wonder if it was a racially motivated attack. You have to consider it as a possibility, Emma,' Dele said, 'especially with the Belafontes now moving in, and Myra's kid is mixed race, too. It could really get some old racist dude's back up, right? All these "foreigners" moving into his precious village,' he said mockingly. He took Emma's hand, looking into her eyes, his own brown eyes sympathetic. 'You have to agree it's more likely than it being Tatjana or even Myra? What motive would they have?'

As he said that, she suddenly saw Jade Dixon's face overlapping with Tatjana's in her mind again.

'Emma?' he asked.

'I don't know,' she said, frowning. 'I really don't know.'

'You look tired, babe,' Dele said.

'I am. All of this has been stressing me out.'

'We'll be able to relax a bit in Dartmouth this weekend.'

They were visiting her mum and stepdad, which sounded relaxing, but was usually anything but for Emma.

'Don't worry,' Dele said, stroking her arm. 'We'll figure this out together.'

She smiled at him. 'I hope so.'

Emma was super organised for the rest of the week. She needed to be on the ball so that whoever was doing this to her wouldn't have another chance to make her slip up. She set her alarm an hour earlier, ensuring she and Isla were ready well on time. They even had time to walk through the woods to school. She did bump into Tatjana on a few occasions but found herself trying to avoid her, which was easy enough because Emma spent most of her time in the playground chatting to Faye. They even met up for a quick coffee one lunchtime. It made Emma wonder if she had been more open to chatting to the other mums, she might have made more friends those first few weeks.

Well, what did it matter? She *had* made a friend.

By the time the weekend came around, Emma felt ready for the trip to Dartmouth. Their window still hadn't been replaced and Emma was finding being in the house slightly claustrophobic. They arrived late in the night on Friday and were up early the next morning, crabbing from the embankment, Isla's favourite thing to do on their visits there.

Emma nursed a takeaway coffee from a bench, looking out at the River Dart as Isla caught crabs with her grandparents and Dele, Harriet watching from nearby.

Emma caught her sister's eye and smiled.

She was tall compared to Emma, all her genes from their dad's side. She was wearing her favourite thick teddy coat, the colour of copper leaves, with a bright-purple hairband in her long blonde hair. She was the kind of woman who drew glances from strangers as they passed, not because she was particularly beautiful – she wasn't – but more because her inner vivaciousness shone through.

Emma leaned her head back, enjoying the autumn sun on her skin. It really was so nice here. It was easy to forget that sometimes – thoughts of her hometown tangled with memories of darker times. She hoped her mum and Ray understood why she didn't come back as much as she should. Being here now made her realise that despite all that had happened here, she ought to make the effort more. It was a child's paradise with crabbing plus a castle and a mermaid statue. But it hurt too much being there, even now, on a beautiful day like this.

It hurt to remember.

Emma shook her head. She wouldn't think of all that. She had other things to think about, like that fake email and those rumours.

She still couldn't shake the feeling that Tatjana might be involved.

But why would she do this?

She got her phone out and found Tatjana's Instagram page again, scrutinising photos of her. She really *was* the spitting image of Jade if you imagined her short hair longer and added a few pounds.

'I caught you!' her mum said, strolling over. 'Checking work emails, I bet?'

'Actually, *Mother*, I wasn't.'

'She looks glamorous,' her mother said, peering over her shoulder at Tatjana's account.

Emma tucked the phone back in her pocket. 'Yep, she is.'

'A friend?'

'Not really.' Emma smiled at her mum. 'You look like you've lost weight, Mum,' she said, taking in her mother's newly svelte figure.

'Weight Watchers is working wonders,' her mother said.

'It suits you.'

'Thanks, darling.'

In fact, everything about her mum's life with Ray suited her. It felt good to see her happy after all these years. They had a lovely flat just a few minutes' walk away from the river. Despite being in a completely different area from the one Emma and Harriet had grown up in on the other side of Dartmouth, it still felt the same in many ways. Same floral sofa, same cat ornaments, same mahogany glass-fronted units, same photos littering the walls with one main photo of Emma and Harriet as teenagers taking centre stage.

Emma watched as Ray helped Isla catch another crab. Ray was a good man. They'd met ten years ago, two years after Emma's mum finally left Emma and Harriet's dad. Her dad, though . . . well, he hadn't been so lucky. Emma knew she'd played a role in his downward spiral. But she really had done all she could. How could you help someone who didn't want helping?

Emma's mother took a seat by her daughter and peered out at the vast estuary in front of them. 'You're lucky, it was hailing yesterday,' she said.

'It always seems sunny here when we come down.'

'Always?' her mum remarked with a raised eyebrow. 'You mean the sum total of five days you've been here with Isla this year?'

'Mum, come on, don't give me a guilt trip, it's a long way to come.'

'I know, it took us four hours each way all the times we've come to visit you this year.'

Emma frowned, swirling her coffee around in her cup. In the distance, she noticed Harriet watching them, her brow creased.

'We're busy,' Emma said. 'You guys are retired now, you have more time.'

Her mother put her hand on her arm and squeezed it. 'Don't worry, love, I understand. I was only joking around. I'm pleased you're here now, that's what counts. God, she gets bigger and bigger every time I see her,' she said as she watched Isla.

'Doesn't she?'

'I remember the first time I held her, seems an age ago.'

'Same,' Emma whispered as she thought back to that time. It had been hard for her mum, as she'd had to wait a couple of weeks before seeing her new granddaughter. But Emma and Dele had been advised not to rush into introducing Isla to people. That first time they met, they decided to go to a park – neutral ground, as the social worker had advised. Isla had been shy at first, clinging to Emma. But it wasn't long before she was giggling as Emma's mother pushed her on a swing. Later, as Emma watched her mother holding Isla close, she'd had to leave the room, as she started crying. It had just been so wonderful to finally see her mother with a much-longed-for grandchild in her arms. Emma remembered hoping in that moment with all her heart that she and Isla would have the same relationship that she had had with her mother, one built on love, understanding and friendship, too.

Emma sunk her head on to her mother's shoulder now, just as she used to when they would sit in this very same spot many years ago. They sat together in silence, taking in the quiet amble of a boat nearby, the flight of a seagull above.

'Have you spoken to your dad lately?' her mum asked after a while.

Emma sighed. 'I sent him a text, no reply.'

'I wish he'd meet someone,' her mum said now. 'A good woman to get him back on his feet.'

'No chance, Mum. You didn't put up with his drinking in the end, why would anyone else?'

'He's a good man, beneath it all.'

Emma wondered if her mum had meant to say 'before it all'.

There was the sound of running as Isla came up, her bucket swinging from her hands. 'Look, Mum, look! Crabs, loads of them.'

Emma fixed a smile on to her face. 'Wow, seven of them! How awesome are you? I don't think I got that many when I was a kid.'

'Dad helped.'

'Yep, that's me, crab-catcher extraordinaire,' Dele said as he walked over with her, puffing his chest out, Harriet rolling her eyes behind him.

Emma laughed, but then her laughter trailed off as she recognised a couple approaching from the distance.

Harriet followed her gaze, face clouding over.

It was their old next-door neighbours, the Coopers. They looked so much older now, and when Emma thought about it, that shouldn't be a surprise; they were probably in their seventies. Emma and Harriet had grown up with their sons, Ed and Charlie, and the two families had been as close as you could get until Emma's parents had to move away.

Emma's mother clutched her daughter's hand, a gesture of reassurance.

'Hello,' she said, smiling at the pair.

The couple nodded at her, but didn't say anything. Instead, their eyes passed over to Emma, and Emma could see the memories in them. She smiled at them, because what else could she do? They gave her a faint smile back, then continued walking.

As they passed by, Emma let out a breath she didn't realise she'd been holding in.

'Who were *they*?' Dele asked, clearly sensing the tension.

'Our old neighbours,' Emma's mother said.

'I see,' Dele said sombrely.

Emma's mum stood up, taking her granddaughter's hand. 'Come on you, let's go put those crabs back.'

'You okay?' Dele asked Emma when her mother was out of earshot. 'I know it's tough coming back here with the anniversary around the corner.'

Emma nodded, watching as the Coopers disappeared from sight.

'Dad, look!' Isla shouted.

'You all right if I go over?' Dele asked.

'Yes, I like watching you both.'

As Dele walked over to his daughter, Harriet came up and sat with Emma. 'You okay?'

'I'm getting asked that a lot today!'

'You just don't seem yourself.'

Emma told her sister about the fake email.

'Wow, the Bahamas, hey?' Harriet said. 'Isn't that where Tatjana is from?'

'Yes! That's exactly what I thought.'

'It can't be a coincidence, surely? That and the rumours. What does Dele think?'

'He thinks it's some old racist dude,' Emma said, quoting him.

'No,' Harriet said, shaking her head. 'No way. I honestly think this Tatjana bird has something to do with it.'

'But why? What reason would she have?'

'Didn't you say she looks like Isla's birth mother?'

'And?'

Harriet looked at Isla, who was now showing some passing children her crab haul. 'What if she *is* Isla's birth mother?'

Emma paused.

'So the thought *has* crossed your mind,' Harriet said, leaning forward, face earnest.

'It sounds mad though, right?'

Harriet chewed on her lip, her bright-red lipstick rubbing off on her teeth. 'Let's think about this properly. If she *is* Isla's birth mother, she could be trying to sabotage you as a mother to – what? Try to win Isla back?'

'Maybe,' Emma admitted, the thought striking fear into her.

'Well, there are the rumours, which I guess could be intended to isolate you. She could have casually mentioned them to this Myra bird who she knew would be pathetic enough to pass them on. But it doesn't sound like the rumours are exactly *serious*. The fake email, though!'

'A school letter was missing from Isla's bag, too, but there could be many reasons for that. I'm just being paranoid.'

Harriet examined her face. 'But your intuition is telling you you're not?'

Emma had to admit her sister was right. Her instincts told her something was *off* about Tatjana.

'A mother's intuition is pretty strong, Emma,' Harriet said.

'Okay, say I'm right,' Emma said, shifting around on the bench to face Harriet. 'Missing a payment deadline and some rumours aren't exactly going to have the authorities rushing to take Isla off me, are they? Plus now Isla is officially ours, social services have nothing to do with us.'

'Unless something serious *did* come to light.'

The two sisters caught each other's eyes. Emma knew what she was thinking. There *was* something that could cause the authorities to consider taking Isla away from Emma, something from the past.

'No,' Emma said, shaking the thought away and crossing her arms. 'I *am* being paranoid. You know how I can be sometimes, like the time I convinced myself I had a brain tumour after I couldn't taste strawberries.'

Harriet laughed. 'Yep, you *are* a daft old bint.' She grew serious again as she peered at Dele. 'Have you spoken to Dele about your suspicions?'

'Not the idea that Tatjana could be Jade. He'd think I was off my rocker.'

'Come on, he's your husband – Isla's dad! You need to tell him, sis. He's a good man. You can't deal with this alone.'

'I have you, don't I?'

Harriet put her hand on Emma's, smiling sadly. 'Talk to your husband. And if your instincts are right, make sure you channel a little bit of me, all right?' Her blue eyes sparked with mischief. 'Play Tatjana at her own bloody game. Nobody's gonna take my niece away from her mummy, am I right?'

Emma took in a deep breath. 'You're right.'

That evening in bed, Dele seemed to sense Emma's mood.

'Okay, what's going on?'

Emma sighed. 'I'm going to say something and I want you to hold off telling me I'm crazy.'

'What's up?'

'Promise!'

'I promise!' Dele said with a crease in his brow.

Emma looked down at her hands, which were crossed over the duvet. 'I know you thought I was mad when I said Tatjana looks like Jade, but I just can't shake the feeling.'

He shifted up on to his elbow, examining Emma's face. 'What are you saying?'

'What if she *is* Jade?'

He laughed. 'How much of your mum's gin did you have tonight?'

'I don't drink, Dele, you know that. I'm just saying . . .'

'You're just saying Isla's birth mother has managed to accumulate a career in fashion, a rich architect husband and a few hundred thousand pounds to build a house in the middle of the forest . . . in the space of nine years? The same girl who was living in a tiny flat with her mum and was claiming the dole every week?'

Emma thought of the young girl she'd met a week before Isla moved in with them. Her black hair a fuzzy mess, dark circles under her eyes. The way she was unable to maintain eye contact apart from the occasional glare.

'I know, but my instincts . . .' She let her voice trail off again.

'Ah, the famous maternal instincts.' Dele was silent for a few moments. 'Okay, let's start with the fake email. Who does it really impact? Isla, right? She's the one who could have missed out on the school trip. If Jade *was* coming back to reclaim her birth child – and I think that's what you're implying?' he asked. Emma didn't say anything and he sighed. 'If she is, why would she want Isla to miss out?'

'To discredit me. Same reason for the missing letter and the rumours.'

'I'm not buying it,' Dele said. 'Sorry babe, but it just doesn't add up.' He was quiet for a few moments. 'Maybe being here has brought up some stuff for you, made your head get all . . .'

'All what? I'm not losing it, Dele. I have cold hard facts. You can't deny the faked email?'

'I can't, but I do *not* think Isla's birth mother is behind it, for Christ's sake. Do you know how nuts that sounds?'

Emma chewed at her lip. 'Yes, but something doesn't *feel* right.'

Dele closed his eyes briefly, taking in a deep breath. 'Okay, let's just go with this for now. So Jade was a heroin addict who dropped out of school when she was fourteen but sure, let's imagine she's turned her life around.'

'It happens, Dele. It's rare, but it really does happen. She was bright – the assessment said that, remember? Before she got involved with her first boyfriend, she was doing really well.'

'Fine then, she turns her life around, qualifies in fashion design with what money?'

Emma shrugged. 'Students get grants.'

'Not any more. Not like people did back in the nineties.'

'But there *are* provisions.'

'Maybe, but it still costs money. Didn't Tatjana say she went to a Scottish university? Why go so far?'

'Because she wanted to get away from it all . . . or maybe she's lying about her qualifications. Faye said she looked up the university and they don't even do a fashion course.'

Dele sighed. 'What next? Ah, that's right, the name change. So Jade changes her name because – what? She was hatching a long-term plan to one day steal Isla away?'

'Maybe,' Emma said, thinking of Isla, who was sleeping soundly in the room next door. 'Or maybe she just did it as a symbol of how she's changed. New life, new name.'

'And then she meets a rich architect?'

'Why not? She's beautiful, successful now.'

'And they just so happen to choose Forest Grove and secure the rights to the land this house was built on within a matter of months? We only moved here ourselves a few months ago, remember?'

He had a point. 'When people are determined, great things can be achieved,' she said, quoting what her dad had once said about Harriet.

'Oh babe,' Dele said. 'Why don't you just chat to Tatjana? Isn't it better to be open about these things?'

'What, you mean go up to her and ask her if she's Isla's birth mother!'

'No!' Dele said, laughing. 'I mean about the rumours, maybe even casually mention the fake email too, gauge her reaction.'

'Yeah, maybe,' Emma said. Dele was clearly completely dismissing the idea that Tatjana might be Isla's birth mother.

But Emma had a feeling Tatjana was the kind of person who was very good at pretending.

◆ ◆ ◆

Emma walked into the school playground on Monday feeling awful. First, they'd got back from Dartmouth super late the night before after being stuck in traffic. Second, she'd been brewing a cold most of the previous day and now it was coming out in true style. Third, it was raining so hard that a huge puddle had formed at the entrance to the school, meaning the bottom of her trousers got absolutely soaked as she carried Isla over it to stop her getting wet.

Emma entered the playground and huddled under a tree as Isla ran off to play with her friends. She couldn't even check her phone; it would get wet.

She was relieved when Shawn joined her.

'Ah, British weather,' he said, rolling his eyes. 'Fraser was bending my ear about this over dinner last weekend, he reckons a storm is coming.'

'I think it's time to move to the Maldives then,' Emma replied, blowing her nose with her tissue.

'You've got a cold, too,' Shawn noticed. 'Faye's off work feeling shite as well.'

'Oh bless her.'

Over the rest of the week, Emma spent the five-minute wait outside school chatting to Shawn, mainly about football and the kids. Shawn always sought her out and Emma wondered if Dele had had a word with him about how lonely she felt. That *was* a very Dele thing to do, though it made her feel a bit embarrassed: poor Shawn having to force himself to talk to his mate's wife. He didn't seem to mind, though. Maybe it was refreshing for him, not being surrounded by gushing mums. Sure, Emma could see the attraction, but she definitely wasn't one of the gushing mums. Shawn was just someone fun to talk to, and it beat standing alone while Faye recovered from her cold at home . . . or chatting to Tatjana, something she was doing her best to avoid.

On Friday morning Emma was looking forward to catching up with Faye. Shawn had told her she was better now and would be dropping the kids off. But Faye wasn't there when the school bell rang. Maybe they were running late?

After making sure Isla got into class okay, Emma strolled towards her car, checking her phone. Lawrence was already keeping her busy with work, Myra sending haughty messages on his behalf at all hours. They were paying a nice amount, though, and Emma's boss had been so impressed he'd given her a bonus, so it was worth it.

As she went to cross the road, someone called out her name. She turned to see it was Faye. Emma smiled.

But then she noticed the look on Faye's face.

She was fuming!

Chapter Seventeen

Emma's smile faltered as Faye stopped before her, face like stone. 'You okay, Faye?' she asked in a shaky voice.

Faye leaned in close to Emma. 'Shawn may play the field at the football club,' she hissed, 'but he doesn't play the field with me, understood?'

Emma stepped back, shocked. 'Excuse me?'

Faye crossed her arms. 'How can I put it more succinctly? Hands off my husband!'

She said it so loud, passing mums paused to watch, curious. Even a curtain twitched in a house nearby.

'I have no idea what you're talking about,' Emma said, cheeks flushing.

'Oh, don't play the fool,' Faye said, looking her up and down in disgust. 'I know what you said to him yesterday.'

Emma wracked her brains. 'I – I didn't say anything.'

'You suggested a drink, just the two of you one evening.'

'I said nothing of the sort! Is that what Shawn said?' She wracked her brains again. Could he have misinterpreted something she had said?

'He didn't need to,' Faye said. 'Someone overheard you.'

Someone? Emma thought. Was this yet another rumour?

She looked over towards Tatjana, who was watching from the edge of the forest with interest.

'And Shawn confirmed it, did he?' Emma asked, crossing her arms.

Faye didn't say anything, just clenched her jaw.

'I swear to you,' Emma said. 'I have *no* interest in your husband. Somebody is trying to mess with you.'

'So you're denying you told people that you fancy Shawn?' Faye asked. 'Or, as you put it, Forest Grove's Tom Hardy.'

Tom Hardy . . .

Memories of the afternoon she'd spent with Tatjana came rushing back. They'd discussed how Shawn looked like the actor Tom Hardy. In fact, Emma was pretty sure it was *Tatjana* who had made the comparison.

That was it – Tatjana *must* have been behind all these attempts to discredit her!

A car horn beeped and Emma looked up to see that she and Faye were blocking the road.

'Nice place to have a chat, ladies,' a familiar-looking woman shouted out from her Mercedes. Emma's stomach sank when she realised it was Kitty Fletcher, the 'parenting guru'.

'Just keep your hands off him, okay?' Faye said, jabbing a finger at Emma. Then she stalked away towards her car.

Emma stayed where she was, stunned, the mums around her whispering as they passed by.

Then Emma noticed Tatjana was still watching her in the distance.

Anger swelled up inside her.

She marched over to Tatjana. 'Tatjana, can I have a word?'

Tatjana smiled. 'Of course.'

'I've been hearing some strange rumours lately.'

A frown appeared in Tatjana's perfect forehead. 'Like what?'

'That I think all working mums are lazy. Plus Faye just accused me of fancying Shawn, for God's sake. She said *I* think he looks like Tom Hardy. The very thing you and I talked about during lunch that time!'

'I don't understand what you're saying, Emma.'

'It can't be a coincidence that all these rumours relate to the conversations we had that lunchtime?'

Tatjana shot Emma an incredulous look. 'You think I passed what was said on to others?'

'I – I don't know. I just can't explain any other reason for it.'

'Well, you have the wrong end of the stick, Emma. I'm not the type to get involved with tittle-tattle – and, frankly, I'm disappointed you'd think that of me.' Tatjana shook her head, then grabbed Phoenix's hand and stormed off towards the forest.

Emma watched her, unsure what to think. Tatjana *did* seem pretty upset at the idea that Emma thought she was behind the rumours. Upset and surprised. But then she *could* be faking it. Hadn't Faye said Tatjana was a fake? And then there was Emma's gut feeling.

A mother's intuition is pretty strong, Emma. That was what Harriet had said.

But intuition wasn't enough. She needed proof – proper proof.

Chapter Eighteen

Welcome to the Mums of Forest Grove Facebook Group

Friday 16th October
9 a.m.

Belinda Bell
Can I please ask the school mums to refrain from arguing right outside my house?

Kitty Fletcher
And blocking the road! They were standing right in the middle of it! I had to beep them to get out of the way.

Ellie Mileham
What happened? I didn't see anything.

Belinda Bell
Two mums were having a bit of a to-do outside the school just now. It's not what I want to be seeing over my morning coffee.

Malorie Cane

Yes, I saw that too and what a surprise, one of the women arguing was the very same woman who blocked our new neighbour's removal van at the beginning of term. I won't say her name on here.

Myra Young

I'll say it! She's not a member here and it's a closed group. It's Emma Okoro and she's been trying to get her hands on one of the other dads, that's what the argument was about.

Pauline Sharpe

Wow! I could tell that woman would be trouble the moment I laid eyes on her.

Vanessa Shillingford

Rubbish! Emma is my neighbour, she's absolutely lovely! This is just conjecture, surely? Kitty, can this thread be taken down? It's none of our business after all.

Belinda Bell

She makes it our business when she's disturbing the peace on our street and is tearing a family apart! It's always the quiet ones. They come across all unassuming and meek, but truth is, they're keeping it all bottled up inside and when it comes out, they explode.

Ellie Mileham

Vanessa is right, this is ridiculous! Please can we close this thread, Kitty?

Kitty Fletcher

I am reluctantly deleting this thread. But before I do, I have to confess, I've had my own suspicions about this woman too. Remember when I mentioned about someone doctoring a MySpace page? It turns out it's more than likely the very same woman. There, I've said it. Now I'm going to delete this thread.

Chapter Nineteen

Friday 16th October
9.25 a.m.

Emma was still shaking when she got into work. She'd tried calling Dele from the car, but he hadn't picked up. She just hoped he didn't hear any rumours before she had a chance to talk to him. She tried his number again, but it went straight to voicemail so she left a quick message. Then she put her phone down and tried to focus on work, but she kept getting flashbacks to that humiliating argument with Faye.

To be fair to Faye, if she really thought Emma was after Shawn, she had every right to have a word. But based on a few rumours? Surely Shawn had tried to tell her it was rubbish? Or maybe he'd completely misinterpreted Emma's friendliness for something else?

As for Tatjana, if she *was* lying, what the hell was she playing at?

Could it really be that she was Isla's birth mother? That was crazy – a crazy idea. She knew she had to try and calm herself down.

After an hour, Dele called her back.

'Hi babe,' she said, rushing into a meeting room and shutting the door behind her.

'Everything okay?' he asked. 'I've had missed calls from Shawn, too. Is something happening at the school? Is Isla okay?'

'Nothing to worry about, Isla's fine,' Emma quickly said. She took in a deep breath. 'It's just Faye. She's – well – she's got it into her head that I have a thing for Shawn.'

'What?' Dele said, incredulous.

'I know, it's crazy. The weird thing is, Faye said I referred to Shawn as the Tom Hardy of Forest Grove. But it was Tatjana who said that to me!'

'What are you saying?'

'That she's behind the rumour,' she said, flinching as she said it. She knew how Dele would react.

'You know how ridiculous this all sounds, Emma?'

'Exactly. It *is* ridiculous!' Emma shook her head, her eyes filling with tears. 'I just wanted you to know before you heard it from anyone else. You know you don't have anything to worry about, right?'

'Course. I better call Shawn back. This is going to be awkward. But look babe, don't blame this all on Tatjana – not until you have proof.'

She took in a deep shaky breath. 'I won't. Text me to tell me what Shawn says. And – and tell him he needs to talk some sense into Faye. I really like Faye and I *hate* the fact she thinks I've betrayed her.'

'Will do.'

Twenty minutes later, she got a text from Dele.

Shawn agrees rumours are ridiculous. He said he was hardly listening to Faye when she asked something about you and him getting drinks, he just sort of nodded as he thought she meant all of us and she just lost it. He's calmed her down, think he's convinced her. Now you just need to convince me . . .

Emma quickly typed back:

Dele! You know I'd never cheat on you! xxxx

You better prove your love to me tonight then. ;-) ;-) ;-)

She rolled her eyes. Well, at least she knew he wasn't taking the rumours seriously. She just wished he'd take her concerns about Tatjana seriously!

She put her phone to her ear again, desperate to speak to her sister.

'Jesus, what the hell is she playing at?' Harriet said when Emma had finished telling her what had just happened. 'Messing with your marriage?'

'I know, she's taking it too far.'

'There's only one reason she'd be doing this, Em.'

'She's Isla's birth mother?'

'Yeah. Why don't you call the social worker you were assigned during the adoption process? Maybe she can put your mind at rest?'

'I wouldn't call her . . . but there is a post-adoption number they gave us.'

'There you go! Give it a call, sis.'

Emma thought about it, then nodded. 'Okay, I'll call. Thanks, Harriet.'

'That's what I'm here for.'

Emma scrolled through her emails to find the number she thought she'd never need to call. It had been given to them after they adopted Isla in case they needed advice or to check anything.

Well, now she needed to check something.

She called the number and after a few rings, a woman answered. 'Hello, Pam speaking.'

'Hi Pam, it's Emma Okoro. We adopted a little girl eight years ago, Isla.'

'Hello Emma, how's everything going?'

'Everything's just great. Isla's – well, she's wonderful. The best thing that ever happened to us.'

'Now this is the kind of call I like to get!' Pam said with a laugh.

Emma scratched at a dent in the meeting-room table. 'I just wanted to ask a question that's going to sound nuts, but I just need you to hear me out.'

'Of course,' Pam said. 'Fire away.'

'Do you keep track of birth parents?'

'As you know, we offer a letterbox option where birth parents can check in on how their biological child is doing,' Pam replied. 'Birth parents are required to come to the offices to collect their letters and photos now, so that's the main way we keep in touch. Are you asking if we've kept track of Isla's birth parents, Emma?'

'Yes, her birth mother, Jade Dixon. But we were told a few years ago that she doesn't come to see the letters and photos we send?'

'I see. Well, I'm afraid that's the only way we keep contact really. More often than not, we do lose track with birth parents. It's sadly just the nature of the unstable lives they lead.'

'I see. Is there any way you could just double-check your records for Isla's birth mother, see if there's been any recent attempts at contact?'

'Can I ask why you want to know, Emma?'

Emma peered out of the window in the direction of Forest Grove. She could just about make out its trees in the distance and the blip of red indicating where the crane was. 'A woman has moved into our village and she looks just like Jade.'

Pam sighed. 'We get this a lot, Emma. You'd be surprised at the number of people who look alike and yet have no connection to each other.'

'It's not just that. Since she moved in, lots of stuff has happened.' She told the social worker about the rumours, the missing letter . . . and most recently, the fake email.

'Hmmm, that can't be very nice for you,' Pam said when she finished. 'I'm sure it's nothing, but let me just do a quick check.' There was a sound of tapping in the background. 'Okay, Jade Dixon. Right, here she is.' Pam sighed again. 'Yes, seems we have lost track of her. As I said, this is very common. Why don't you tell me more about the woman who's moved into the village?'

Emma raked her fingers through her hair. 'Her name's Tatjana Belafonte. It seems – if she *is* Jade – she's really turned her life around. She's a fashion designer now and she's married to an architect. They've built a huge house in the woods and—'

'Whoa, wait a minute,' Pam interrupted with a small laugh. 'That's quite a leap, Emma. From a drug addict with violent criminals for boyfriends – as I can see from her records – to a fashion designer with an architect husband? You realise how unlikely that is, don't you?'

'It does happen.'

'Sure, but it's rare. Look, I'll make a note to do a little digging to try to track Jade down, just to put your mind at rest. How does that sound?'

'That would be great, thanks.'

'But try not to worry. It would be *very* unlikely, considering what you've told me about this woman. Focus on enjoying your beautiful girl.'

'I will,' Emma said. *As long as Tatjana lets me.* 'Sorry for taking up your time.'

'Hey, don't apologise. It's very normal at this stage, you know,' Pam said. 'Nearly ten years down the line, everything's going well, so you're waiting for the rug to be pulled out from underneath you. You'd be surprised at the number of parents I have getting in touch around this time.'

But did those parents have someone who looked just like their child's birth mother messing with them?

'Thanks,' Emma said. 'I appreciate it.'

She ended the call. Even with Pam's reassurances, she was still convinced her instincts were right about Tatjana. In fact, having it confirmed that Jade had disappeared off the map made her even more certain. From the training that she and Dele had had when they were going through the adoption process, they learnt that many birth parents went on to have other children and continued, sadly, to be known to social services. How could Jade have just dropped off the radar?

She sighed and walked back out of the meeting room.

It was Emma's turn to leave the office early that evening. She approached Forest Grove Primary with trepidation. She had no doubt other parents would have seen Faye haranguing her . . . and there was every chance she would see Faye or Shawn in the playground, too. Not to mention Tatjana. Thank God it was half-term next week.

When she got to the school playground, the first person she saw was Lawrence.

For a moment, Emma thought about telling him her suspicions about Tatjana. But he was Tatjana's husband – and what's more, he was her client!

Surely Tatjana must have told Lawrence about her run-in with Emma, so Emma tried to avoid him by heading to the other end of the playground.

But it was too late. He'd seen her and was striding over, his hands in his pockets.

'Hello, Emma, how are you?' he asked. 'Tat has a cold, so I'm doing the school run today.'

She explored his face for any indication that he knew about her row with Tatjana. There was nothing. 'Poor thing,' she said. 'I'm fine. How's the house?'

'Very nearly done. We'll see you at the Halloween party in a couple of weeks, I hope?' he asked. 'I think everything will be pretty much ready for it.'

Emma hesitated. How could she be a guest in their house when she knew Tatjana was trying to undermine her?

She was about to make an excuse, but stopped herself.

Maybe it would be *useful* to go? She could do some snooping. If Tatjana was Jade, then surely there'd be some evidence of it in the house?

'Absolutely,' she said. 'We can't wait!'

Chapter Twenty

Saturday 17th October
12 p.m.

I have to admit, Isla, your fake mother is surprising me. Garrett just called to tell me his source informed him that Emma called social services yesterday. Clearly, she has some suspicions.

Truth is, I've underestimated her. It's not just the call she made to social services, it's the way she's got you back on that trip, too, which surprised me. The school is rather strict about missing deadlines and yet a few days later, I learn she somehow managed it.

Of course, ultimately, that's good for you, Isla. I didn't mean to upset you – it was rather horrible seeing you so upset at dinner the other night when you learnt the deadline had been missed. But then I also admired the way you shouted at your useless fake mother!

In fact, she was a little too confident at that dinner. Getting Lucy invited was meant to unsettle her! But Lucy just seemed to go into herself and Emma got more and more confident.

It unnerved me so much, I ended up drinking. I don't like it when I do that. I have a tendency to lose control when I drink, as I've learnt to my detriment and to others', too.

When Emma was in the restaurant's bathroom alone, I was tempted to have it all over and done with. Get her out of your life.

But then I heard the tinkle of your laughter and it reminded me: no matter what happens, you will not think badly of me, not like the way I felt about my parents. It's always been my rule: no matter how tough things get, no matter how the buzzing in my head begins to feel like a needle wheedling its way into my skull, never ever must I lose control in front of my children.

If I do have to resort to drastic measures, then it will be done without you there to witness it, my love, so don't worry about that.

All you need to know is I will make sure you're mine, no matter what it takes. And I'm hoping what I have planned for Halloween will send your pretend parents right over the edge . . .

Chapter Twenty-One

Saturday 31st October
7.25 p.m.

Emma positioned the long white-haired wig on her head, checking her make-up in the mirror. She was going as Daenerys Targaryen from *Game of Thrones* to the Belafontes' Halloween party. It was her sister who had come up with the idea.

'Badass Mother of Dragons,' Harriet had said.

It was easy enough to put together. Emma had a long black dress and black boots. All she needed was a dark-red cape and a black scarf criss-crossed over her chest to turn it into a war-like costume. The wig was an easy find from a fancy-dress shop in Ashbridge that morning and there wasn't much to think about when it came to the make-up: just some bronzer, eyeliner and nude lipstick.

As she looked in the mirror in her full outfit, she actually felt as if she was going to war, a warrior about to battle for her child.

'You look awesome,' Harriet said as she applied a thick line of eyeliner. When she'd heard about Emma's plans to do some snooping, she'd insisted on coming along, too.

'Every detective needs a sidekick,' she'd said.

She was going as an evil fairy, her favourite Halloween guise. She was even wearing the very same dress she wore at the Halloween party they'd held at their London flat years ago.

'She's ready!' Dele shouted out from Isla's room. He'd been helping her get ready for the past thirty minutes. Isla had come home on the last Thursday of term with the costume she'd designed as part of her Design Divas sessions, but she had kept it hidden because she wanted it to be a surprise. Emma had been tempted to accidentally 'lose' it, whatever it was. She really hated the idea that Tatjana had been helping Isla make her costume. But she didn't want to upset Isla, especially as Emma had already decided that her daughter would not be going to Design Divas any more.

Emma and Harriet walked down the hallway and into Isla's room.

'Ta da!' Isla said.

The first thing Emma noticed was that Isla was wearing a long black wig, so long the plaits came down to her feet. The dress she was wearing was a deep-purple colour and reached to her knees in opulent loops of material.

'Wow,' Emma said, not sure what else to say, as she really didn't have a clue who Isla was supposed to be.

'I know, doesn't she make a great *Rapunzel*?' Dele said point-edly, giving her a look.

'Ah, yes,' Emma said. 'An *awesome* Rapunzel.'

'Whoa, I am loving the dress, Isla,' Harriet said as Isla did a twirl.

'It's a modern take on Rapunzel,' Isla explained as she smoothed her fingers over her wig. 'Tat came up with the idea.'

'Tat, hey?' Harriet said, raising an eyebrow at Emma.

'We made her black, though, like me, Daddy and Tat,' Isla said. *Me and Daddy and Tat.*

Emma tried not to look at Harriet, who was shaking her head in dismay.

'It's very cool,' Emma said as she smiled down at Isla. 'You look amazing.'

'And so does Mum, doesn't she?' Dele said. 'My Khaleesi,' he added, wiggling his eyebrows.

'Who?' Isla asked.

Harriet laughed. 'Mother of Dragons, child!'

'It's from a programme we watch,' Dele said. 'It's very cool, trust me. Not as cool as Zombie Dad though!' he said, gesturing to his outfit: old skinny jeans with some fake blood on them, a ripped shirt and green eyeshadow on his face. Somehow, it worked.

'Right, shall we go then?' Emma said.

'Do you mind driving so I can have a drink?' Dele asked. 'I would suggest we walk, but . . .' He pulled a face as he peered outside, and Emma followed his gaze to see it was raining.

Great.

'Sure,' she said reluctantly. She hated driving, especially at night in conditions like this. But it wouldn't be fair on Dele to say no. She didn't drink, after all, and it would be good for him to have a few drinks. 'Come on then!' she said to everyone.

They all went outside and piled into the car.

As Emma drove carefully through the forest, Harriet leaned forward, grasping on to the back of Emma's chair. 'Do you remember when we did spooky walks through our local forest at Halloween when we were kids? God, we had a great childhood, didn't we?'

Emma nodded, smiling.

'But then that all changed when we grew up,' Harriet said.

Emma frowned. She didn't want to think about that.

'Ooops, sorry,' Harriet whispered, pretending to zip up her mouth. 'Must follow Dad's rules. No talking about it.'

But it was too late; unwanted memories were flooding Emma's brain. The bounce of headlights on the ground. The thunderous clatter of the rain. The screams . . .

She clutched tight on to the steering wheel and shook her head. Why did Harriet have to bring all that up right now? She needed to focus on the task at hand: tonight was all about finding out if Tatjana Belafonte was in reality Jade Dixon.

'Mum, look!' Isla said, pointing up at the trees. Huge glow-in-the-dark spiders and bats were hanging from the branches, fake cobwebs strung from twig to twig.

'Wow, Forest Grove knows how to do Halloween,' Harriet said. As they drew up to the new home of Lawrence and Tatjana Belafonte, she let out a low whistle. 'Now that is quite some house.'

Harriet was right, it really was quite something. The whole exterior was lit up an eerie green with moving silhouettes projected on to it, from witches on broomsticks to howling werewolves. The area in front of the house had been made to look like a graveyard with tombstones either side, a path winding through it lit up by red spotlights. Michael Jackson's 'Thriller' was blasting out from inside, mingling with the sound of children's laughter and adults talking.

'They really *do* know how to do Halloween,' Dele said as he looked at the house with an open mouth.

'This. Is. Awesome!' Isla declared, clapping her hands.

Emma parked the car next to the Belafontes' Jaguar.

'Bit scary for kids though,' Harriet said.

'Might spook out some of the more sensitive kids,' Emma agreed, frowning. 'It's a bit over the top.'

'Come on, be nice,' Dele said in a low voice.

Harriet raised an eyebrow as Emma rolled her eyes. 'Aren't I always?'

They walked in through the open door. It was already crowded inside, people chatting and dancing as kids darted here and there.

Emma felt a stab of apprehension. After that confrontation with Faye and all the rumours going about, she wasn't looking forward to this.

But it seemed her long white wig was a good disguise and nobody seemed to notice her.

The downstairs area of the Belafonte house was completely open plan, a large kitchen to the right of the vast hallway with state-of-the-art blue units, a dining room laden with all sorts of Halloween-themed food. Across from the kitchen to the left of the house was a living room area with a big blue sofa, the long stretch of wall behind it made up of wooden panels with a series of woven circles featuring patterns in black, blue and white. Large stylishly illuminated pumpkins stared back at them from every surface, in stark contrast to the tiny pumpkin Emma had carved with Isla, which looked more surprised than scary.

'This place is amazing,' Harriet whispered, peering up as they passed under a balcony walkway which was lined with a long glass panel looking down into the ground floor, fake spider webs hanging from it.

Emma noticed Lawrence and Tatjana with their boys at the back of the living room, chatting to Myra who was dressed as a vampire in a long red dress, her dark hair dyed black and straightened.

To her horror, Emma realised that Tatjana was also dressed as Daenerys Targaryen. But her outfit hadn't been cobbled together like Emma's. Instead, she wore an official costume, a long white Grecian-style dress that suited her figure perfectly. Her white immaculate wig looked amazing against her dark skin and she even had a pretend baby dragon on her shoulder.

Was this another thing she'd done on purpose to undermine Emma?

'Awkward,' Harriet said, pulling a face.

'You look *much* better,' Dele whispered in Emma's ear, when he noticed her looking at Tatjana. 'Short and curvy like the real Khaleesi.'

Emma smiled, but she still felt rubbish. She had to admit, Tatjana looked absolutely stunning.

Lawrence caught their eye. He was dressed as Jon Snow from *Game of Thrones* with a thick fur cloak over a black battle outfit, a fake moustache and black wig completing the look. Their sons, who were running around the house, Zeke bashing Phoenix with a fake sword, were dressed as little dragons, one green, one blue.

'How lovely,' Harriet whispered sarcastically into Emma's ear, 'a little dragon family.'

As she said that, Lawrence waved them over.

'You go,' Harriet said. 'I'll go scope out the joint. I'll holler if I see anything.'

Harriet walked away, disappearing into the crowds, and Emma followed Dele and Isla as they headed over to Tatjana and Lawrence. Myra walked past them, looking Emma up and down as she went by.

'Your twin!' Lawrence said to Tatjana as he took in Emma's outfit.

'You know nothing, Jon Snow,' Dele said in a terrible Northern accent.

Lawrence and Tatjana laughed, Tatjana smoothing her hand over her long white wig as she looked down at Emma with a glacial smile on her face. Emma didn't return her smile, but instead held her gaze as if to convey the fact that she was on to her.

Tatjana turned to Isla. 'Look at this masterpiece we made!' she said, putting her arm around Isla's shoulders. 'Doesn't the dress look divine, darling?' she asked Lawrence.

'Brilliant,' Lawrence said. 'What a talented young girl.'

'Isn't she just? What do you think, Emma?' Tatjana asked, her cold gaze returning to Emma. 'A little Rapunzel, taken from her birth parents and locked away in a tower by a *wicked* woman who forces the poor child to call her mother.'

Emma's mouth dropped open as Dele's brow creased. She was about to say something when Isla grabbed her hand. 'Nobody's going to take me away from my mum and dad!'

Tatjana's smile faltered.

Emma pulled Isla even closer. 'Never,' she said, her eyes on Tatjana. 'You're all mine.'

Tatjana's jaw tensed. 'Drinks?' she asked. 'We have Melted Witch Martinis for the adults!' she said, gesturing to a table of luminous green cocktails.

'Absolutely,' Dele said.

'Emma?' Tatjana asked.

Emma tried to contain her annoyance. Tatjana *knew* that she didn't drink!

'I'm the designated driver,' she said.

'You *drove*?' Tatjana asked.

Dele pointed outside with a laugh. 'Have you seen the weather? We don't live in the posh houses, you know, we're a good ten-minute walk away.'

Lawrence laughed. 'Fair enough. Tatjana, get Emma one of the juices Myra brought, will you? Myra's been a godsend,' Lawrence said, looking around at the decorations. 'I'm not sure how we would have got everything ready in time without her.'

Tatjana frowned slightly. 'I did some of them, too.'

'Of course, darling,' Lawrence said.

Tatjana walked into the kitchen where Myra was. She took a pumpkin-shaped cup from Myra and brought it over to Emma.

'Pumpkin Mocktail,' she declared as Lawrence and Dele talked about football. 'It's delicious.'

Emma accepted the large cup, taking a sip. She reluctantly had to agree it really *was* delicious.

'Ah, there's Levi,' Lawrence said, taking Tatjana's hand. 'Come meet him, will you? Have a fab time!' he said to Dele and Emma. 'Eat, drink and be merry!'

He pulled his wife away as Isla spotted Tegan and darted off to play with her.

'You *must* have noticed that?' Emma asked Dele. 'You can't deny that Rapunzel remark and the way she looked at me was odd.'

'I don't know,' Dele said. 'You're probably reading too much into it.' But this time, he didn't look convinced. Was he beginning to doubt Tatjana, too?

They both watched as Isla filled a plate with party snacks, chatting away to her friends and Myra's son Justin as Myra looked on.

'Look,' Dele said, rubbing the back of his neck, 'I've been thinking. Why don't we call that post-adoption number that was given to us, just to put your mind at rest about Jade? I can tell it's been worrying you.'

'I already called them,' Emma admitted.

Dele slammed his drink down. '*What*? You didn't consult with me first?'

'I didn't want to bother you! It's like you said, it sounds mad. I needed to get all the evidence together and—'

'Evidence?' he said. 'Jesus, listen to yourself, you're treating this like a police investigation.'

'Maybe it should be. Think about it, Dele, what if I'm right about her?' she said, pointing to where Tatjana was now, strangely quiet, staring out at the forest as Lawrence chatted to a couple.

'And what if you're not?' Dele said, disquiet in his brown eyes. 'Look, I'm just concerned this will backfire and it'll end up making *us* look bad. It was hard enough trying to convince them you were okay after everything that happened. We had to get all those records to prove you'd had counselling sessions, remember, and that your head was in the right place?'

Emma turned away, her face flushing. Dele put his hand on her cheek, making her look back at him.

'*I* know you're fine now,' he said gently. 'But they might think it's happening all over again, like it did all those years ago and—'

'I'm not imagining it, Dele!' Emma said. 'I just wish my husband had a little more faith in me. I'm going to do some exploring. You go chat to your football buddies.'

She shoved him away and headed to the kitchen, weaving in-between the crowds as she sipped her Pumpkin Mocktail. In the kitchen she picked at some ghost-shaped crisps, then downed her drink before grabbing another from the table. She could see Tatjana chatting to Lucy and Myra now, probably all gossiping away about Emma.

Well, while she's distracted, I'm going to see what I can find, Emma thought.

She looked around her, then quickly headed up the long glass staircase. As she walked down the hallway, she peered into the rooms. There were two children's bedrooms, one with the solar system on the ceiling and bed covers depicting the planets, the other an animal-themed room. At the end of the hallway she saw what was clearly Tatjana and Lawrence's bedroom: it stretched across the back of the house and looked out to the forest.

Emma looked over her shoulder then walked inside, closing the door behind her and using the torch from her phone to search around in the semi-darkness.

If someone found her in here, she could just say she was lost and looking for the bathroom.

The queen-sized bed was draped with a faux-fur brown-and-white throw, the walls papered a bronze colour. The floor was dominated by the same wooden floorboards as the entire house, and the bedside tables were made from mirrored glass. It was just as she imagined it would be: opulent, beautiful and stylish.

She went to Tatjana's side of the bed, signalled by the battered old Agatha Christie novel on the bedside table with a distraught woman on the front. There was a photo of the boys on the table, too, along with a glass of water.

She opened the little drawer on Tatjana's side. Inside was an expensive-looking moisturiser and some tablets – Sertraline, according to the label. Wasn't that an anti-depressant?

Then she noticed a small notepad with an embroidered bird of paradise on the front.

Emma peered towards the door again. She wouldn't be able to explain rifling around in the host's bedside drawer, would she?

'Oh well, needs must,' she whispered, feeling unusually brave.

Emma quickly pulled out the notepad, flicking through it.

It was full of lists. At first, she thought they might be shopping lists, but on closer inspection she realised they were step-by-step handwritten guides to things like 'How to fit into Forest Grove' and 'How to help the boys at school'. Under the 'How to fit in' list, she'd written the dress code: wellies, Boden raincoats, jodhpurs.

Jesus, Emma thought.

She flicked through to the last page and then gasped at what she saw.

How to undermine E
  1. Highlight her incompetence
  2. Isolate her
  3. Create marriage troubles

'What the hell . . . ?' Emma whispered.

This was proof. Tatjana *was* trying to undermine her.

165

There was a sound from the hallway outside. She quickly took a photo of the page with her phone and shoved the notepad back into the drawer. As she did so, she noticed, under a photo of Zeke and Phoenix, another photograph of a smiling, proud-looking black man in his fifties.

She quickly closed the drawer just as the door to the bedroom opened.

Chapter Twenty-Two

Saturday 31st October
8 p.m.

There she goes, creeping her way upstairs.

Where is she heading, I wonder?

She really is turning out to be a lot sneakier and yes, a lot braver than I thought.

I go to follow her.

'How did you get that spider's web draped on to the trees?' Shawn asks.

I turn to him, forcing myself to smile. He really is such a Luddite. I really have no idea what Faye sees in him. Now I've spent more time getting to know her, I like her. She pulled herself up from her working-class background, just like me.

Maybe if she had adopted you, Isla, I could rest easy.

But no, instead it's the dullest couple on earth and here I am, talking to another of the dullest men I've ever met.

What do the other school mums see in him? Shame my attempt to make Emma seem like one of those mums failed; Emma and Dele clearly seem happy enough together. Having said that, I haven't seen Faye and Emma talk tonight so that's a bonus.

'Ladders are marvellous things,' I say.

They all laugh. God, they can't even tell when I'm being rude. Or maybe they can, but they're just too polite to say anything.

'Excuse me a moment, will you?' I say.

I slip away, weaving in and out of the gathering crowds. How many people are here? It must be over a hundred. I hadn't expected there to be this many people. I was hoping it would be a smaller affair so I could focus on you, my darling.

But you're too busy having fun with your silly little friends.

Maybe I should just have it over and done with now? Did anyone really notice Emma walk upstairs, alone? Did they even see her come in? I nearly missed her with that ridiculous cheap wig of hers.

Nobody would suspect me if her body was found in the woods in the night, finger marks on her neck, the life drained out of her.

Then she'd be gone, forever, and I could take what is mine. Her wimp of a husband wouldn't be able to cope. I know his sort, crumbling with grief, unable to look after his child.

Or maybe I've underestimated him, too? Maybe he would cope? Then what? No matter how much digging I do, I can't find anything negative from his past.

Emma, however, that's a different story. I had a very interesting call earlier and I was very much hoping I'd have something concrete so I could put the nail in her coffin tonight, but alas, not yet.

Yes, maybe it really would be better – neater – if she was just gone?

I check behind me. Nobody's noticed. I glide upstairs, hand sliding along the polished wooden rail. I see her disappear into our bedroom, a shadow.

She shuts the door behind her.

Sneaky little thing.

I walk up the hallway and place my hand on the doorknob.

Chapter Twenty-Three

The door crept open.

Emma held her breath as someone walked in.

It was Lawrence.

'Oh Lawrence, you scared me!' she declared.

In the semi-darkness, his eyes blinked at her. He didn't move, just watched her.

'I got lost,' she said with a nervous laugh. Had he heard her rifling in the drawers? 'This isn't the bathroom, is it?'

He flipped a switch, flooding the room with light.

'Just our boring old bedroom,' he said with a charming smile.

She quickly looked back towards the drawer again, thinking of the notepad within.

'Are you okay?' Lawrence asked, walking up to her and putting his hand on her shoulder, squeezing it. 'You look like you've seen a ghost.'

She stumbled slightly and he held her elbow.

'I feel strange,' she admitted, realising she *was* feeling slightly woozy. 'Maybe I haven't quite shrugged off my cold.'

'I have to admit, you don't look great. Let's get you downstairs.'

He helped her down the stairs and led her to one of the stools in a quiet corner of the kitchen.

'Do you want me to find Dele?' Lawrence asked.

She noticed her sister Harriet watching her with a concerned expression on her face.

'No, I'm fine,' Emma said. 'You go have fun.'

Lawrence hesitated for a moment, then smiled and wandered off, heading over to the dance floor where Isla was busting some moves with her friends.

Harriet walked over to Emma. 'You okay?'

'I don't know, I feel odd. I think I'm getting a cold, the whole village seems to have had it.' Emma smiled. 'But hey, guess what? I found something.' She took out her phone and showed her sister the photo of Tatjana's list.

Harriet shook her head in amazement. 'That woman!'

'I know, right!'

'You *have* to confront her with it.'

'I will.' Emma searched the crowds for Tatjana, but she was nowhere to be seen. In the distance she noticed Faye standing with Shawn. Faye caught her eye and turned away as Shawn's face flushed. Then Lucy came up to Faye, putting her hand on her shoulder, her face sympathetic as she narrowed her eyes at Emma.

Emma suddenly felt self-conscious.

'Hey, are you sure you're all right?' Harriet asked softly.

'Yeah, fine.' She went to get another Pumpkin Mocktail.

'Whoa, wait!' Harriet said. She leaned over Emma's drink and sniffed it. 'You do realise there's vodka in that, don't you?'

Emma looked at her in surprise. 'What?'

Harriet pointed to a small sign on the table, which Emma hadn't noticed before:

PUMPKIN PUNCH, A TRULY WICKED MIX OF VODKA, RUM AND CIDER – PLUS, OF COURSE, PUMPKIN! BEWARE ITS BEWITCHING POWERS!

Tatjana had lied about it being a mocktail!

She shoved the drink away from her. 'Jesus Christ, Tatjana *gave* this to me. She knows I don't drink!'

'Do you think she did it on purpose?' Harriet asked.

'She must have. But I'm driving. It's so dangerous!'

'Maybe that's the whole point? Look at the weather! She could have hatched the plan when it started to rain and she realised you'd be driving,' Harriet said, gesturing to the rain outside. 'It would make sense you'd drive. I mean, that would be truly irresponsible, wouldn't it? A mother driving her daughter home while drunk?'

Emma stood up, searching the room for Tatjana. This was the final straw!

Harriet pointed towards the stairs and Emma followed her gaze to see Tatjana heading up the long glass staircase. Emma followed her, taking two steps at a time until she got to the landing. Tatjana went into her bedroom and shut the door. Emma paused for a moment then entered the room too, finding Tatjana sitting on the bed.

Emma walked towards her, adrenalin rushing through her.

Tatjana didn't look up as Emma approached. It was as if she was expecting her.

'You gave me that drink on purpose, didn't you?' Emma shouted at her. 'Despite it being alcoholic, you gave it to me! I'm driving Isla home tonight – or was that the whole point?'

Tatjana winced, looking away.

'Admit it, Tatjana!' Emma said, striding towards the bed. 'You might as well, I know everything anyway. I know you're behind all the rumours. The fake school email. No surprise the host is based

171

in the Bahamas, is it? And then there's this,' she said, going to the drawer and yanking it open, getting out the notepad and showing her the last page.

Tatjana's eyes widened. She opened her mouth to say something to Emma. But instead she jumped up and shoved past her, running from the room.

'Listen to me!' Emma shouted as she chased her to the glass balcony. 'You can't deny it! I know everything, *Jade*.'

Tatjana froze just before she got to the stairs, her hand on the rail.

'I know it's you,' Emma said. 'I know you're Jade Dixon.'

Tatjana shook her head. 'No.'

'Liar!' Emma shouted again. Her voice echoed around the vast area, the people in the room below looking up at them. 'You're lying,' Emma said. 'Tell everyone you're lying,' she added, gesturing to the crowd below. Dele walked over, shaking his head at her. But Emma was fed up with this, she was fed up with all of those people down there treating her like she was some kind of pariah.

Myra and Lucy appeared from the crowd and rushed upstairs towards Tatjana, Myra putting an arm around her.

'Why are you upsetting her, Emma?' Myra hissed.

'Because she's been spreading rumours about me!' Emma replied. 'The stuff about me saying working mums are lazy. Let me guess, where did you hear that from?'

Myra didn't say anything, just frowned.

Below them, the guests had stopped pretending they weren't listening. They drew closer, watching the drama on the stairs.

'And what about me fancying Shawn?' Emma asked Myra, the alcohol she'd accidentally consumed giving her courage. 'Did you hear that from Tatjana too, then pass it on to Lucy?' She looked at

Lucy. 'I mean, we all know who to talk to if we want a rumour or two spread. Tatjana got *that* right.'

'Emma,' Dele said in a low voice.

'That's just rude,' Lucy said, folding her arms as Tatjana remained silent, taking in deep breaths. Below them, Faye walked forward, watching with interest.

'Anyway, why would Tatjana want to spread rumours about you?' Myra asked.

Emma turned to Tatjana. 'Yes, why is that, Tatjana?' She wanted *her* to say it. 'Why did you fake an email so I missed paying for the school trip to Warwick Castle? Why did you pretend the Pumpkin Punch was non-alcoholic, so I'd drive my daughter home drunk?'

Some of the parents below raised surprised eyebrows, whispering to each other.

'That's complete rubbish, isn't it, Tatjana?' Myra said.

But Tatjana didn't say anything. Instead, she just burst into tears. Emma almost felt sorry for her, but then she remembered what this woman had been trying to do to her all this time.

Lawrence shoved his way through the crowds then and rushed up the stairs towards his wife.

'What's going on, darling?' he asked.

Tatjana looked up at him and shook her head. 'I'm sorry,' she whispered.

He turned to Emma. 'Emma? What's going on?'

'Your wife is trying to sabotage me.'

He frowned. 'Maybe we should find somewhere quiet to talk?' He gestured towards a side room and the three of them walked inside, Lawrence shutting the door behind them before Dele could enter. Tatjana leaned against the wall, her face expressionless, as Lawrence raked his fingers through his hair, standing in the middle of the room, which was some kind of small office.

'So?' Lawrence asked.

'Your wife has a vendetta against me,' Emma said.

'Tatjana?' Lawrence asked.

She looked up at him. 'It's not true.' But her voice came out feeble, unsure.

'What makes you think this, Emma?' Lawrence urged, an expression of concern on his handsome face.

Emma told him everything – about the faked email, the nasty rumours and the notebook she'd found in Tatjana's bedside table, plus the alcoholic drink she'd given her. But she stopped short of saying that Tatjana was Jade. She didn't have enough evidence yet.

Lawrence's eyes widened. 'Jesus, Tatjana, is this true? Why?'

Tatjana sank down on to a chair, looking shell-shocked.

Emma frowned. Tatjana really looked broken.

What a charade!

Lawrence went to his wife, kneeling down in front of her and taking her hands. 'Darling, I know you're going through some stuff – but this?'

Some stuff. What did that mean?

Tatjana's shoulders slumped and she started sobbing again. Emma was surprised – *touched*, even – to see a tear slide down Lawrence's cheek.

This apparently perfect couple clearly had some issues to work through.

'I'm sorry,' Emma said, backing away. 'I'll give you both some privacy. We can talk when this all settles down.'

Then she left the room.

When she got out, an anxious Dele was hovering by the door. 'Jesus, Emma, what the *hell* is going on?'

'I found this in Tatjana's bedroom drawer,' she said, showing Dele the photo of Tatjana's list on her phone.

'*E* could be anyone,' he said as he looked at it. 'And anyway, what are you doing snooping through her drawers?'

'I had to! Don't you understand? Tatjana has a vendetta against me. That pumpkin punch she gave me, for example? It's *full* of alcohol. How do you feel about me driving our daughter home *drunk*?'

The expression on his face faltered.

'She didn't even *deny* it, either,' Emma said. 'She *is* behind all this, Dele.'

'Why?'

As he asked that, Lawrence walked out of the side room, gently closing the door behind him, his face drawn. He noticed them both and walked over.

'I'm so sorry, she just admitted to it all,' he said with a sigh.

'All?' Emma asked. Did he mean her being Jade, too?

'The fake email, the nasty gossip, even destroying some letter about dress-down day,' he said. 'And yes, she lied about the punch being non-alcoholic.'

Dele dragged his hand over his face, looking shocked. 'Jesus. Why would she do this to Emma?'

Lawrence hesitated for a moment and glanced at the chatting guests below. 'Tat has always struggled with mental health issues,' he said quietly. 'I thought things would change when we moved here, but it seems that isn't the case.'

'But why target me?' Emma asked.

Lawrence turned to Emma. 'She becomes *fixated* on people. If they don't reciprocate, she can get a bit . . .' His voice trailed off.

'A bit what?'

'Dark.'

Emma felt goosebumps.

'The fact you didn't see her again after you had lunch,' Lawrence said, 'I think she might have taken it personally. She brought it up a few times. She really admires you, Emma. You're everything she wants to be.'

Emma looked at him in surprise. 'Are you kidding me?'

'Seriously! You shouldn't downplay yourself,' Lawrence said as Dele nodded. 'You're a successful businesswoman, you juggle it all so well.'

'I'm obviously very good at faking it then,' Emma said. She felt Dele's hand take hers.

'And so is Tatjana,' Lawrence replied, sadly.

Is she faking an identity as well?

'I think it goes back to her mum rejecting her,' Lawrence said. 'She walked out when Tat was just ten. Tat didn't see her for years, then shortly before they were due to meet, her mother passed away.'

Emma frowned. That wasn't the case with Jade's mother. Evie had always been there, even though she and Jade had a tempestuous relationship.

'She told you this?' Emma asked Lawrence.

Lawrence sighed. 'Her dad did.'

Emma frowned again. 'You know her dad?'

'Yes, of course. He's the one who helped me set up my business. Amazing guy. Set up his own business too, despite a difficult upbringing in Hastings. Quite an inspirational man.'

Suddenly, Emma's conviction that Tatjana was Jade started to falter. Sure, Tatjana could be lying to Lawrence about her background, but then he *knew* her dad. Why would he lie?

It was beginning to make more sense that Tatjana was struggling with mental health issues and had somehow become fixated on Emma.

'Has she done this kind of thing before?' Dele asked. 'Faked stuff, spread rumours?'

'Sadly, yes,' Lawrence replied. 'An old university friend of hers got a job at the fashion company where Tat was interning. Tat got a bit jealous. Her friend was doing really well, so Tat tried to sabotage her. Sent a fake email to the boss. Spread rumours that she was sleeping with him.'

'Shit,' Emma whispered. 'I really thought . . .'

'Thought what?' Lawrence asked.

Dele gently squeezed her hand.

'Nothing,' she said, realising how truly ridiculous the idea was now, that Tatjana was Jade. She took in a deep breath, relief flooding through her.

It was good news: Isla's birth mother wasn't trying to steal her back!

But poor Tatjana! Despite all she'd done to Emma, she felt sorry for her.

'She needs help, Lawrence,' Dele said.

Lawrence's face looked pained. 'I know.'

'Is she seeing a therapist?' Emma asked.

'She was seeing a great one in Scotland, but when we moved here we didn't think she'd need one any more.' He took in a deep breath. 'I wish I'd insisted now.'

'I know someone,' Emma said, suddenly desperate to help. 'He's in London, but it's only an hour by train. He's very good. I – erm – I've used him, in the past.'

Lawrence looked at her with interest. 'Really?'

She nodded, getting her phone out and finding the therapist's number. 'I'll email his number to you.'

Lawrence's phone pinged and he looked at it. He was silent for a few moments, deep in thought. Then he looked up and gave her a charming smile. 'This is really good of you, Emma.'

'It's fine, really.'

'I don't want this to affect our business relationship,' he added, an earnest expression on his face. 'I won't blame you if you decide not to work with me after all this.'

'Lawrence! Of *course* we will continue to work with you,' Emma said. 'This isn't your fault. If Tatjana can get the help she needs, then that's great.'

He nodded, giving her a kind look. 'I'll make sure of it.'

Chapter Twenty-Four

Welcome to the Mums of Forest Grove Facebook Group

Saturday 31st October
11 p.m.

Kitty Fletcher
Can I just take the chance to say what a wonderful time I had at the Belafontes' tonight? I'm just sorry I had to leave so early because of this silly cold I have. Tatjana is simply an amazing host, Lawrence is so charming and their children are impeccably behaved. They're a true asset to the village! And that house too, just beautiful.

Pauline Sharpe
Erm, Kitty, were we at the same party?

Kitty Fletcher
We were, Pauline! We had a chat, remember?

Belinda Bell
I think Pauline's referring to the time after you left, Kitty. Some rather interesting revelations were made about Tatjana.

Ellie Mileham

You know she's a member of this group, Belinda?

Belinda Bell

Not any more! I just checked, she's left.

Kitty Fletcher

She has indeed. What on earth happened?

Belinda Bell

Turns out she's been stalking Emma Okoro.

Kitty Fletcher

What nonsense!

Lucy Cronin

I'm afraid Belinda's right, Kitty. I was right there when it all came out and Tatjana didn't deny it. She faked an email to make Emma miss a school trip payment deadline and spread some rather nasty rumours. Even worse, as I learnt later, she gave Emma an alcoholic drink, pretending it wasn't alcoholic – and Emma was driving!

Kitty Fletcher

Gosh, I didn't know about that bit. I wouldn't be surprised if Tatjana's the one behind my doctored MySpace page.

Vanessa Shillingford

Can we close this thread please? It's not fair on Tatjana. She's clearly going through something at the moment and as much as I don't approve of her actions, especially as they impacted on my lovely neighbour Emma, my guess is she has some mental health issues to deal with.

Belinda Bell

Pfft. Not that old excuse. You know, I always knew they were trouble when they moved in. Plus their eldest son is a little lout, he hit my grandson only last week!

Rebecca Feine

I thought it was Emma you thought was trouble, Belinda? Make your mind up! And please be careful what you say about kids on here.

Myra Young

Lawrence is lovely, I can say that with complete confidence as his PA. Please don't tar him with the same brush. Yes, Zeke is a handful but he's just a very spirited little boy. Lawrence is devastated about this and is doing all he can to help his wife. I suggest we give them some privacy and turn the comments off on this thread, Kitty.

Kitty Fletcher

Agreed. Consider this thread CLOSED for business. In the meantime, I am going to look into the possibility that Tatjana Belafonte was behind the fake MySpace page.

Chapter Twenty-Five

Saturday 31st October
11.30 p.m.

Emma lay in bed, unable to sleep. She and Dele had left the Halloween party with Isla straight after their chat with Lawrence. They had decided to leave the car and walk back through the woods after those Pumpkin Punches Emma had drunk. She couldn't find Harriet, but then she was used to her sister disappearing at parties.

They'd tried to make the walk back fun and spooky, but Isla was quiet. She would have heard some of the commotion, but she didn't ask what it was all about. Emma was pleased she didn't. She was struggling to wrap her head around it all herself!

After Isla went to bed, Dele and Emma sat in the living room.

'I should have taken you more seriously about Tatjana, babe,' he said with a sigh. 'I'm sorry.'

'You *were* right about her not being Jade, though,' Emma said. She had finally admitted this to herself now, after their conversation with Lawrence. He said Tatjana had grown up in Hastings and her mother had died when she was young. It just wouldn't add up if she was Isla's birth mother, who had lived in London all her life and whose mother was certainly alive when they adopted Isla.

'I can't blame you for thinking it, though,' Dele said, holding her hand. 'I should have listened.'

'Well, it's over now.'

'Not for Tatjana. I hope she gets the help she needs.'

Emma nodded. 'Me too.'

They had gone to bed, but now Emma lay awake, thinking about Tatjana. The truth was, she was concerned about her. Yes, Tatjana had had this awful irrational vendetta against her, but she was clearly mentally ill. Hadn't Emma herself struggled once?

At least Tatjana had a good husband like Lawrence, just as Emma had in Dele at that time. He'd get help for her.

'Hey, you.'

Emma looked up. They kept the bedroom door ajar to listen out for Isla, and now Emma could see her sister standing in the darkness of the landing. She got out of bed, quiet so as not to disturb a snoring Dele, and went out to join her.

'So Tatjana was behind everything?' Harriet whispered.

'Yep. Everything.'

'Are you going to call social services, then? You have your proof now.'

Emma shook her head. 'She's not Jade.'

'Come on. Are you serious? What about your instincts? The way she fawns over Isla? I saw it at the party, it was ridiculous!'

'I was wrong. There is *nothing* linking her to Jade Dixon.'

Harriet looked at Isla sleeping in her room, curled up on her side, her thumb in her mouth. 'So that's it,' she asked with a furrowed brow, 'you're just going to drop it?'

'Of course I am!' Emma loved her sister, but sometimes Harriet just didn't know when it was time to let go of something. Isla stirred in her bed. 'Look, Harriet, I'm tired. I need sleep.'

Harriet shrugged as she backed away. 'Fine then. But don't say I didn't warn you – if Tatjana does turn out to be Jade.'

On Monday, Emma braced herself as she entered the school playground with Isla. She wasn't sure how people would react. She was convinced half the village knew about it now, there were so many people at the party.

The first person she saw was Lucy, who was talking in a huddle with some of the other mums. When she saw Emma, she headed straight for her.

Great, Emma thought.

'I am *so* sorry,' Lucy said as soon as she got to her, Isla and Poppy going off to play together. 'I should never have been taken in by Tatjana's lies.'

Doesn't explain why you were a spiteful little cow, Emma wanted to say.

Instead, she smiled. 'Don't worry, it's in the past.'

'Phew,' Lucy said, pretending to wipe her brow. 'I was so worried you'd hate me.'

'Hmmm,' Emma said.

'I mean, look at them.' Lucy gestured to Isla and Poppy, who were doing some kind of dance move in the middle of the playground. 'They're so great together. You know, we really need to sort a playdate.'

All these months after I moved here? Emma wanted to say.

Instead she nodded. 'Sure.'

'So did you ever find out why Tatjana had it in for you?' Lucy asked, lowering her voice to a whisper as she leaned in close to Emma. 'Myra thinks it's because she had a thing for Dele, whereas Michelle reckons it's—'

'I have *no* idea,' Emma quickly interrupted her. 'There's no point speculating. She'll have her reasons.'

'Well, everyone feels so awful for you.'

Emma looked around her at the other parents, who were giving her sympathetic looks.

Funny how opinions could change so quickly in Forest Grove.

'Oh God, there she is,' Lucy said, crossing her arms as she looked towards the forest.

Emma followed her gaze to see Tatjana emerge from the trees holding Zeke's hand as he tried to get away from her. People in the playground turned to look at her, whispering.

'I can't believe she's here today,' Lucy said, shaking her head in disgust.

Myra walked over to join them.

'Can you believe she's here?' Lucy said to her, scandal in her eyes. 'I thought she'd at least pretend to be sick or something, let the dust settle, you know. It's not like she hasn't got the money to get a childminder.'

'Quite,' Myra said.

Emma looked at Myra in surprise. She was Lawrence's PA! But that wouldn't necessarily stop her from disliking his wife, would it?

Emma stood awkwardly watching Tatjana, too. She didn't want to be part of this witch hunt, and yet Tatjana had tried to ruin her reputation.

'That kid needs a firm hand,' Lucy said, as Zeke shoved Tatjana away then ran up to a tree, grabbing at one of the hanging branches. 'Look at him! No respect for nature and she's doing f-all about it!'

Tatjana closed her eyes, pinching her nose.

Emma couldn't help it, she felt sorry for her! Lucy and Myra were right. Tatjana shouldn't have had to come in today. It was less about her having the gall to show her face, as they'd implied, and more about how vulnerable she must be feeling after Saturday night.

Couldn't Lawrence have brought Zeke in?

'God, look at her,' Lucy spat. 'To think I called her a friend.'

'I know I work for Lawrence, but between us, I never really liked his wife,' Myra said, narrowing her eyes in Tatjana's direction. 'Prancing around in those expensive clothes of hers.'

'I know, right?' Lucy said. 'Like a Gucci coat is appropriate for forest life.'

Myra and Lucy were too busy laughing to notice when Emma backed away from them. She did *not* want to be involved in their malicious gossip.

'Funny how people can change their tune, isn't it?'

Emma turned to see Faye standing close to her. They watched Lucy and Myra still gossiping.

'I mean, it's pretty awful what Tatjana did,' Faye said, 'but I hate the way they pretend they weren't both fawning over her this time last week.'

Emma nodded. 'Yep, that's why I had to walk away.'

'I noticed.' They watched Tatjana grab Zeke's hand and pull him across the playground towards the school, her eyes down. 'I actually feel sorry for the woman,' Faye said. 'Can you believe it?'

Just then Tatjana looked over and caught Emma's eye.

'I'm glad I'm not the only one,' Emma said as she frowned and turned away from Tatjana's gaze, face flushing. 'I mean, she has issues, doesn't she? Lawrence should have made her stay at home, poor thing.'

Faye gave her a look. 'I'm surprised *you're* being so nice about her.' Then she sighed. 'Look, I've been meaning to message you. I spent half of yesterday composing text messages then deleting them.' She swallowed, looking uncomfortable. 'It's clear Tatjana was behind the rumours about you and Shawn and I'm sorry, okay? I was a psycho bitch, I should have waited for the facts before I laid into you.'

'Yeah, you should've,' Emma said, then she gave Faye a small smile. 'I forgive you though.'

Faye smiled back. 'Can we continue where we left off? Maybe lunch some time?'

Emma nodded. 'That would be great.'

The school bell rang out and they both turned to watch as Tatjana hugged her son goodbye, holding him for a few moments longer than usual as he tried to shove her away. She let go and Zeke ran off to the queue without a backward glance.

Tatjana stood watching him for a while, clearly trying to hold back her tears.

Then she looked over at Emma, a tear falling down her cheek, before turning and heading back towards the forest.

'At least her little vendetta is over now,' Faye said, putting her hand on Emma's arm. 'You can try to relax.'

Emma nodded, but inside something didn't feel right.

Chapter Twenty-Six

Monday 2nd November
9.15 a.m.

Tatjana really needs to snap out of it! It's bad enough she's made a complete mess of this. I'm having to take it all on myself now – I just can't trust Tatjana to follow through. She's been utterly useless lately after a brilliant start – and even worse, she expressed sympathy *for Emma yesterday.*

I think poor Zeke senses all the tension as he's playing up more than normal. I gave him a quick slap and Tatjana completely overreacted. She started ranting and raving, telling me he was just being this way because of how obsessed I am with you.

Well, I am, you're my daughter!

And don't be alarmed by me mentioning that slap. You know I wouldn't do that to you, darling. From what I've seen, you are impeccably behaved, despite your snowflake parents.

When Tatjana calmed down, we had a little chat. As I reminded her, she was onboard with all of this when I first raised the subject of getting you back a year ago. She wouldn't ever say this out loud, but Tatjana is desperate *for a girl – and after making it very clear that there would be no more babies (the mess! The sleepless nights!) the next best thing for her was you. She completely fell in love with you when I showed her all your photos and the videos I've had taken.*

Who wouldn't?

We were all ready to put our little plan into action, had even found a gorgeous penthouse flat in one of the best streets in Islington to be near you, but then your pretend parents put a spanner in the works and decided to move you to Forest bloody Grove.

Tatjana loves London, so the thought of becoming a country bumpkin filled her with horror. I had to promise her a house like nothing she's ever seen. It helped when we visited Forest Grove — it was actually rather lovely. And when Tatjana saw the plans for the house, she suddenly decided she loved the idea of moving there. Funny what the promise of living in a huge house can do to a woman like her.

When we got to work, Tatjana was very enthusiastic. She loves her little projects. I think that's why she was so drawn to me at first. A messed-up boy that needed taming.

As for why I was drawn to her, it's pretty clear really: she looks just like your birth mother, Jade. Or a version of Jade that could have been if she'd had more self-control with the drugs.

Yes, yes, I played my part in Jade's addiction, I admit. But if I hadn't sold drugs back then, there would have been no money because of my useless parents, and my little brother would have had no home.

It was a case of necessity, Isla, not desire, as it always was back then. I hope you understand that?

Anyway, seeing Tatjana that day outside her flat was fate — I truly believe that. She was looking for me just as much as I was looking for her. Her mother had passed away, you see, and she'd just got back from an awful lunch with her father, exhausted from keeping up her lies about being at Edinburgh University, when in fact she was at a poky little college studying fashion instead.

She needed someone who knew her for all she was, but still loved her. And I needed to fill the gap Jade had left. Her father's money helped, too. Luckily, he's an old-school socialist, a man who believes in finding diamonds in the rough. He took me on as a project, too, cleaned me up, turned me into the kind of man his daughter deserved. Suddenly, the poor little rich girl grieving for her useless mother was a happy little rich girl with a handsome new man.

Except lately, she's begun to doubt me. I knew it from the moment I found the dossier she'd created on Jade. Photos of Jade's mother, of her father. She tried to tell me she wanted to learn more about her future daughter's background, but I knew she was lying. She was looking into me, trying to figure out where Jade was . . . why she seems to have disappeared off the face of the earth.

That's the problem with women like Tatjana, we're just playthings to them. The novelty wears off too quickly.

I'll make sure you're not like that, Isla, even with all my money at your fingertips. You have the right genes to ensure you aren't a fly-by-night type.

At first, when I met your mother Jade, I thought she would be like that, too. She saw me for what I was, accepted it, didn't try to change me.

But then she changed. I know now it's because she was pregnant. She didn't even give me a chance. She couldn't believe I would ever change. If only she could see me now!

I will never forgive her for not telling me you were growing inside her. She just let me move away with no knowledge that I would become a father in a matter of months.

When I returned two years later, your grandmother Evie told me about you. I was a father! When she told me Jade had given you up for adoption, I went mad! So mad that yes, I admit, I may have hurt her.

I tried my best to track you down, but in the end, I'm ashamed to say, I gave up.

And my father-in-law's money made things a whole lot easier. Sure, I had a little money from my days dealing drugs. Yes, I'll admit to that, Isla. I dealt drugs. But I never used them! That's the thing about dealers, the good ones anyway – we don't touch the drugs ourselves. So I kept clean while your mother went downhill. Even got good A levels despite the God-awful school I was at. Used my money from dealing to get the hell out of my estate, start a degree in architecture at some second-rate university as far away as I could get in Scotland.

When I met Tatjana, her dad helped finance the rest of my training to become an architect over the years, set up a business as I trained, become the man I was meant to be. For once, I understood it is possible to pull yourself up from the gutter. I saw all my potential and it made me feel superhuman! My little business designing office spaces started to make money, proper money.

I was able to hire Garrett, my private investigator. That first video he sent me from your tenth birthday party last year was one of the best things I've ever seen. I knew then that I had to get you back. I felt such a strong ache in my heart for you, Isla. I started with your fake father, digging into his past, watching him. But he's just too boring, too average, too safe.

Your fake mother, on the other hand . . . She was a true gift to me. She makes it just too easy.

But now my plans are falling apart after Saturday night's disaster. My idea was to get Emma so drunk she'd be caught drink-driving her daughter home, either by other villagers or by a conveniently placed police officer. But no, she figured it out . . . and saw those bloody notes Tatjana had made.

Don't worry though, Isla, all is not lost.

What a little gift it was to find out that your fake mother saw a therapist . . . and for her to even give me his name. A whole new path has opened up to me. Just now, I had a phone call from Garrett that was very interesting indeed.

It turns out Emma was admitted to a private mental health facility in her twenties. Of course, there's an obvious reason why. I know that from her history and what happened then.

But why the private *facility? Why the hush-hush?*

I have a feeling that when I get the answers to my questions, finally you will be back with your real daddy. In the meantime, let's have a little fun at your fake mummy's expense . . .

Chapter Twenty-Seven

Wednesday 11th November
8.25 a.m.

Isla jogged downstairs, dark hair bouncing around her shoulders.

'Shoes on,' Emma said, yanking on her own boots.

'Okay, chill, Mum,' Isla said.

Emma smiled, shaking her head. She was already talking like a teen and yet she was three years away from being one. Nope, make that *two* years, because she was turning eleven soon. They'd been writing invites the night before for Isla's pamper party. Fifteen girls all cooped up in the house with make-up and hair accessories!

It would be exhausting but fun, thought Emma as she helped Isla put on her coat. As long as Isla was happy.

They both ran out of the house towards the car.

Halfway down the path, Isla stopped dead in her tracks, a look of horror on her face.

'Oh no, Mum!' she declared.

'What's wrong?' Emma asked.

Isla pointed to the front of the car.

Emma followed her gaze, then let out a gasp.

A large black crow was tangled up in the grille of the car's bumper.

'Oh Jesus,' Emma said. 'Don't look at it.'

But Isla's horror had now turned into fascination. 'Is it dead?' she asked in an awe-filled whisper, refusing to look away. 'Why is its neck like that?'

'It's definitely dead, darling.' Emma glanced at her watch. They'd be late if they didn't leave soon, but how could she drive to school with a dead crow tangled in her bumper?

And how on earth had it got there in the first place?

Maybe she'd driven into it in the dark on the way back from work the night before, but surely she'd have felt the impact?

'Wait there, darling,' Emma said, 'and *please* stop staring at it.'

Emma ran back up the path and let herself in, scrambling around in the under-stairs cupboard for a plastic bag. Finally finding one, she darted outside again, locking the front door behind her.

'Get in the car, Isla, I'll sort it,' Emma instructed.

'Can't I watch?' Isla protested.

'No, darling! Get in the car.'

Isla's shoulders slumped and she jumped into the car, craning her neck so she could watch her mother go about the delicate operation of removing a dead crow from her bumper.

Emma wrapped the plastic bag around her hand and crouched down in front of the bird. Up close, she could see its wing had got jammed under the grille, its head bent backwards, one beady lifeless eye staring up at her.

'Poor thing, how on earth did you do this to yourself?' Emma said, flinching as she wrapped her plastic-covered hands around the crow's wing, turning her head away so she didn't have to watch. It took several pulls to yank it out and when it finally did, a speck of its blood landed on Emma's coat.

She tried not to gag as she wrapped up the bird. As she was about to tie up the bag, something caught her eye.

She frowned, peering closer.

Was that a *necklace* wrapped around its neck?

Emma shook the bag a little to make the crow turn, and let out a gasp as the necklace came into full view.

It was made of black tweed, a pale-pink gemstone hanging from it.

Emma reeled back in horror, dropping the bag, the dead crow spilling out of it.

She knew that necklace!

Chapter Twenty-Eight

Emma steadied herself with her hand on the hard ground as she continued staring at the necklace.

Memories came flooding back to her.

Another time and another necklace just like this one, tainted with blood.

She shook her head, putting her hand to her mouth.

What was happening? *Why* was this happening?

'Mum?' Isla called out from the car. 'What's wrong?'

Emma quickly wiped the tears from her eyes. 'Nothing, darling!'

She gulped in some deep slow breaths to calm herself, then carefully untangled the necklace from around the crow. She scooped the bird back up with the bag, twisting the handles around to secure it before standing up on shaky legs and throwing it in the outdoor bin. She looked at the necklace then tucked it in some tissues, placing it in her bag.

She took another breath, catching sight of her reflection in the window and the haunted look in her eyes.

She wiped a trembling hand across her brow then fixed a smile on her face, turning back to Isla. 'All done!'

'Was it gross?' Isla asked as Emma got in.

'Yep,' Emma said, struggling to get out more than one word.

She started the engine and swerved out of the drive, nearly crashing into a passing car.

'Mum!' Isla declared.

Emma grimaced, raising a hand to say sorry to the other driver.

'That was close!' Isla said.

'Sorry, darling,' Emma replied, doing all she could to hold on to her sanity as she thought of the necklace.

It couldn't be a coincidence. Could it be Tatjana? She'd been behind everything else, after all. And yet was she really capable of going to the trouble of finding a dead crow – or worse, killing one – then attaching an exact replica of the necklace to it, before shoving it into the grille of Emma's car?

Even worse, that would mean Tatjana knew what had happened all those years ago. Emma allowed herself to consider if her original instincts were true and Tatjana *was* Isla's birth mother.

What had happened could be used as ammunition against Emma – ammunition that could lead to Isla being taken away from her!

Emma looked at Isla, tears filling her eyes.

When they got to school, it took every ounce of Emma's strength not to burst out crying. She held Isla close as she walked through the school gates and Isla didn't protest, as if sensing her mother's torment. Every now and again, she peered up at Emma with worried eyes.

Emma saw Tatjana and Lawrence right away when they got into the playground. Lawrence had begun accompanying Tatjana on the school run over the past few days. Emma supposed it made sense if he was worried about his wife 'playing up'. She was tempted to march up to Tatjana right then and ask her if she'd done it – but what then? She would have to explain why the necklace was so significant.

Could she risk that?

So instead, she lowered her head and pulled Isla even closer, grateful to her daughter for sticking so close by her instead of running off with her friends.

When the bell went, Isla gave her mother a big hug. 'I love you, Mum,' she said.

'I love you too, darling.' She hugged Isla tight again, then watched her join her friends in the queue.

When Emma turned, she noticed Lawrence walking towards her.

Great.

She just wanted to get back to her car and try to understand what she'd just seen. But Lawrence Belafonte was her client, so instead she had to fake a smile.

'How are we doing this fine morning?' he asked in a jolly voice when he got to her.

'Fine!' she lied. 'How are you?'

'I'm great. I wanted to chat to you actually. Shall we walk back to your car together?'

She looked in the direction of Tatjana, who was watching them with a dark look on her face.

Lawrence followed Emma's gaze. 'Tatjana's heading back home, so don't worry, it'll just be me.'

Emma fell into step with Lawrence as they headed towards the car park.

'I wanted to let you know Tatjana has an appointment with that therapist you recommended,' he said.

'Oh, that's good.' Only then did Emma wonder if she'd made a mistake, putting Tatjana in touch with someone from her past.

Maybe, somehow, that was how she had found out about the necklace?

No, no, Emma, she pleaded with herself. *Tatjana is not Jade!*

Lawrence examined her face. 'Is everything okay, Emma? You seem . . .' he paused. 'Upset about something.'

Her cheeks flushed. 'No, I'm absolutely fine.' As she said that, her voice wobbled, tears flooding her eyes.

Lawrence put his hand on her shoulder. 'Emma, what on earth is wrong?'

'I found a dead bird in the grille of my car this morning.' She glanced at the front of her car where the crow had been, her voice quivering with emotion as she thought of the necklace in her bag. 'It was horrible.'

He grimaced. 'I can imagine.'

Emma looked towards where Tatjana had disappeared among the trees.

Lawrence followed her gaze. 'Oh God, you don't think it's Tatjana, do you? She's incredibly squeamish about things like that, plus we've been away visiting her father – we only just got back an hour ago!'

Emma frowned. That *would* make it difficult for Tatjana to stuff a dead crow into her grille. Not impossible, but difficult.

She took a deep breath. She needed to get a hold of herself. 'No, no, it's fine, just a silly bird flew into my poor car. Right, I must start my day. I'm very busy, thanks to you. Not that I'm complaining!' she quickly added with a nervous laugh.

He laughed too. 'Yes, at least all the work I've given you will keep your mind off a dead crow.'

She nodded but inside, she knew *nothing* would take her mind off that.

And she was right. She simply couldn't focus all day long, and all that night too, her sleep was filled with nightmares she thought were long gone.

It was the same every night that week and by the end of it, she was absolutely exhausted.

When she got into work on Friday, she had a message waiting for her to call her manager Saul as soon as possible. He was actually supposed to be on holiday, so it was bound to be something urgent.

'Hi Saul, you called?' she asked when she called him.

'Ah, Emma. Yes, I did. I've been having a look at the Belafonte Designs social media streams.'

'Okay,' Emma said hesitantly.

'There are rather a lot of typos on their feeds and one of the images is blurry,' he said, clearly hating to have to tell her this.

Emma put her hand to her face. She was usually so good at double- and triple-checking her content – what was going on?

'Can you have a word with whoever's been in charge of scheduling content?' Saul asked. 'Is it the new girl, Aisha?'

'No, Aisha's great. It was me,' she admitted.

'You?' he asked in surprise.

'Yes, Lawrence Belafonte insisted nobody else should have control of his accounts via our scheduling tool.'

'I see. You really should have told me that, Emma. It's been a while since you've had to do that kind of work. You're out of practice. No wonder you're making mistakes! Do you think you can fix this?'

'Of course.'

'Fine, I'll send you a list of the mistakes I noticed.'

After he'd said goodbye, Emma slammed the phone down, putting her head in her hands. How could she have made mistakes? Maybe it was because she was *so* exhausted. She needed to sort out her sleep, otherwise she'd only make more mistakes. She didn't even have Tatjana as an excuse now. She quickly set about editing all the posts Saul had emailed her about. Unfortunately, only LinkedIn and Instagram posts could be edited; Twitter didn't have an edit function yet.

As she checked them, she frowned. They were odd mistakes, strange grammatical errors that she would never make.

When she was done correcting everything, she was even more exhausted. At least it was an early finish for her that day. She'd pick up Isla and they could go straight home, get in their PJs and watch a film in bed with popcorn. Then she'd have the whole weekend to think about that necklace she'd found on the dead crow, maybe tell Dele. Isla had already mentioned the crow to him, but they didn't know about the necklace. Until then, she'd just need to somehow get through the afternoon.

After lunch, she got a call from Myra. 'Emma, we've just had a disgruntled former employee post a derogatory comment on Instagram about Belafonte Designs,' she said in her clipped tones.

'Oh really?' Emma said, scrambling to find their account in her social media management tool. A reminder for something popped up on her screen and she quickly closed it, focusing on finding the comment which had been posted just a couple of minutes ago.

AVOID THIS COMPANY LIKE THE PLAGUE! Pay terrible, plus the MD Lawrence expects you to work all the hours under the sun and is a bloody tyrant despite the way he acts to the outside world. WORST COMPANY EVER!

'You have to delete it,' Myra said.

'I wouldn't recommend deleting it,' Emma replied. 'It's bad form, really. The employee will probably notice it and it'll wind them up even more. It looks far better to compose a response.'

Myra paused. 'Fine,' she snapped. 'Just get it sorted.' Then she put the phone down in her customary rude way.

Emma started to compose a response, managing to do it within five minutes. She pressed 'post', then smiled.

Later, as she drove out of the building, she was greeted by an epic traffic jam. She sat in it for ages, but luckily, she was still just in time to pick Isla up from school.

But when Isla came out from her class, she looked miserable.

'We missed you this afternoon,' her teacher Miss Morgan said when Emma walked over.

'This afternoon?' Emma asked. 'What do you mean?'

'Our weekly parents' talk. You were coming in to chat about your job, remember?'

Emma closed her eyes. How could she have forgotten? She thought of the reminder that she'd dismissed in a hurry to sort out that disgruntled employee. It must have been about the talk. 'I am so sorry, it *completely* slipped my mind.'

'It's fine, it happens,' Miss Morgan said with a smile. 'We can reschedule you?'

'Yes, absolutely. Thank you.'

Emma took Isla's hand, feeling the other parents' eyes on her. In the distance, she noticed Tatjana watching her too, her brow creased.

Well, this was something she *couldn't* blame Tatjana for. It was all her own fault!

As for that dead crow and the necklace, she didn't know what the hell to think about it all.

Over the weekend, she deliberated whether or not to tell Dele about the necklace. But she just couldn't bring herself to. They'd had so much drama lately; she didn't want to lay this on him. So instead she called her sister during a walk in the forest, while Dele took Isla to her guitar lesson.

'That's messed up,' Harriet admitted after Emma told her about the dead crow.

'Yep, someone must know. The necklace is just too much of a coincidence.'

'But how?' Harriet asked. 'Dad sorted it, right?'

Emma nodded. 'But the truth always gets out, doesn't it? I always bloody knew it would.'

'Don't be silly. You're jumping to conclusions!'

'Then how do you explain the necklace?' Emma shouted, kicking at a pile of leaves in frustration.

'Okay, calm down,' Harriet said. 'Who do you think is doing this? Tatjana?'

Emma looked towards the Belafontes' house. 'I don't know, she's supposed to be getting help and she seems so – so *vulnerable* lately.'

'Who else can it be though, Em? Surely this is ringing alarm bells about her again?'

'But *why* is she doing this?'

'You *know* why.'

Emma shook her head. 'No, Lawrence said she grew up in Hastings and her mum died. Tatjana's *dad* told him.'

'So what? Her dad is Jade's birth *grandfather*, maybe he's in on it too?'

'Either way,' Emma said as she stepped over a log, 'that still doesn't answer the question about how she knows about the necklace.'

'There were photos from us earlier in the night – they were in the local paper, remember? It's easy if someone does enough digging.'

'Jesus,' Emma said, her scalp tightening in fear. 'This is just awful.'

There was a sound from nearby. Emma froze, peering around her, but there was no one there.

'Don't panic! This doesn't mean she knows *everything.*' Harriet's voice softened. 'She's messing with your mind. Just – just rise above it.'

'You don't get it, do you?' Emma said. 'If it is Jade, then she's trying to find a way to discredit me as a mother – and oh boy, is this the *ultimate* way.'

'But what happened has nothing to do with your parenting skills!'

'You sure about that?'

Harriet was quiet.

'Anyway,' Emma continued, 'I *lied* to the authorities. I didn't disclose pertinent information during the adoption process.'

'That's not enough for them to take Isla away.'

'True, but the nature of it . . .' Emma came to a stop and leaned her hand against a tree, gulping in deep breaths as she thought about that night.

'Emma, calm yourself. Follow my breaths. In, out.'

Emma did as her sister said and found herself growing calmer. 'Maybe I should just come clean,' she said.

'No!' Harriet shouted. 'They'll take Isla away from you.'

'Maybe that's what I deserve.'

'Don't think like that. It was a *mistake.* Look, we just need to figure this out together.' She paused. '*I* know! Why don't we try to track Jade down ourselves, just so we know for sure?'

'Like how?'

'Do you know where she used to live?'

'I wasn't supposed to, but we pretty much guessed when the social worker said it was the roughest estate in North London.'

'You mean Rowgham Estate?'

'That's it.'

'Yeah, I read some reports about it. Why don't we visit it? Even if she's not there, we can ask questions. Talk to her mum. Any skank of a boyfriend of hers. Friends. Be a regular Nancy Drew.'

Emma thought about it. Maybe Harriet was right. She just needed this little niggling voice in the back of her mind telling her that Tatjana was Jade to go away, then she could try to pull herself together.

'Okay,' she said. 'Let's do it. Let's visit Jade's estate.'

Chapter Twenty-Nine

Sunday 15th November
2 p.m.

Well, it's official, your fake mother is losing it. I just saw her in the woods and she was on the verge of having a full-on breakdown!

She's making this too easy for me! A little shove in the right direction and she's falling apart at the seams without any real help from me. But then she has *got a lot to contend with. A past heavy with secrets which I'm doing everything I can to remind her of.*

Tatjana doesn't approve, of course. She said the dead bird was too much. But it was a nice touch, don't you think?

I saw you looking at it with interest, Isla. Good, I'm pleased you're not squeamish. I was worried you'd get upset, but you seemed fine with it. Your fake mother, however . . . well, it worked a treat. I'd parked around the side of your street and waited for Emma to come out of the house so I could drive past on the way to school just in time to see the look on her face when she saw the necklace! It was worth it, even with Zeke asking over and over from the back why we were driving to school instead of walking.

That was a particularly clever touch. In one of the articles I found online about what happened all those years ago, there was a photo 'taken on the very night of the tragedy' as the caption said and in it, that necklace.

It was easy enough to find something similar – a cheap thing off eBay – and I was all set. Then all I needed was the bird. I told Tatjana I found it dead on the lawn. She didn't need to know I killed it myself. One throw of a rock and it was done. I thought about asking Tatjana to attach it to the car, but I knew she would mess it up. That wasn't exactly pleasant, I can tell you, going out in the dead of the night with a dead crow in my hands.

I'm still punishing Tatjana, you see, like forcing her to continue doing the school run last week, despite her pleas for me to do it. In the end, I've had to accompany her this week because, honestly, she looks like she's going to lose it just like Emma is. I wouldn't want her blurting anything out, would I?

These women are so weak! You won't be like that though, Isla, I'll make sure of it.

Don't worry, it won't be long until we're together. Garrett is in Dartmouth right now, and said he just needs a little more time to get all the facts.

In the meantime, I'm going to continue pushing Emma over the edge. It's such fun to watch, after all, and what I have planned next is particularly *exciting* . . .

Chapter Thirty

The large tower block where Isla once lived with Jade and her grandmother loomed above Emma as she drove towards it. She'd booked the day off work, telling Dele she needed a duvet day after so many sleepless nights. The plan was to get in and out of London in time to pick up Isla from school.

'Wow, that is *quite* some sight,' Harriet said as Emma drove them through the estate. She'd appeared that morning raring to go. Emma was grateful. She needed her.

Emma looked out at the rubbish-strewn public gardens and the skulking characters who looked as if they hadn't had a good meal in weeks.

'It makes me feel sad that Isla spent her first year here,' Emma commented. 'It's such a contrast to Forest Grove.'

'Yep, weird to think my gorgeous niece started life here.'

'Or maybe we're being snobs,' Emma said. 'Who are we to judge? Maybe these people are perfectly happy.'

'Nope,' Harriet said, shaking her head resolutely. 'I read a lot about this estate when I was working at the think tank.

Back then, it was crying out to be renovated and it looks like that never happened. So crime rates just grow, the poverty just deepens.'

Emma peered over at her sister as Harriet gazed outside with a sad look on her face. She was so passionate about the injustices in society. She'd bang on about how hard it was for people to break the chain of poverty and instability passed down from generation to generation. In the end, it had been one of the factors that made Emma and Dele want to adopt: they wanted to give a child the chance to break that chain before it was too late and another generation was forced to endure a difficult life.

'Do you really think Jade got out and transformed herself into an accomplished young fashion designer?' Emma asked as they passed a teenage girl sitting on a brick wall, sullenly staring at her phone. 'That would take quite something.'

'The chance of seeing the child you gave birth to again would be quite some motivation,' Harriet replied.

'I hadn't thought of it like that.'

They passed a car with no wheels and Harriet raised an eyebrow. 'Feast your eyes on how your car will look later.'

'Bloody better not, I just got these wheels replaced.'

She turned into a small car park outside the flats and parked next to a white van with rusting panels. She looked up at the tower block again. 'There must be hundreds of flats in there.'

'And you have no idea which one Jade lived in?'

Emma shook her head. 'No. I don't even know for sure if she lived in this particular block!'

'This is going to be a looooong day.'

'We better hurry up then, I have to pick Isla up later.'

They got out of the car and walked up to the tower block, the smell of weed swirling its way towards them.

'They're making it easy for us,' Harriet said, pointing at the main door into the flats, which had been propped open with a brick.

Emma shuddered as she thought again of little Isla being here: the lack of security, the cloud of drugs.

They walked into a small foyer. It actually looked as if it had been renovated lately, the smell of new paint on the walls, even a large canvas on the wall showing a circle of laughing children. But Emma was pretty sure she could see a needle in the corner of the reception area and there was a splurge of what looked like bloody fingerprints beneath the painting.

'So we take it floor by floor then?' she asked her sister.

Harriet nodded, silent as she took it all in.

They walked to the lift, then sighed as they noticed the 'out of service' notice.

'As if life isn't bad enough already for these people,' Emma said.

Harriet pointed to a door to the side with a stairs symbol on it. 'I hope you've been doing your leg lifts?'

'Ha, like I have time for exercise!'

They opened the door to see a child of about Isla's age sitting on one of the steps, playing with a Barbie doll. Emma's heart sank as she took in the girl's blonde matted hair and the bruise around her eye. She exchanged a look with Harriet and her sister shook her head sadly.

Emma walked up towards the girl. 'Hello.'

'Hi,' the girl said, peering up.

'Do you know anyone by the name of Jade who lives here?' Emma asked her.

The girl shook her head.

'Okay, thanks.'

They went to pass her, but then the girl tugged on the hem of Emma's jeans. 'Old Vea talks about some lady called Jade, though. She has a picture of her in her flat.'

Emma paused. 'Old Vea? Where does she live?'

The girl pointed to the door leading to the first floor. 'Number one-oh-seven.'

'One hundred and seven?' Emma asked. The girl nodded and Emma and Harriet smiled at each other. At least they wouldn't need to walk up twenty flights of stairs to find out if 'Old Vea' knew Jade.

They thanked the girl, then went into the corridor, finding the flat they were looking for. The door was painted a different colour to the other doors, a pretty peacock blue. But the paint was faded and cracked in places.

Emma knocked on the door.

There was the sound of movement, then the door opened a few centimetres, two brown eyes peering out from the gap. Through the glimpses she caught, Emma could see it was a black woman in her late forties, thin and short with gaps in her teeth and short frizzy black hair. She was wearing a long black-and-red dress and furry puppy slippers at the end of her bare pockmarked legs.

'Hello?' a croaky voice asked.

'Hello, are you Vea?' Emma asked.

'Sorry, not doing any readings today.'

Emma took in a breath. Jade's mother had made money doing tarot cards.

Was this woman Jade's mother . . . Isla's grandmother? She *had* been called Evie.

The woman went to shut the door, but Emma put her hand on it. 'I'm not here for a reading. I'm looking for Jade.'

The woman's eyes narrowed. 'My Jade?'

My Jade.

It *was* Jade's mother.

'Yes,' Emma said, trying to keep her voice steady. 'Does she still live here?'

'Oh, she's long gone.'

'How long?'

The woman's eyes flooded with tears. 'Since they took our darling Isla away.'

Harriet put her hand on her sister's back to reassure her.

'Do you know where she went?'

'Nope,' Evie snapped. 'Just disappeared.'

Chills ran down Emma's spine. 'May I come in to have a chat?'

'Why? What you after?' The woman stared at Emma suspiciously.

'Nothing! I'm just – I'm friends with Jade. We've lost touch. I'd love to chat to you about her.'

The woman examined her face, then she peered behind her in Harriet's direction. 'You have quite the aura about you,' she said.

Emma wasn't sure if that was a good or a bad thing.

Evie opened the door. 'Fine. Come in.'

Must be a good thing.

They both walked in and Emma tried not to put her hand to her nose. The small flat stank of cigarette smoke, alcohol and some kind of meaty stench. She looked down at the filthy carpet, imagining Isla crawling all over it as a baby.

'Scuse the mess,' Evie said. 'Takes an effort to tidy now with me old cranky bones. I used to keep it in better shape when I did all my readings, but those have tailed off too now I have my bad back.'

'We don't mind,' Harriet said, her expression suggesting the opposite as she peered around her into a dark untidy bedroom.

The woman led them into a small living room with two battered brown leather sofas. Between them was a coffee table strewn with dirty mugs and women's magazines. On the walls were posters featuring illustrations of mystical-looking women in various poses holding crystal balls, and a pack of tarot cards lay sprawled on the floor.

Evie gestured towards a large photo of a pretty girl who looked like an older version of Isla. 'There she is,' she said. 'My girl.'

'Jade,' Emma said. She walked to the photo and picked it up. It was an old photo, probably from around the same time she'd met Jade all those years ago. She explored her face. Yes, carrying less weight, with short hair and a better lifestyle to make her skin and eyes glow, she could easily be Tatjana.

'So you haven't heard from Jade in nine years?' she asked as she put the photo back down.

'Nope.' Evie lit up a cigarette. 'How do you know her?'

'We went to school together.'

Emma felt bad about lying, but what would Jade's mother think if Emma told the truth? And what if it got back to social services? Dele had been right, Emma needed to be careful: she didn't want them to start looking into *her*.

Evie gave her a cynical look. 'You don't look like a Rowgham Comprehensive type of girl.'

'I'm so sorry you've lost contact with Jade,' Emma said, ignoring that statement. 'Have you reported her missing? Nine years is a long time.'

'Why?' Evie said. 'That girl always used to go missing, don't you remember? In the end, the police wouldn't even come out to see me when I reported her gone.'

Yes, Emma did remember from the reports she'd read about her before adopting Isla.

'Has anyone else seen her?' she asked.

'I hear rumours,' Evie said, taking in a long puff of smoke.

Harriet leaned forward. 'What kind of rumours?'

'Some people tell me she worked on a cruise ship, others that she moved to Australia.' Evie laughed, smoke spilling from her mouth. 'Some even told me she married a rich man!'

Emma and her sister looked at each other.

'As long as she isn't with that scum boyfriend any more, I don't mind who she married.' Evie drew her breath in through what remained of her teeth and shook her head. 'Bad news, that boy. Knew it from the moment I met him. I have a sense about these things.' Her eyes slid over to Harriet again, then away. 'The bruises Jade would come home with! He even hit me once.'

Harriet's mouth dropped open as Emma shifted uncomfortably in her seat.

'I'm so sorry to hear that,' Emma said.

'He had a spell on my girl,' Evie continued, leaning forward. 'She was *addicted* to him, like she was addicted to the drugs he sold.'

Emma swallowed. 'Was he Isla's father?'

'Of course! Don't you believe those rumours about Jade putting herself about. She told social services that, so they didn't question who the father was.' Evie smiled. 'Clever girl, meant they wouldn't contact him. No, my Jade wasn't a slut like some of the other girls were. Once she met someone she loved, she was loyal, like her good ol' mum.'

Emma closed her eyes for a moment. So Isla's father was a violent drug dealer. She shouldn't be surprised; they'd been warned it might be the case. But still, to hear it confirmed . . .

'What's his name?' Emma asked as casually as she could.

'Nathan . . .' She paused, thinking about it. 'Bellford, that's it!' she eventually said. 'Long time since that family moved away. Bloody psychopath, he was!' she spat.

'Why do you call him a psychopath?' Harriet asked.

'You know he killed a man?' Evie said, eyes narrowing. 'Of course, the police could never prove it. That boy was clever, that's why he was so dangerous. Was a surprise how clever he was really, considering the family he came from, two junkies and a backward boy for a little brother. But Nathan, he had something,' Evie said, tapping her head. 'Even with all the beatings he took off his father, who was a huge man, he somehow kept some brains about him.' Her face clouded over. 'Used it in the wrong way, mind, building himself up to be some drug lord here, then killing a boy who tried to get Jade away from him. They say the boy fell while they fought, that it was an accident, but we all know the truth. That was what he was like, Nathan. Jade once told me: once you was his, there was no stopping that, even if it meant killing someone else.'

Emma shivered as Harriet looked at Evie, alarmed.

Isla's father was a murderer!

'Does he still live here?' Emma dared to ask.

'No, thank the Lord. His family moved out before Isla was born.' She put her hand to her thin chest. 'Oh that precious little baby, why did they take her away?'

Emma watched as Evie shook her head. It must have been difficult for her to lose her granddaughter. From what Emma had read, Evie had done most of the caring. But she had her own demons. It just wouldn't have been the right place to bring up a child.

Emma thanked the stars Isla was able to escape this place and the awful violent man who was her father.

'I'm sure Isla has a wonderful life now,' Emma said, suddenly desperate for Evie to know that in some small way her granddaughter was fine. 'I'm sure she's a very happy girl.'

'She is,' Evie said with a sure nod. She reached for her tarot cards. 'I seen it in these, how happy she is. Bright as a button, too. I dream about her a lot, you know.'

Emma smiled, tears filling her eyes. 'Really?'

'Yes, I dream of her on a red swing in a big beautiful forest.'

Emma blinked in surprise.

'People say I'm a fake,' Evie said, leaning forward, 'but those who come to be read by me know. Like you. You're hiding something deep, I can sense it. There's a *guilt* in you, a dark twisted rope connecting to the past that you need to cut. You want me to do a reading?'

Emma quickly stood up. 'No, but thanks for your time.'

'Here's one for free then,' Evie said, pointing a finger at her. 'You carry a burden around with you. Until you let that burden free, you'll never feel right in your skin.'

'Shall we let ourselves out?' Emma asked, backing away.

'Whatever,' the old lady said, waving her hand about.

'She's good,' Harriet said as they stepped into Evie's hallway.

'Hmmm,' Emma whispered, not wanting to dwell on just how good she was. 'It's interesting how she said that Jade just "disappeared".' She used her fingers to make speech marks. 'Disappeared and started a new life as a fashion designer?'

'Or she's . . .' Harriet paused.

'She's what?' Emma asked.

'Dead?'

Emma stopped walking. 'Jesus, Harriet.'

'It's been years, Emma! And she had a violent ex, right? Isla's birth dad?'

'No,' Emma said, shaking her head. 'You told me yourself a million times how people slip between the holes in society. Let's just get out of here, okay?' she said, peering behind her into the living room at Evie, who was watching her intently. 'It's giving me the creeps.'

As they walked past a bedroom door that was ajar, Emma froze.

On the bedroom wall was a portrait of an old black man . . . the same man that Tatjana had had a photo of in her bedside drawer!

'What's up?' Harriet asked, looking between her sister and the portrait.

'Tatjana has a photo of that man! I'm sure of it!' She quickly took a photo of it with her phone, then looked back towards Evie. 'Sorry, one last question,' she called down the small hallway.

The woman looked up from the tarot cards she was gathering up from the floor. 'Yes?'

'That picture of the man in your room. Who is that?'

Evie's face softened. 'That's Devon, Jade's father.'

'Thanks,' Emma said. 'And thanks for the chat. Take care.'

Then she let herself out, adrenalin coursing through her.

'That's it!' she said as they walked down the exterior corridor. 'A solid connection! How else can Tatjana explain having a portrait of Jade's father unless she *is* Jade?'

'You hit the jackpot, sis,' Harriet said, smiling at her. 'You did it!'

'*We* did it,' Emma said. They smiled at each other. Then Emma sighed. 'I now just need to prove Tatjana *has* that photo. That's going to be tough, considering we're not talking.'

Harriet shrugged. 'Just arrange to meet up at her place. Make out you want to clear the air, then pop to the loo and take a picture.'

'Good idea. I'll talk to her tomorrow morning.' She looked at her watch. 'Right, shall we get some lunch, then I can head back to pick Isla up?'

'Why don't we go see Dad?' Harriet suggested, peering into the distance towards his flat, which was a twenty-minute walk away.

'You go if you want,' Emma said, not in the mood to spring a surprise visit on her unwelcoming father.

'Yeah,' Harriet replied, blowing her sister a kiss as she backed away. 'I will. Let me know how you get on.' Then she walked off.

On the drive home, Emma felt a sense of elation. She knew for certain that Tatjana was Jade now, and she just needed to get evidence of that photo from inside Tatjana – or Jade's – bedside drawer.

But her mood soon changed when fifteen minutes away from Forest Grove, there was a huge pile-up, leading to massive delays.

'Shit,' she said, looking at the time. Nearly three. 'Shit, shit, shit.'

She tried calling Dele, but he didn't answer. She even called Faye – no luck with her either. *This* was why she needed to make more friends. More mums to be on hand to help out, but instead, she had nobody!

When she called the school, it went to voicemail, so she left a quick message, then just tried to hold in her frustration as her car moved ahead at a snail's pace.

Forty minutes later and twenty minutes late, she screeched into the school car park, for once annoyed it was nearly empty as it made it even more glaringly obvious how late she was. She ran through the gates and headed to Isla's classroom, but when she got there it was deserted!

She hammered on the locked door. 'Hello, it's Isla's mum!' she called out.

No answer.

Her throat went dry. Where the hell could Isla be? What did they do when parents ran late? Surely it happened every now and again? Why hadn't they called her?

She ran to reception, starting to panic now. Thankfully, the head teacher was still inside. She knocked on the glass window and Mrs Gould walked over, opening the door.

'Everything okay, Mrs Okoro?'

'Isla,' Emma said, out of breath and anxious. 'I was stuck in traffic. I left a message. Is she here?' she asked, craning her neck to peer into the semi-darkness behind the head teacher.

'Mrs Belafonte has her,' the head teacher replied. 'She said she'd call you.'

Emma looked at her in horror. 'What the hell? She's not on my pick-up list.'

'She is, Mrs Okoro. You sent a new one in in Isla's bag last week.'

'I didn't!' Emma backed away, shaking her head.

Tatjana had taken Isla!

Chapter Thirty-One

Monday 16th November
3.55 p.m.

Emma drove at a breakneck speed towards the Belafontes' house in the forest, her anger and worry fuelling her. Had Tatjana taken Isla to her house . . . or had she taken her away somewhere? If Tatjana *was* Jade, her mental state had surely declined over the past week – what lengths would she go to?

Emma thought of what Lawrence had said again.

She can get a bit . . . dark.

'Oh God,' she whispered to herself.

Her ring tone echoed around the car. It was Dele. She pressed the hands-free button to answer.

'Hi babe, you called?' he asked.

'Tatjana picked Isla up from school! I was stuck in traffic so I was late and when I got there, Mrs Gould said Tatjana had taken her home and – and that we'd filled in a new pick-up permissions form with her name on it, but we bloody didn't! And now I know Tatjana *is* Jade and God knows where she's taken her!' Her words came out in a tumble, tripping over each other.

'Whoa, calm down, calm down,' Dele said. 'Tatjana is definitely Jade? What proof have you got?'

'I'll explain later. Just believe me.' Emma drew up to the grand house in the woods. 'There's no car out front! I'll call you in a minute.' She hung up and jumped out of her car, jogging to the house.

It was empty. No lights on, no people, no sound.

Emma felt tears prick at her eyes. She should have followed her instincts from the start. She should never have let it get this far. Tatjana – *Jade!* – had taken her daughter.

She felt bile work up as she hammered on the door.

'Tatjana!' she shouted. 'Isla!'

Suddenly, she saw movement inside. Then Lawrence appeared from a door at the back of the house with Isla behind him.

'Isla!' Emma shouted through the glass.

Lawrence walked towards her and opened the door, his phone in his hands. 'We've been trying to call you. It was constantly engaged.'

Emma ignored him, shoving past him and running to Isla, pulling her into a hug. 'Oh darling, my baby.'

'Mum, what is *wrong* with you?' Isla said, squirming to get away. Tatjana appeared at the end of the room then with her two boys. She looked like she'd lost even more weight, and had a strange pallor to her skin.

'How dare you pick my daughter up?' Emma hissed at her.

'Why's this lady mad at you, Mummy?' Zeke asked Tatjana.

'It's okay darling, it's just a misunderstanding,' Tatjana said, her eyes flicking to Lawrence, then away again.

'Hardly a misunderstanding!' Emma shouted, her words echoing around the hall and making the three children flinch.

Tatjana stepped away from Emma, putting her hand to her chest in surprise.

'Mum!' Isla said, looking deeply embarrassed.

'You were twenty minutes late, Emma,' Lawrence said calmly, his hand on Isla's shoulder. 'The poor girl was standing out in the rain!'

'But I never gave you permission to pick her up!' Emma said, eyes still on Tatjana. 'I know you bloody put your name on that permission form.'

Lawrence looked at Tatjana, his face stern. 'Did you, Tatjana?'

Tatjana's brown eyes widened. 'I – I . . .' She clapped her mouth shut with her hand, shaking her head as she looked at her husband.

For a moment, despite everything, Emma felt sorry for Tatjana. She was clearly damaged . . . and clearly *very* vulnerable.

But then that only made her more dangerous, surely?

'Jesus *Christ*, Tat,' Lawrence hissed. He turned to Emma. 'I am so sorry about this. I will make it up to you, I promise.'

Emma looked at them. Should she just tell them about her visit to the tower block now?

But the kids were there.

'We need to talk,' she said instead. '*Without* the kids.'

'Of course,' Lawrence said.

'Let's catch up in the morning before school and arrange a time,' Emma said. 'For now, I want to get my *daughter* back home.'

Then she grabbed Isla's hand and walked out, slamming the door behind her.

Chapter Thirty-Two

Monday 16th November
4 p.m.

That was interesting. Your fake mother has quite *the temper on her, Isla. She's surprising me in so many ways. Like how quickly she's figuring things out – such as the permissions slip I slipped into your book bag the other day before school, when you left it on the side to play with friends.*

And now this, a pure rage that boils inside her.

You looked very shocked, Isla. I understand. It can be horrible to see a parent lose their temper like that. I used to see it a lot at your age, and before, too. Of course, we all have our moments, we're only human. God knows I do! But never in front of my children! That's the rule!

I learnt that first-hand. I still have nightmares about what I witnessed as a child, I'm not ashamed to admit it. Your grandparents – your real ones – had no understanding of the simple rule of discretion. It was all out there in the open. I did my best to protect my brother from it, but it was hard. It still saddens me to think he had to endure the very worst of it, in particular the time my mother threw a pan of boiling water over our dad and then, feeling bad afterwards, rubbed oil into his wounds.

I wouldn't wish that on my worst enemy and my dad really was my worst enemy. His screams still pierce my dreams at night. My brother's, too, according to his carers.

I know it's not the same, the way Emma is. It's more how open *she was with her anger. It worried me, I'll be honest. If she can't abide by that one rule – discretion – then what hope is there?*

It makes me even more determined to help you escape from her.

In the meantime, I wait while Garrett digs, digs, digs. Not that I don't have enough occupying my mind with Tatjana falling apart at the seams. Honestly, I thought she had some grit about her! If she is to be your stepmother, then she really needs to pull herself together. I have ways to make her do that – all behind closed doors, of course. But I'm still concerned I will lose control of her like I did of your birth mother, and then what choice will I have?

Chapter Thirty-Three

On the drive home, Isla refused to look at Emma.

'I hope you understand why I'm so angry at Tatjana?' Emma said.

'No,' Isla shot back. 'It was nice of her. It was freezing standing outside with Miss Morgan!'

Emma sighed. 'There are strict rules about who schools can allow you to go home with. She faked a permission slip, Isla, and that's just the tip of the iceberg.'

'What do you mean?'

Emma looked at her daughter. 'It doesn't matter.'

Isla rolled her eyes. 'God, Mum, most of the kids in my class walk home on their own anyway, what's the big deal?'

'Well, we don't allow that.'

Isla crossed her arms and glared out of the window. 'We don't live in London now, Mum. Kids aren't getting stabbed on the streets.' She paused. 'Is it because I'm adopted?'

Emma pursed her lips. Isla rarely brought up the fact that she was adopted, even though Emma and Dele had been transparent with her from the start.

'Of course not, darling,' Emma said. 'Why would it be?'

She shrugged. 'No reason.'

'So what did you do at their house then?'

'Lawrence showed us a model of a house he's building. He was going to make us hot chocolates until *you* turned up.'

When they got home, Isla ran straight upstairs, slamming the door to her room.

Emma sank on to the sofa, putting her head in her hands. The gloom of the windowless living room seemed to press in around her. Maybe she'd been too hard on Tatjana in front of the kids. Isla shouldn't have had to witness that. She'd always made that promise to herself, that Isla should never have to endure the anger and turbulence that marked the first year of her life. Even though there had been no violence directed at Isla as far as the social workers knew, she had had to witness it between Jade and her mother, according to police reports. Emma knew from the training they'd received during the adoption process what an impact that could have on a child. In fact, she saw it herself in those early months when Isla moved in with them, the way she flinched when she heard an argument on TV.

Emma sighed and walked upstairs, gently knocking on Isla's door. She walked in to find Isla curled up on her bed, watching her iPad. Emma sat beside her, putting her hand on her leg. 'I'm sorry you had to see me getting angry earlier.'

Isla scowled and continued staring at her iPad. Emma gently took it away from her. 'Darling, please look at me.'

Isla sighed and forced herself to look at her mother. 'I am!'

'I was *so* scared when I turned up at the school to find you not there. When people get scared, they get angry.'

Isla scowled. 'That doesn't make sense.'

'You know how next door's Jack Russell burst your football and I said it was probably because it was scared seeing the ball heading right for it over the fence?'

Isla nodded.

'Well, it was like that for me. I was scared and I got angry.' She put her arms out. 'I really need an Isla hug right now.'

Isla's pretty face softened. She leaned over and hugged her mother.

'What's wrong with Tatjana, Mum?' Isla said. 'She's so different lately. They even stopped Design Divas. Is she, like, *ill* or something?'

'Yes,' Emma said, stroking Isla's hair. 'Not in an obvious way, like a broken arm, but in her head.'

'Oh yeah, Miss Morgan taught us about mental health at school. It's not people's fault, they're sick.'

Emma nodded.

Tatjana was sick. *Jade* was sick. Her unhealthy mind was telling her all she was doing was right, as long as she got her daughter back.

'I love you *so* much, you know that, right?' Emma whispered to Isla.

'I love you too, Mum.'

Emma smiled. 'Shall we get into our pyjamas?'

'Yay!' Isla said.

A couple of hours later, when Dele got in, Emma and Isla were sat on the sofa in pyjamas, snuggled up while watching a film. He walked straight over to Isla, giving her a kiss.

'Lots of drama today, hey?' he said, peering over her head at Emma with a serious expression. 'Shall I make you two snugglies dinner?'

'Yes please!' Isla said.

Later, after Dele had helped Isla dry her hair, he sat across from Emma and she knew it was time to talk. To *properly* talk. He looked exhausted; this was clearly all getting to him just as much as it was getting to her.

'Isla said you got angry with Tatjana,' he said.

Emma sighed. 'Yes, she took our child and she faked a permission slip.'

'We don't know that for sure.'

'Oh come on, Dele. Mrs Gould said she got a new slip from us last week.'

Dele wiped his hand over his tired eyes. 'You said on the phone you definitely know she's Jade.' He sounded wary, cynical.

'Yes, I spoke to Jade's mother today.'

Dele looked up in surprise. 'What?'

'I visited the estate she grew up in.' She leaned forward, grabbing Dele's hand. 'I needed to know for sure, Dele, and now I do!'

'Wait, rewind,' he said, moving away from her. She could see he was trying very hard to contain his anger. 'Why did you visit her mother? Do you understand what you've done, Emma?' he said. 'Going to the estate where our adopted daughter's birth mother once lived, grilling her mother. Do you realise how *bad* that looks?'

She thought of the dead bird. She wished she could tell him about the necklace. But memories of her father came back to her.

Never ever tell anyone. No matter what. This stays between us or you could lose everything.

'You know that dead crow that was in the grille of my car?' she said carefully. 'I think Tatjana did it.'

Dele put his head in his hands, stifling a cry. 'This is *madness*, Emma.'

'You have to trust me. Look,' she said, getting her phone out and showing him the portrait in Evie's bedroom. 'This is Jade's father.'

He took the photo and examined it. 'And?'

'And I found the very same photo in Tatjana's bedside drawer.'

'Did you take a photo of that?'

Emma shook her head. 'I plan to, though.'

He closed his eyes for a few moments. When he opened them, they were sad. 'I think it's time you saw your therapist again.'

'No,' Emma said, shaking her head. 'No, I am *fine*.'

'You're not, Emma. You're really not.'

He went to hold her hand, but she pushed him away. 'Jesus, Dele, don't you get it?' she shouted as she shoved the phone into his hands. 'Tatjana has a photo of Jade's father in her drawer.'

He properly looked at the photo and sighed.

'A black man.' He handed her phone back to her. 'It's easy to get us confused,' he said with a sarcastic lift of the eyebrow.

'Dele! It's him, I *swear* to you.'

'Fine, we go talk to them right now. Vanessa next door can look after Isla.' He stood up and went to the front door, but Emma went after him, grabbing his arm and pulling him back.

'Can we get Isla's birthday out of the way first?' she pleaded.

'Why wait?'

She didn't want to tell him she was worried that Tatjana knew what had happened to Emma all those years ago, and that confronting her might bring it all to the surface. She didn't want that ruining Isla's birthday.

'Please,' Emma said. 'Let's just get the birthday out of the way on Saturday.'

'Fine. But after that, we need to sort this out,' Dele said in a firm voice.

Emma nodded. She just needed to hope nothing awful happened before then.

Chapter Thirty-Four

Welcome to the Mums of Forest Grove Facebook Group

Saturday 21st November
7 a.m.

Kitty Fletcher
Just to let everyone know, there appears to have been a crash on Birch Road by the roundabout. There's lots of debris in the road. Doesn't look like anyone was hurt, thank God.

Pauline Sharpe
Oh no! What kind of car? My Roger left for work ten minutes ago.

Malorie Cane
It's a red Fiat, looks like an older make. It's in a right state, wrapped around a lamp post. I heard the bang in the middle of the night, presumed it was one of those RAF sonic jet booms like we had the other month.

Belinda Bell
I heard it too and presumed the same, Malorie. That's why I didn't call the police. Didn't want to get told off for wasting

time again! I can hear sirens, so presume the police are on their way now?

Vanessa Shillingford
Surely someone was driving the car? Maybe they went into the forest, confused after being injured? Are the police checking?

Rebecca Feine
Good point, Vanessa. I'm sure the police are on top of it but I'll be keeping an eye out when walking the dogs in a minute.

Myra Young
Me too. I'll get Justin ready early and we'll have a proper look.

Lucy Cronin
I'll join you with the kids, Myra.

Kitty Fletcher
Be safe everyone!

Chapter Thirty-Five

Saturday 21st November
7.05 a.m.

Emma stared at her face in the bathroom mirror. She looked awful! No surprise, considering she'd hardly slept the last few days. Dele was giving her the silent treatment, casting her worried glances. Luckily, they were so busy sorting Isla's birthday party and gifts out, the days had gone quickly.

And now the big day was here: Isla's eleventh birthday and her long-awaited pamper party. Emma's mum was coming up with Ray, and Emma was hoping to see her sister, too. Dele's parents were arriving the next weekend for what Isla was calling her second birthday.

Emma looked at the time. Dele and Isla were still sleeping. She looked in on Isla. Eleven years old and yet when she slept, she still looked like that two-year-old they brought home all those years ago. Emma's eyes flooded with tears. She was exhausted by the battle of the past few weeks, the rollercoaster of emotions and the second guessing. But now she was sure of it: Tatjana was Jade. All that was left was to take a photo of that picture she had in her drawer and confront her. That *had* to wait until after the birthday, though. Now it was all about Isla.

She padded downstairs, smiling as she passed the birthday banners and balloons Dele had set up the night before for Isla to wake up to. He'd taken the day off so at least one of them would have time to get everything sorted. In the living room was a pile of presents, but Isla's main one, from her mum and dad, was waiting all wrapped up in the garage to present to her after everyone had left. It was a mannequin bust for Isla to create her own clothes on, and Emma couldn't wait to see her face when she opened it.

Emma made herself a coffee and stood at the window, peering outside towards the treetops in the distance, listening to the patter of rain on the windows. She imagined Jade on this day eleven years ago, probably in the later stages of labour, considering Isla was born at nine in the morning. She was clean from drugs when she had Isla. Did she feel hopeful, excited? Was she confident of a happy future with her daughter?

And now what? Was she, too, staring out at the forest with a coffee in her hands like Emma, hopeful she'd get Isla back?

As Emma thought that, a police car scooted past, its sirens on. She went to the front window and saw her neighbour Vanessa poking her head out of her front door, craning her neck to watch the car pass.

Emma opened the window and leaned out. 'Wonder what's going on?' she asked Vanessa.

'A car crashed down the road,' Vanessa replied.

'Oh no. I thought I heard a bang last night. Has anyone been hurt?'

'No one was found in the car according to the Facebook mums' group. Some people are going to check in the forest – they're worried whoever was driving it might still be out there, injured.' Vanessa looked up towards where her three teenage boys were no doubt still sleeping. 'Probably a teenager. A Fiat like that is the kind of cheap car a teenager would have, isn't it?'

Emma blinked. 'Fiat?'

'Yes, that's the make of the car. A red Fiat.'

Emma's legs went weak. 'Wh-where is it?' she managed to get out in a trembling voice.

'The roundabout by Birch Road,' Vanessa answered. 'Someone said . . .'

But Emma didn't wait to hear the rest of her sentence. Instead, she pulled on her boots then ran outside, jogging down the street in her PJs until she got to the roundabout.

And there it was: an old red Fiat with a 52 number plate, toppled over in the middle of the roundabout, one door swung open, a tyre missing.

A red Fiat just like the one that had changed her life all those years ago.

Chapter Thirty-Six

I look at the photo of Emma with her sister Harriet as Garrett sits across from me. The girls have their arms around each other, laughing into the camera, people dancing in some cheap-looking nightclub behind them. Harriet is far more beautiful than Emma. Confident, too. You can just see it from the way she smiles into the camera, that glint in her eyes.

How must that have felt for Emma, a plain shy blip of a girl, to grow up with a bright spark like Harriet? And yet Emma was the one who ended up with the supposedly perfect little family life Harriet had dreamed of.

I place the photo down and read the report again. 'Well, this is an interesting twist in the tail,' I say.

Garrett nods in agreement. He's a very ordinary-looking man. Short. Thin. Nondescript hair. You wouldn't take him for a private investigator, but maybe that's what makes him so good. He blends into the crowd.

In the distance, I watch as the Fiat is lifted into the air. 'Suddenly, that little car takes on even more significance. You did a good job with that, by the way.'

Garrett nods. Not usually his line of work, but a couple more thousand pounds put his way and he suddenly decided crashing a car into a roundabout in the dead of night could easily be in his repertoire. All he needed to do was drive it there, then leave the engine running, pop off the handbrake and voila, down the hill towards the roundabout it rolled.

I wonder if Emma has seen it yet? It's just up the road from her; the police cars and the commotion will surely have drawn her out. If not, she's sure to hear all about it from the other mums at Isla's party today. I'll enjoy watching that.

The door to my office opens. Tatjana steps in, her eyes darting to the photo of the two sisters, then away again.

'You didn't knock,' I snap.

She lowers her eyes. 'Sorry. I just wanted to see if either of you wanted a coffee?'

'No,' I say, waving my hand at her to go away. 'Just go get the boys ready for Isla's party.'

'Are you sure it's a good idea we go?' she asks as Garrett tries to look busy with his phone.

'Yes, I am sure,' I say. God, what is wrong *with her lately? Of course I want to go to your birthday, my love!*

She looks at the photo again, then walks out.

I turn back to Garrett, closing the folder holding all the information he's gathered about that fateful night.

'Yes, I think we have enough here,' I say. 'You've done a great job. All sewn up just in time for my daughter's birthday. The rest of the money will be in your account by this afternoon.'

He nods, standing up. 'It's been a pleasure, Mr Belafonte.'

'Hasn't it just?' I say, shaking his hand.

When he leaves, I look back at the photo and smile. That's it, darling, game over for your pretend parents.

Chapter Thirty-Seven

Emma tried to stop her hand from shaking as she buttered some bread. Her sister watched from the corner of the kitchen, a worried look on her face.

Emma had told Harriet about the red Fiat when she'd arrived an hour ago.

'I'm sorry all this is happening to you, Emma,' she said.

'I just need to get this party out of the way,' Emma replied tightly, 'then I'm going to confront Tatjana.'

'You mean Jade.'

'Yeah, Jade.' She stabbed her knife into the butter and smoothed it over another slice of bread as she looked out towards where the red Fiat had been. Thank God it had been removed before her mum and Ray had turned up. The awful memories it would have brought back for their mother!

It confirmed everything, as far as Emma was concerned. Someone was sending her a message: they knew what had happened, maybe even knew the very worst of it – though how, Emma wasn't sure. And that someone *had* to be Jade – or Tatjana, as she was calling herself now.

Tomorrow, Emma would go to the Belafontes' house and insist on talking to Tatjana. Mother to mother. Hopefully she could sneak a photo of the picture she had of Jade's father. That would be a bonus when she went to social services with her suspicions, and maybe the police too. She had to be careful. She didn't want to stab herself in the foot in the process.

Isla let out a giggle in the next room. The two sisters turned, watching as the birthday girl held up a slogan T-shirt her grandparents had got her. Beyond her, the large dining room had been made into a pamper area with make-up and hair 'stations', a local beautician setting up ready for the onslaught of fifteen excited young girls.

'Funny, isn't it,' Harriet said as she took it all in, 'how you used to say you'd be quite happy without kids and I was always the one who wanted a family? Now look at us.'

Emma frowned. 'Did you?'

Harriet nodded. 'Always. A busy shambolic family full of artistic little pixies.' Then she sighed. 'No chance of that now, hey?'

The doorbell rang out and Emma dragged her eyes away from Harriet, quickly walking to the door and blinking rapidly so the tears filling her eyes disappeared. Poppy was standing outside, her dad trying to take shelter from the storm that was whipping up already.

'Looks like that storm I predicted is coming,' Fraser said.

In more ways than one, Emma thought.

'See you in two hours?' he asked.

She nodded.

The next hour was filled with excitable girls screaming in delight as they gushed about each other's make-up and hair dos, bursting all the adults' eardrums as they did. Some of the parents had stayed, too, something Emma wasn't used to. Back in London, it was just a given that parents would drop kids off, but then she hadn't made that clear on the invites.

As Emma darted back and forth, getting drinks and snacks, she caught glimpses of her sister watching from the corner of the room behind their mother's chair, a glass of wine in her hand.

Harriet was right. She *had* had the chance to have children snatched away from her, and it was all Emma's fault.

Emma shook her head. *Don't think about that today, not on Isla's birthday.*

Her mother strolled over. 'Everything all right, sweetheart? You seem . . .' She let her voice trail off.

'You know what kids' birthday parties are like, Mum,' Emma quickly said. 'I'm a bit stressed, that's all.'

'I just thought I'd check, with the anniversary coming up and everything.'

Emma's jaw tensed. 'I'm fine, Mum! Can we not talk about that right now?'

To her relief, the doorbell went. Emma walked off, watching as Harriet went over to their mother and put her hand on her shoulder.

Emma planted a smile on her face and opened the door. But the smile was quickly wiped away when she saw Tatjana standing on the doorstep with Lawrence and their two boys.

'Sorry we're late,' Lawrence said with a bright smile. He peered behind Emma. 'Where's the birthday girl?'

'Good, you're here,' Dele said, joining Emma and ushering them in.

Emma shot him a look.

'I bumped into Lawrence when I picked Isla up from school yesterday,' Dele explained. 'I thought it would be nice if they came too. Come in, come in.'

Lawrence walked in as Tatjana followed, holding their boys' hands. Tatjana wouldn't meet Emma's eye as she passed and instead looked down at the ground. Emma watched them walk into the living room in disbelief, unable to get her head around the fact that Dele had invited them!

Isla came running out, smiling as she saw the new arrivals. Then her smile faltered as she looked at Emma, clearly thinking of how angry she'd been with Tatjana the day before. Emma tried to adjust her face into something pleasant instead of showing the rage she was feeling inside.

Think of Isla, she told herself. *Don't ruin her birthday.*

Lawrence looked down at Isla. 'Hello, birthday girl,' he said.

She looked up at him shyly. 'Hello.'

'Eleven now, hey?' he said. 'What's all this then, a pamper party?'

'Yep. We have a beautician and everything,' Isla replied.

Zeke and Phoenix grimaced.

'Oh, don't worry,' Isla said, taking their hands. 'She does face painting too, do you want to be dinosaurs?'

'Yes!' they both said, Zeke letting out a roar as he ran towards all the girls, who screamed in delight.

'Look at her with them, isn't she just wonderful?' Lawrence said to Tatjana. She nodded faintly, her eyes cast downwards.

Tatjana – or rather Jade – was acting so timid, but Emma was sure it was part of her game plan.

Dele went to follow them into the dining room, but Emma grabbed his hand, pulling him back. 'What the hell?' she hissed.

'I thought it would be good. Help mend some bridges.'

'Are you fucking kidding me?'

One of the mums peered over, raising an eyebrow at Emma's use of bad language.

'Look,' Dele said in a harsh whisper, 'Lawrence and I had a good chat yesterday in the school playground. We agreed it's all got a bit out of hand. Don't worry!' he quickly added, 'I didn't mention your theories about Tatjana, not yet anyway. But honestly babe, I did some gentle probing and the facts don't add up, she just isn't Jade.'

Emma shook her head as she watched Lawrence chatting to her mum and Ray, Harriet watching Tatjana with a surprised look on her face.

What the hell? she mouthed.

Other parents looked surprised, too. After all, they'd witnessed the drama between Emma and Tatjana at the Halloween party!

Emma took in an angry breath as she turned back to her husband. 'This was a mistake, Dele, a big mistake.'

'Why? You said you wanted to talk to Tatjana, this will be your chance!'

'At our daughter's birthday party?'

'After Isla's gone! Your mum and Ray can take her out and we can all sit down and chat like adults. No more sneaking around. I've had enough of all this, it needs to be nipped in the bud.' He walked into the living room. 'Drinks?' he asked Lawrence and Tatjana, ignoring Emma's death stares. 'We have everything, including wine.'

'A glass of wine would be great, actually, to celebrate this wonderful girl's birthday,' Lawrence said as he smiled at Isla. 'Tatjana will have an orange juice, won't you darling?'

Tatjana nodded. Emma could see her eyes were red, her cheeks hollow. She had a lot of make-up on, even more than usual.

Emma frowned. Was this really the face of a woman who'd arranged for a car to be crashed into a roundabout the night before? Because surely that was what had happened. A strategic move to unsettle Emma and send her a message.

Maybe this was just proof that Tatjana was spiralling out of control.

Emma gritted her teeth, then walked into the kitchen, yanking open the fridge to get out their drinks.

How could Dele *do* this?

'Emma?' a small voice asked.

Emma glanced around to see Tatjana entering the kitchen.

She turned to her, crossing her arms. '*What* are you doing here, Tatjana?'

'It was Lawrence's idea,' Tatjana said. 'I swear, I . . .'

Lawrence walked into the kitchen then, putting his hand firmly on Tatjana's back. 'Go check on the boys, will you?' he asked her.

Emma quickly poured Tatjana her orange juice. 'Here,' she said, shoving the glass into her hand as she glared at her.

Tatjana took it and hurried out.

Emma sloshed some wine into a glass for Lawrence, then quickly poured one for herself, too.

Yes, it broke all her rules, but she bloody needed it!

'I hope you don't mind us coming,' Lawrence said. 'Dele and I just thought it would be the best thing to do. He mentioned you're still concerned about Tatjana, but I want to reassure you, she *is* getting help.'

Clearly not enough.

'It's fine,' she said instead, taking a huge gulp of wine. 'It's not really something I want to discuss at my daughter's birthday.'

'Of course,' Lawrence said, following her gaze towards Isla, who was helping the beautician paint Phoenix's face. 'I thought you didn't drink?' he said, eyeing Emma's glass.

'Like you said, it's a special occasion.'

He smiled. 'It certainly is.'

Isla came running in then. 'Mum! Let's open presents! Dad said it's nearly time for everyone to go.'

'Ah yes, presents,' Lawrence said. 'Better go get ours. I'm afraid it's a big one.'

He disappeared down the hallway as Emma followed Isla into the living room, standing beside her sister while Dele gathered all the presents into the middle of the room.

'I can't *believe* they're here,' Harriet said.

'I know,' Emma whispered under her breath.

Lawrence walked back in with a huge box that was taller than Isla.

'Wow!' Isla said as she gawped at it.

'Let's open your friends' presents first,' Emma said, trying to hide her irritation at the fact that Tatjana and Lawrence had brought a present that dwarfed everyone else's.

They all gathered around as Isla unwrapped her presents. There was the usual mixture of reverse-sequin notepads and crafting kits. When it came to Tatjana and Lawrence's ridiculous-sized present, Emma searched around the room for Dele, but he wasn't there. She wanted him to see how wrong it was to invite them! They were already taking over with their present.

Isla let Zeke and Phoenix help her rip off the paper, revealing a plain brown box.

Isla's face dropped and Lawrence laughed.

'Here, let me open it for you,' he said.

He leaned close to Isla and pulled the tape off the side of the box. Then it sprang open, revealing a huge mannequin bust.

The same one Emma and Dele had got Isla!

Emma looked at Tatjana. 'You knew!' she shouted at her. 'You somehow knew we've got Isla one of these for her birthday and you've *ruined* things on purpose!'

Everyone in the room went quiet.

'Emma!' her mother said as Harriet looked at her sister sadly.

'Mum?' Isla asked. 'What's wrong?'

'We've got one of these for you too, darling,' Emma said in a trembling voice. 'We were *so* excited about you opening it.'

'Oh well, she'll have two now!' Lawrence said.

Parents in the room exchanged looks.

Emma glared at him. Didn't he *get* it?

Dele walked in then.

'Have you seen this?' Emma said, gesturing to the mannequin bust. 'Have you seen what they got her?'

Dele frowned as he looked at it.

'Well, I think it's time we went now,' one of the mums said, peering at the clock as the doorbell went, marking the arrival of more parents to pick their kids up.

'Great, thanks for coming,' Dele said to everyone. He helped a sad-looking Isla hand out the party bags as he eyed Emma, who was still glaring at Tatjana.

'Can you take Isla upstairs to get changed?' Dele asked Emma's mum. 'She got juice all over her dress.'

Emma's mother nodded, looking at the two couples. Then she took Isla upstairs as Ray and Harriet disappeared into the kitchen to do the washing up.

'Shall we have that chat now?' Lawrence asked.

'Actually, I'd like to save that for another time,' Dele replied.

Emma looked at him, confused. 'I thought you said we'd all talk after the party?'

'No, another time,' Dele said, his eyes deep in hers. 'I mean it, Emma.'

She fought back tears. What was going on?

'The boys are exhausted anyway,' Lawrence said, picking up a sleepy Phoenix. 'Another time is fine. Come on,' he said to Tatjana, taking her hand and pulling her away.

When the Belafontes had left the house, Dele pulled an A4 padded envelope from his coat pocket.

'This was posted through our letterbox,' he said. 'It was addressed to me . . . and Isla,' he added.

'What is it?' Emma asked.

He pulled a USB stick out and a document with the title: *Transcript Of Interview With Colin Evans.*

Her dad!

Dele looked into Emma's eyes. 'I haven't had a chance to read the whole transcript yet but . . . is everything you told me about what happened to Harriet true?'

Emma's eyes flitted down to the USB stick he was holding, then back to her husband again.

This was it. This was the moment she always knew deep down inside would happen, the moment she'd been dreading for the past fourteen years.

The truth was all finally coming out.

She knew it the moment she saw the necklace on that dead crow.

She just never expected her dad to be the one to let it out.

Why would he *do* that?

Emma looked towards the kitchen where her sister was now watching them through the glass door with sad eyes.

'Emma?' Dele asked.

Emma turned back to Dele.

'How did Harriet really die?' he asked.

Harriet blew Emma a kiss, then she faded away, and Emma was alone again, her sister just a distant memory.

Chapter Thirty-Eight

'I'll explain everything,' Emma said, trying to understand what her father might have said, why he said it . . . and to whom. 'But not here – not with Isla in the house.'

Dele nodded. 'Then we walk.' He went to the kitchen, poking his head in. 'We're just going out for a walk, Ray,' he said.

'In this weather?' Ray asked.

'It's not raining any more. Can you guys keep an eye on Isla?'

Ray nodded. Emma could see that he wanted to ask if everything was okay, but he was always so careful not to interfere.

Emma and Dele grabbed their coats, then stepped outside. It was cold, almost dark beneath the weight of the black clouds above, a storm brewing within them. They walked silently down Forest Grove's main road until they entered the woods, and beneath the canopy of branches Emma finally felt able to talk.

'Most of what you know about the accident is true,' she said sadly. 'There's just one missing detail, a vital one.'

The accident had happened a year after Emma met Dele; a year after her sister's engagement party. Harriet had defied all the cynics and had actually stayed with her fiancé Alba, returning to Dartmouth for her hen party with Emma.

Harriet had kept in touch with all her old school friends. Despite all the new friends she'd made in London, it was those early friends she'd had when she first started school that remained the closest ones. That was the thing with Harriet: when she made a friend, it was for life. It was difficult for Emma. Difficult seeing just how easily Harriet and her friends fell into their old ways again. As she'd watched them doing their silly dance routines in the local nightclub during Harriet's hen night – Harriet dressed in a little black dress and a bright-pink sash screaming 'BRIDE2B' – Emma had felt even more left out.

'Here, have some of this,' her sister had said, stumbling over to her with a shot of something.

'Wait,' Emma said, grabbing her arm to make her stay before she darted off to dance again. 'Sit, just for a moment, will you?'

Harriet had smiled, sitting next to her big sister. 'I'm so pleased you're out with us,' she'd slurred.

'Me too,' Emma had lied. 'Here, I have something for you.'

She'd reached into her bag and pulled out the necklace she'd got her sister: a black tweed necklace with a hand-cut pale-pink gemstone. 'It's a rose quartz,' she explained. 'It means unconditional love. Sister love.'

'Aw sis, you didn't have to!' Harriet had said, taking it and rubbing her thumb over the jewel as she smiled.

'I just want you to remember me when you're living with Alba, that's all.' It was hard for Emma knowing her sister would be moving out soon, leaving her alone in that flat they'd shared.

'What are you talking about?' Harriet said. 'We'll see each other all the time. You, me, Alba and Dele. Double-date central.'

Emma had smiled. 'I know. I just wanted to get something for you, that's all.'

247

Harriet had given her a hug. 'Well, I love it! Now come dance. I want you completely off your face within thirty minutes – deal? I need Crazy Emma to come out to play tonight.'

Emma had laughed. 'Deal.'

Over the next two hours, Emma did as her sister commanded, drinking shot after shot. She hardly remembered that part of the night, just the non-stop dancing, the big hugs with her sister, even her sister's friends saying what a laugh the usually reserved Emma was when she was drunk.

Emma distinctly remembered thinking, *Maybe this is what I need to do more, get absolutely hammered. Maybe then I'll have more friends.*

When the night came to an end, Emma and Harriet walked home alone together. The club was just a twenty-minute walk from their parents' house. It was unseasonably mild for November but clouds were gathering above so they hurried as they walked.

'You're fun when you're drunk,' Harriet had said, her heels dangling from her hands as she walked barefoot along the promenade, their house within sight now.

'Oh charming, I'm not fun usually?' Emma had said as they crossed the road.

'You know what I mean!'

'Maybe I should drink more often then.'

'You don't need drink!' Harriet said, taking her sister's hand and gently squeezing it. 'You just need to let your inhibitions go a bit more. I know more people will be drawn to you that way.'

Emma had come to a stop, stung. 'Thanks, *Harriet*,' she'd said. 'So people aren't drawn to me?'

'Oh Em, you're so *sensitive* sometimes,' Harriet said, rolling her eyes. 'Forget I even said it.'

'No,' Emma had said. 'Tell me what you mean.'

'You *know* what I mean. You just need to let your hair down.'

'It's easy for you to say. I'm not like you.'

'Come on, yes you are! Crazy Em is just like me!' She swirled around, laughing up at the sky. 'Crazy, crazy, crazy!'

Emma had watched her, her eyes filling with tears. Harriet was so clueless. She had no idea how lucky she was. She had no idea how painful it was to watch her from afar and try so hard to be like her, but fail miserably.

'You just have to shake it out,' Harriet had said, coming to a stop and shaking herself, her blonde hair shimmying around her. 'Shake, shake, shake. Be adventurous. Lose your inhibitions.'

'Fine, then,' Emma said, grabbing her sister's hand as she marched her to their parents' house just as rain began to fall. 'Let's go.'

'Go where?' Harriet had said, giggling.

Emma fumbled around in her bag, finding her car keys. 'That club in Totnes, the one that stays open until four.'

Harriet burst out laughing. 'That club is full of mentalists.'

'Exactly! You told me to be more mental!' Emma said, spinning around as Harriet laughed.

'But it's agggggges away.'

'I'll drive,' Emma said, pulling her sister towards her car . . . a small red Fiat.

Harriet came to a stop, shaking her head. 'Em, that's ridiculous. You're drunk.'

'I'm not,' Emma lied. 'I stopped drinking after that first shot, which was hours ago.'

'Really?' Harriet asked.

'Sure. Come on, before we get soaked,' she said as rain started coming down harder. 'Let's be crazy!'

Harriet shrugged. 'What the hell? It is my hen night, after all.'

Emma walked to the car, struggling to operate the handle, she was so drunk. When she eventually did, she slid into the driver's seat as her sister threw herself into the passenger seat, giggling. 'This is going to be awesome,' she said, 'a last night out before I run off and make babies with Alba.'

Emma switched the engine on. Above them, a curtain twitched and she looked up to see their father watching them. For a moment, she thought about switching the engine off and going back inside.

Oh God, how she wished she had!

But instead, she just gave her father a defiant look. *Now who's the one with some spark about them?* she thought.

Then she slammed her foot on the accelerator and the car shot out of the drive, speeding down the road, windscreen wipers going back and forth as Harriet clutched on to the door handle. 'I haven't even got my seatbelt in, Em,' she'd said, trying to shove it in, but too drunk to get it right.

'Here,' Emma had said, leaning over. 'I'll do it.'

She was so focused on trying to sort her sister's seatbelt out, she didn't even notice she'd swerved over to the other side of the road . . . and was heading right for a lamp post. She just felt the impact, heard the screech of wheels, saw the world spin as the car turned over.

'As you know, Harriet died straight away,' Emma said now to Dele as he tried to digest what she was telling him. 'She wasn't wearing a seatbelt. I was, though. I didn't get hurt at all. I don't remember much of what happened after that. Just what Dad told me. How he ran out, how he saw it all . . . saw Harriet.' She muffled a sob with her hand. 'I don't know how he managed to wrap his head around it all so quickly, probably all his years in the police. But he knew if I was seen in the driver's seat, it would be over for me. So he pulled me out, and – and he moved Harriet over to the driver's side. Then he told me never *ever* to say I was in that car. He'd lost one daughter, he didn't want to lose another.' Emma frowned. 'And yet he *has* told someone, clearly.'

'Jesus,' Dele whispered, hands on either side of his face in shock.

'He made me run back inside before anyone saw me. Our neighbours came out just as I walked inside – the Coopers, the ones you saw in Dartmouth the other day?' Dele nodded. 'I always wondered if they saw me. They never said anything if they did. The sound of the woman's screams when she saw Harriet . . .' Emma shuddered. 'I'll never forget them.'

'It all makes sense now,' Dele said. 'Why your father is the way he is. Why didn't you *tell* me?'

'I promised my dad. I – I was scared. Only he and I know.'

Dele looked at the USB stick and transcript. 'But now he's told someone else . . . someone else who wants *me* to know. Why?'

'Tatjana,' Emma whispered.

'Maybe,' Dele admitted.

'So you believe me now?'

'I don't know. Jesus,' he said, pacing back and forth. 'If she *is* Jade, then this would suit her, having you out of the picture – because you know if this gets out, you'll go to prison, right?'

Emma pressed her lips together. Of course she knew.

She pulled her phone from her pocket. She needed to call her dad, find out what the hell was going on. But when she tried his number, it went to voicemail. The message she left was simple: 'Call me, Dad . . . please.'

'We should go see Tatjana,' Dele said when Emma put her phone down. 'We can talk to her, *reason* with her. Maybe if Lawrence knows, he can help us talk to her too?'

Emma was silent. She couldn't think properly.

'Come on,' Dele said, taking her hand and leading her deeper into the forest towards the Belafontes' house. She could see how rattled he was about this. He knew the seriousness of it and the implications for their little family.

251

So did Emma, of course she did. But in that moment, all she felt was numbness. It was the same after the crash. She'd seen her sister dead in front of her, the unfamiliar dullness of her eyes, the horrific gash at the back of her head. It felt like she was sleepwalking when she'd gone back to the house in darkness and sat in her room. Even when she heard her mother get up in the room next door at the sound of their neighbour's screams – so loud they penetrated the earplugs she always wore at night – Emma didn't feel anything. She wasn't able to process her emotions. She simply went mute.

'She's grieving,' was an easy way to explain it away. But it was guilt. Guilt so profound and nightmarish, all she could do was shut down as it spread inside her.

The funeral was the first time she imagined Harriet sitting beside her and making quips about what her friends were wearing. Emma began to *feel* something, the numbness dissipating when she imagined her sister there next to her. So she kept her sister close, so strong, feeling so *real,* until one day her dad came down to the kitchen in the middle of the night to find Emma talking to Harriet.

Or to nothing, as he saw it.

He got her 'proper help', as he called it. Not the NHS therapist she'd been assigned, but a private psychiatrist based in a centre in London, which Emma ended up staying in for a few weeks. But all that did was make her learn how to pretend better . . . pretend that she didn't imagine Harriet with her all the time, because, my God, that was better than accepting that she was gone forever.

Harriet did disappear for a while, though, when things became settled and a busy family life took over for Emma. But in moments of crisis or worry – like the past few weeks – Harriet would return, and Emma would take comfort in her presence.

Emma peered behind her now, seeking her sister among the trees, but she was nowhere to be seen.

'They're not in,' Dele said when they got to the Belafontes' house. 'Do you have Lawrence's number?'

Emma nodded, getting out her phone. She was starting to feel that way again: numb. Sleepwalking. Not quite there.

But then she thought of Isla. Isla needed her here, right here. But then maybe some detachment could help her now? Maybe it could help her protect her family.

'Maybe we're going about this the wrong way?' she said.

'What other way *is* there?' Dele asked desperately.

'Maybe – maybe I need to just come clean, tell the police, tell social services.'

'No!' Dele said.

She grabbed his arm as raindrops started to fall on their heads. 'It would be better coming from me than Tatjana, right? Tatjana – *Jade* – wants to have Isla for herself. That includes taking her away from you, too, because surely she knows you'd never allow her to have Isla. At least if I tell the authorities before she does, I can make sure you're untouched. *You* will be with Isla, even if I can't be.'

As she said that, her voice broke. She clenched her fists, forcing herself to pull it together. This was the way it had to be now.

'Please, no, Emma,' Dele said, tears starting to fall down his cheeks. 'You might go to prison. Think of Isla.'

'I don't deserve Isla anyway. I killed her aunt, didn't I?'

Dele pulled her into his arms. 'Oh, darling, all these years,' he whispered. 'You've carried it all these years.'

'I should never have driven in that state. I killed her.' She realised her voice sounded monotone, emotionless.

Dele tilted her chin up, examining her face. Could he see that familiar numbness descending upon her? 'It was an accident,' he said.

She pulled away from him. 'I'll call the police on Monday. It's the only way.'

He shook his head but it *was* the only way, she needed to convince him of that. She stroked his cheek. 'I love you so much, Dele. You don't deserve all this.'

'Neither do you.'

'That means a lot, your faith in me. So you need to trust me now when I say it's the only way.' He went to open his mouth to say something but she put her finger to his lips. 'Can we just go home now? I want to spend some time with Isla – it is her birthday after all.'

He paused for a moment then reluctantly nodded, and they walked back home.

That evening, Emma sat in the living room alone with her headphones on, ready to listen to her father's 'interview'. She looked up at the ceiling towards her and Dele's bedroom. Isla was asleep with Dele upstairs, both curled up together on their bed. When they'd got back from the walk, Emma had tried to act normally. Her mother had watched her with hooded eyes, clearly worried about her. She probably thought it was because the anniversary of Harriet's death was a week away. If she only knew it was so much worse than that . . . that Emma had killed Harriet.

When they'd kissed goodbye after dinner, her mother had stroked her cheek. 'You look exhausted.' She'd wanted to collapse into her mother's arms then, tell her that yes, she was exhausted. But instead she'd just smiled. 'I'm fine, Mum.'

Emma pursed her lips together now, stifling a sob as she looked at the USB icon on her desktop. Then she clicked on it, pressing play.

The first thing she heard was her father's voice. The sound of it sent a heady mixture of emotions through her: love, guilt, anger, sadness. She noticed there was even more of a slur in it, too, deeper than the slur that had always been there for as long as she remembered.

'I haven't told a soul about this,' he said.

'Now's the time,' said a woman whom Emma didn't recognise.

'I don't know . . .' Emma's dad said, seemingly reluctant.

'Come on, it'll do you good,' the woman encouraged.

A sigh, then: 'Fine. But this stays between us two, all right?'

'Of course,' the woman replied.

Over the next twenty minutes, Emma listened as he told his side of the story of what had happened the night Harriet died, the unknown woman audibly encouraging him to keep talking whenever he seemed unable to. He talked about how he'd seen the look of determination in Emma's eyes before she'd got in the car with her sister. How he'd run outside to stop them, chasing the car down the road. And then the awful sound of the impact.

As Emma listened, she sobbed. To hear him reliving it, to hear the obvious torment in his voice . . . it was so difficult.

The only good thing was it sounded as if he had no idea he was being recorded by this mysterious woman. He hadn't *meant* to expose Emma.

After Emma finished listening, she got her phone out again, staring at it.

'Call him again,' a voice whispered to her in the darkness. 'Talk to him.'

She looked up to see her sister watching her. Or what she imagined to be her sister.

Then she called her dad again.

Chapter Thirty-Nine

Saturday 21st November
8.45 p.m.

I look up at the window of your house, Isla. There's a storm building in the dark skies above, the branches of the trees in your garden whipping themselves into a frenzy.

But I am calm because I know you will be mine soon, Isla, now that the terrible truth is out of what your fake mother did.

She killed her own sister!

I thought about going to the police first, but my history with them isn't the best. No, it felt like a good chance to leave the evidence there at your party and to watch the beginning of the end with my own eyes.

If I know your fake father as well as I think I do – from the research I've had done on him – his overzealous commitment to morality and truth will have him encouraging Emma to go to the police. Then the police will have no choice but to arrest Emma and her alcoholic father.

I then have everything in place to sweep in and take over. I spoke to a new solicitor today, a very well-regarded solicitor with offices in Knightsbridge. He says it will *be a challenge, but with my impeccable record over the past few years, plus the fact I didn't even know Jade had a child, I stand a very good chance of getting you back.*

Yes, yes, I know, even with Emma in prison, Dele might still have a claim to you. But look what I can offer you! Not just all the money and luxuries you need, but also a family. Me, your biological *father. Your biological brothers. And then Tatjana who, yes, is a challenge at the moment, but with time she will be fine. How can a lone father with a wife in prison for causing death by drunk driving match up to me?*

The solicitor I spoke to earlier agrees that this all puts me in a very good position, and soon everything I've worked for over the past few months will come to fruition.

Soon, you will be all mine, Isla.

Chapter Forty

Emma's dad's phone rang and rang, and at first she thought he wouldn't pick up again. But eventually he did.

'Hello,' he said in his familiar gruff voice.

'Dad . . . it's Emma.'

No words, just the sound of his breath on the other end. Then finally: 'You okay?'

'You told someone what happened, Dad,' she said bluntly.

'What?'

She could tell in his voice he had. 'I have a recording of it, Dad, right here. You told someone.'

'A recording?'

'Yes. Who did you tell?'

He was quiet for a few moments, then he sighed. 'April. Bloody April.'

'Who's April?'

'The landlady of my local, I've known her a few months. We sometimes . . . well, you know. She stayed over the other night and we got into this deep talk. Are you definitely sure she *recorded* it?'

'Yes. It's clear when you listen to the audio.'

'That bitch!'

'You told me never to tell anyone! Why did you tell her?'

'I had to,' he said, his voice breaking. 'It's been tearing me apart, keeping it all inside, what with the anniversary coming up.'

'So you told some woman you've only known a few months?'

'It just came out! She kept telling me she could sense something was torturing me. She convinced me to let it all out.' His voice cracked. 'And she bloody *recorded* it?'

Emma put her head in her hands. 'Oh, Dad.'

She heard him take a sip of something, probably his favourite: neat vodka.

'You sound so much like Harriet, you know . . .' He let out a sob and Emma squeezed her eyes shut. Should she be surprised by the way he was, after all these years carrying a burden like this? She knew how he felt; that burden lay so heavy on her shoulders, too.

Still, to tell some woman he scarcely knew when she hadn't even told Dele!

'Someone's using this against me, Dad. I think this landlady you know was paid to get the information out of you and record it.'

Her dad was quiet for a few moments, then he sighed. 'She does need the money. Got herself into pretty bad debt, might even lose the pub. It'd have come out by now though, wouldn't it?' he said. 'Surely the police would have come knocking already? You'll be fine.'

'She's biding her time,' Emma said, peering out towards the forest.

'She? Who's she?'

'Isla's birth mother. She's going to use this information to finally get what she wants: Isla.'

She heard a glass crash to the floor. 'What?'

Emma was too tired to explain it all. 'It's a long story, Dad. I just need to focus on making sure she doesn't get what she wants;

259

that Isla stays with Dele. Maybe this is the best way, anyway. After what I did to Harriet.' She pinched her lips together, tears squeezing from her eyes. 'I don't deserve to be a mum.'

'Don't you say that! You're a good mother! A *great* mother.'

Emma laughed bitterly. 'How do you know that? We never see each other any more. You haven't even *met* your granddaughter!'

'I see it in your letters, in those photos you take. Those little pictures Isla draws, too.' So he *had* been reading her letters. 'Clever kid. *Happy* kid. I always knew you'd be a good mum.' She could hear the smile in his voice.

'I'm really not, Dad. The past few weeks . . .' She sniffed, wiping tears from her eyes. 'I'm so busy. I forget things. I – I feel so overwhelmed.'

'Oh Emma, you've always been like this, doubting yourself. If you had an ounce of your sister's confidence . . .' His voice trailed off. 'Look, you took that little girl from a real bad start in life and you gave her something she might not ever have had: a stable happy home. Trust me, she wouldn't have had it with that father of hers hanging around.'

'Isla's father?' she asked, wiping her tears away. 'How do you know about him?'

'I still have my contacts. I had to check out my granddaughter's background, didn't I? Spoke to a few people on the estate. It was clear who the father was, despite Jade Dixon pretending she put it around. He's bad news, love, all the Belafontes are bad news.'

Emma's blood turned to ice. 'Belafontes?'

'Yep. Isla's dad was Nathan Belafonte.'

'But – but Jade's mother said he was called Nathan *Bell*ford.'

'Nah, she's getting confused. No, he's definitely called Nathan Lawrence Belafonte.'

Emma jumped up as the truth suddenly dawned on her.

It wasn't Jade who wanted Isla back . . . it was Isla's birth father, Nathan Belafonte.

Or Lawrence, as he was calling himself now.

'I have to go,' she said.

'But Emma!'

'I'll call you when I get all this sorted.'

She hung up and paced the living room, thinking of Lawrence, the smiling pleasant man she knew – her client, the rich architect. Could he really be the violent, thuggish man Jade's mother told her about? The psycho, as she had referred to him?

Were Jade – or Tatjana, as she called herself now – and Lawrence working together? Not just one birth parent but two?

A mother desperate to have her daughter back was bad enough. But add to that a violent man capable of murder . . . it was a whole new level of threat.

She thought of Dele and Isla sleeping upstairs. Should she tell Dele? No, she mustn't wake them. This was her mess.

Instead, she pulled on her raincoat and grabbed her keys, then stepped out of the house, jumping in her car and driving into the forest.

The weather was wild when she turned down the drive towards the Belafontes' house, leaves whipping up around the car and the tall trees creaking ominously above her. When she parked outside the grand house in the woods she saw that all the blinds were closed. No surprise, considering it was gone ten at night.

She stared at the large imposing house, imagining Lawrence and Jade in there right now, plotting to take Isla from her.

She shivered.

Had she made a mistake coming here? But she needed to talk to them face to face: Isla's biological parents, the people who were trying to take her daughter away. The thought of it gave her a courage she didn't usually have.

She took a deep breath and got out of her car, marching up to the front door and knocking on it.

After a few moments, Tatjana – *Jade* – answered it. Emma was struck again by how thin she looked . . . and, even worse, she was sure under the harsh light of the hallway she could see a faint bruise around her eye.

When she saw Emma, she tried to close the door, but Emma stuck her foot in the gap, stopping her.

'I know that Lawrence, or should I say *Nathan*, is Isla's birth father,' Emma hissed. 'I know you're Jade.'

'I'm not. You've got it all wrong.'

'Liar!'

'I mean it, Emma. I'm not Jade.'

Emma looked at her in surprise. Something in Tatjana's eyes told her that she was telling the truth. Emma blinked. She'd been wrong all this time? She quickly recovered herself. It didn't matter. She needed Tatjana's help. She wasn't denying who Lawrence was, after all.

'Is Lawrence in?' Emma asked, trying to peer behind her.

Tatjana shook her head. 'He's gone to London.'

'Can *we* talk then?' she asked.

Tatjana swallowed, then shook her head. 'I can't talk to you.'

She went to close the door again, but Emma placed the flat of her hand against it.

'You have to,' she pleaded. 'If it's true what you're saying, if you aren't Jade, then surely you can see how wrong this is? He's trying to take my daughter away and you know it! Imagine if someone tried to take your boys?'

Emotion flickered on Tatjana's tired face.

'Please!' Emma said. 'I really need your help. You *know* him. As one mother to another, I'm begging you.'

'He's the father of my kids, Emma. Don't you get that? I'm sorry,' she added, her voice breaking. 'All I'm going to say is that I am *not* Jade Dixon.'

Then she slammed the door shut.

Emma sighed. It was pointless. Lawrence had complete control over her.

She ran through the rain and jumped back into her car as she tried to figure out what the hell to do next.

Then there was a knock on the window.

She looked up to see Tatjana standing outside, cardigan wrapped around her, the heavy raindrops wiping away the foundation on her face to reveal the stark purple hue of the bruise around her left eye under the moonlight.

'Can I come in?' Tatjana shouted over the rain.

Emma nodded, leaning over to open the passenger door for her.

Tatjana got in and sat down. She was shivering, her clothes soaked through. She looked so vulnerable sat there with that awful bruise and her wet clothes. Emma felt a burst of sympathy and guilt.

'You're really not Jade, are you?' Emma asked.

Tatjana shook her head. 'But I *was* behind some of it,' she replied. 'The missing school letter. The fake email. The gossip. I – I actually enjoyed it.'

'But Lawrence put you up to it, right?' Emma said, her eyes sliding to the bruise on Tatjana's face.

Tatjana lifted her fingers and touched the bruise, wincing. 'Not at first,' she confessed. 'It was exciting. I was going to do something so *amazing* for the man I loved – I was going to get his daughter back!' She tensed her jaw, turning to look out into the darkness. 'It went so well at first, he was so – so *proud* of me. He told me how clever I was, how creative. It's been a long time since he said those things to me.'

Emma remained quiet, letting her talk.

'Of course, in the back of my mind, I knew he was using me,' Tatjana continued. 'But that's fine, we're married, sometimes partners use each other, don't they?'

She turned to look at Emma for reassurance, but Emma just shook her head. 'It shouldn't work like that, Tatjana.'

Tatjana's face hardened. 'You think I'm weak.'

'Not at all! Lawrence coerced you into this. Even if it *seemed* like you were enjoying it, that was part of his manipulation. The strongest of people can be made to do the worst things when it comes to coercive control.'

'I used to be strong,' Tatjana agreed. 'I've always been proud of that. Fact is, Lawrence got to me at my most vulnerable, that's all. My mother had just died and it sent me into a spin. I wasn't myself.'

'I get it,' Emma said with a sigh.

'Your sister?'

Emma nodded, wondering just how much Tatjana knew about her past.

'It's like losing a crucial defence in your armour, isn't it?' Tatjana said.

Emma smiled sadly. 'That's a good way of putting it.'

'Well, that was how it was for me. Lawrence snuck in through the gaps. You can't blame me for falling for him, can you?' she said. 'So handsome and charming, even before my dad's money made him what he is today. Honestly, it was bliss in those first few months. He seemed to love the fact I wanted to run my own business. He would go on and on about how strong and fierce I was, and how he loved that about me.' Her face flickered with anger. 'But when we married, it was those very things he tried to stamp out of me.' She played with the hem of her top. 'I honestly just didn't have the strength to fight back. We had Zeke pretty quickly after we married so I was exhausted.' She swallowed hard, face clouding over. 'You know the first time Lawrence hit me, it was because he said I was being too weak with Zeke when he had tantrums? He stamped all the strength from me, then hit me for being too weak. I know I should have left that first time. But the boys!' She looked at Emma, eyes pleading. 'You understand, don't you? You build a family and you will do *everything* to hold it together, even if it means sacrificing your own happiness?'

'Oh God, do I understand,' Emma said, her own eyes filling with tears. 'I really do. That's why this has been tearing me apart.'

'I know that now. I didn't really understand the impact on you initially. The way Lawrence talked about you . . .' She let her voice trail off. Emma didn't want to ask what she meant. She just assumed Lawrence had bad-mouthed her. Why else would Tatjana agree to taking Isla away from her? 'I only saw you and Dele through his eyes at first,' Tatjana continued with a sigh. 'He was so adamant Isla needed to be taken away from you and become part of *our* family.' She smiled slightly. 'I've always wanted a girl, you see, and when he showed me a photo of Isla, I could see how much she looks like Lawrence and me, too, in her way.'

Emma nodded. She could see Lawrence in the shape of Isla's face, now she thought about it. The little gestures. It had been right there all along, but she'd been too fixated on Tatjana being Jade.

'I got so excited about having a little girl as part of our family,' Tatjana said as she stared out through the hard rain at the house. 'When we moved here and saw how beautiful the village is, it made me even more excited. That day we first met, that Monday?' Emma nodded. 'After, we walked to the park nearby with the boys, the one with the hedgehog huts, and Lawrence went on and on about how wonderful it would be to push his daughter on the swing there. He wouldn't even let the boys go on the red swing. He said that one was for Isla. He made me imagine this beautiful girl in our life. He made me *want* it as much as he did!'

Emma scrunched her hands together. It was hard listening to Tatjana talk about her Isla like that.

The smile disappeared from Tatjana's face. 'But the more I got to know you, the woman Lawrence made you out to be didn't match the one in front of me. And the more I saw of you and Isla together – the more I saw of Dele too, the way you all are as a family . . . I started to doubt everything Lawrence had said about you.' She looked into Emma's eyes. 'You're such a good mum, Emma.'

Emma thought of what her dad had said earlier: *You're a great mother, Emma. You just need to believe it.*

'So are you,' Emma whispered, putting her hand over Tatjana's.

The two women smiled at each other, then Tatjana pulled her hand away from Emma's and shook her head.

'I'm not a good mum,' Tatjana said firmly. 'I should never have done all that to you.'

'You did it for the boys.'

'That's why I *shouldn't* have done it. It was wrong and yet I didn't realise that for so long. How can I teach my boys the difference between right and wrong if I don't know it myself?'

'Lawrence manipulated you, he brainwashed you, this is what men like that do!' Emma looked at Tatjana's bruise again. 'You need to get away from him before he hurts you again . . . before he hurts the boys!'

'He wouldn't do that! He told me I'm the only one he's done this to.'

'He's lying. He hit Jade too – her mum told me. You *must* leave him.'

'But I have nothing without him,' Tatjana said in a voice barely above a whisper. 'I've let my business wind down really. My dad's business is struggling, so it's not like he can help any more. The only money I have access to now is Lawrence's money.'

'You'll find a way. You're strong, remember? The Design Divas class is amazing. All the kids love it. You can do more of those!'

Hope flared in Tatjana's eyes, then she frowned. 'Why are you being so nice? I've been horrible to you.'

'You've told the truth. That's all I wanted. And now all I want is for Isla to stay with Dele, even if I do end up going to prison. Lawrence will *not* get Isla!'

Tatjana looked down at her hands, which were curled into fists in her lap. 'He's so convinced he will, though. He honestly thinks with the right amount of money, anything is possible. Two solicitors have told him how unlikely it is with his violent past, but he just won't listen.' She lifted her eyes to Emma again. 'He went to London right after Isla's party to meet with a new solicitor, one who'll no doubt be charging a ridiculous amount.' She shook her head. 'My father did this to him, made him think that money can buy absolutely anything. Like hiring that private investigator and getting all that stuff about your sister. That was the final straw for me, when he said he was using that against you. I just didn't want to be involved. I *did* try to convince him, you know. I said it was unfair, that you're a good mother and that's in the past – but he got angry.' Her fingers flickered up to her bruise. 'I did try,' she whispered. 'There's nothing else I can do.'

'There is! I – I know I'll probably lose Isla.' As Emma said that, the reality of it hit her again. She clenched her jaw to stop herself from crying. 'What's important now is we have to stop Lawrence getting custody of Isla.'

'But how?' Tatjana asked.

Emma gestured to the bruise on Tatjana's cheek. 'You need to go to the police about this.'

Tatjana shrank away from Emma, shaking her head. 'No. I can't go to the police, I can't do that to the boys. I can't have them thinking their father is a monster.'

267

'He *is* a monster!' Emma said, her voice echoing around the car. 'What else is a man who does this to his wife? And God knows what's happened to Jade – you know she's missing, don't you? I thought that was because she was you, assuming a new identity. But now I know she isn't, what the hell happened to her?'

She thought of how Evie had been convinced that Lawrence had murdered someone.

Could he be behind Jade's disappearance?

'You have to go to the police, Tatjana,' Emma said, more desperate than ever now. 'For the boys. For Isla.'

Tatjana was quiet for a long time, then she nodded her head. 'Okay.'

A few minutes later Emma drove away from the big house in the woods, watching in the wing mirror as Tatjana ran inside through the rain. She'd promised Emma she was going to get out that night while Lawrence was away. Emma was pleased. She didn't want Tatjana to suffer for all this. Plus with Tatjana on her side, giving evidence against Lawrence – if she did in the end – it would surely mean he would have no chance of getting custody of Isla, no matter how much he paid some London solicitor.

As she drew up to her house, the storm was at full throttle, leaves swirling around the rain-drenched roads, wheelie bins toppling over.

She let herself in, then stopped, frowning.

All the lights were on.

'Hello?' she called out, quietly in case Isla was still sleeping.

Dele ran out from the living room, his face full of panic. 'I've been trying to call you!' He peered behind Emma. 'Where is she?'

'Where's who?'

'Isla!'

Emma's skin went clammy. 'She's not with me. What the hell is going on, Dele?'

'Jesus!' He raked his hands through his hair. 'We fell asleep. I woke up, she wasn't with me. I checked her room, then I came down, neither of you were here, so I – I just thought you'd gone out for some reason.'

'Oh God,' Emma said as she noticed a broken window in the kitchen. 'Lawrence has taken her!'

Chapter Forty-One

Welcome to the Mums of Forest Grove Facebook Group

Saturday 21st November
10.40 p.m.

Malorie Cane

The police just came into the pub. They're searching for little Isla Okoro! She's gone missing from her house. They seemed incredibly worried. Vanessa, you live next to them, any news?

Vanessa Shillingford

Yes, I can confirm Isla is missing. My husband and boys are out helping Dele and Emma search for her, I'm at the house with the police in case she comes back, but to be honest, I don't think this is a case of her running away. There's a broken window in their kitchen.

Lucy Cronin

Oh God, has someone taken her? I can't believe she's out there in these weather conditions! I'll get Fraser to go and help with the search. They need to get the police helicopter out!

Rebecca Feine

They have, judging from the helicopter that just flew over my house! This is awful, I'm going to go out with the dogs.

Belinda Bell

Me too. Did Dele check the garden? Or the toilets?

Rebecca Feine

Erm, yes, I think he would have done all that, Belinda.

Malorie Cane

I told the police they must make sure they check CCTV! And do a search of the forest. They'll need to take torches, it's very dark out there.

Vanessa Shillingford

I think the police will be on the case with the torches, Malorie. So worried for little Isla. Such a lovely girl. Emma and Dele must be beside themselves. Gavin is going out in his car now, did the police mention any particular area we should search?

Myra Young

I just had an officer knock at the door. They asked me if I'd seen Lawrence, which seems a strange thing to ask.

Belinda Bell

Well then there's our answer. The man has abducted her!

Ellie Mileham

We shouldn't rush to conclusions.

Belinda Bell

Really? I knew they'd be trouble the moment they moved in.

Kitty Fletcher

I quite agree with Belinda. I always knew something wasn't right about them, Lawrence in particular. From the moment I saw that crane in the middle of the woods followed by the Belafontes flouncing around the village with their designer clothes and those obscene cars of theirs – I mean, really, who needs a car the size of a lorry to drive around a little village like ours? I just knew they'd be trouble!

Ellie Mileham

You've changed your tune, Kitty! Last week Lawrence and Tatjana were the best things that ever happened to Forest Grove and Emma Okoro was the worst.

Kitty Fletcher

Things come to light, don't they? Right, I'm going out to check my garden, you never know, there are a lot of hiding places in there. Stay safe everyone!

Chapter Forty-Two

Emma's windscreen wipers splashed manically, going back and forth to clear the rain and the splatter of leaves from her windscreen as she scoured the streets for Isla and Lawrence. She was taking the east of the village while Dele took the west. She could already see lots of villagers out, their torchlight bouncing against the flooded roads. Police, too, with their helicopter above and the glimmer of their blue lights in the distance. They'd suggested Emma and Dele stay in the house in case Isla returned, but she knew Lawrence wouldn't bring her back, so it was up to them to *get* her back.

Emma just had to hope Lawrence hadn't got too far with Isla. The main road had already been blocked, so all that left was the village and the surrounding area.

'You will not take my daughter, Lawrence!' she shouted out loud, her voice echoing around the car.

'No, because you will *not* let him.' She turned to see Harriet sitting beside her, eyes scouring the darkness, too. 'Think, Emma, think. Where would he take Isla if he can't get out of the village?'

Emma took a moment to mull it over. 'He isn't at their house, the police checked.'

'Then where else?'

That was when it came to her: Tatjana had talked about a swing Lawrence wanted to take Isla to.

He wouldn't even let the boys go on the red swing. He said that was for Isla.

Emma slammed on her brakes, turned the car around, its tyres screeching on the wet leaf-slimed road, then headed towards the closest entrance into the forest.

She turned down the forest track, tyres bumping along as the trees thrashed above her.

The hedgehog playpark appeared in the distance. She parked in the small car park, then darted out into the rain, her jumper and jeans getting soaked through, her red hair clinging to her face. As she ran into the forest she nearly slipped but managed to stop herself, grabbing on to a nearby branch.

Above Emma, the trees creaked, the dark skies ominous.

Isla will be so scared, Emma thought. *So confused and scared.*

That thought made her run even faster until the park came into view.

It was all made of wood apart from the silver of the slide and the stark red swing beneath a solitary street light.

As Emma drew closer, she realised she was right. There was Isla, wrapped in Lawrence's thick blue raincoat as he pushed her back and forth on the swing.

Emma stayed where she was for a moment, hidden from view as she caught her breath.

She had to approach this carefully.

She got her phone out and quickly typed a message to Dele: *He's at the hedgehog park. Am here. Tell police.*

Then she stepped out from the shadows.

Chapter Forty-Three

Saturday 21st November
11 p.m.

I understand this is difficult for you, Isla. But I wish you wouldn't cry so much! It's making a challenging situation even worse. It wasn't meant to happen like this, me breaking into your house and snatching you away. I know how terrifying that was, my love, to hear your name called, then see me in the darkness staring down at you!

But I have run out of options.

The solicitor I spoke to emailed me while I was watching your house to tell me he couldn't take me on, despite how enthusiastic he'd seemed when we met for an early dinner. There was no point, he said, it would be impossible for me to get you back with my history.

And then Tatjana left me a message. She has left me, taken my beautiful boys!

Oh please stop sobbing, Isla. I told you I'm your father. Your real father!

But then girls can be like this, can't they? Not quite as robust as boys.

That's fine, I can get used to it.

'Don't worry, we'll be back in my car soon,' I say as I push you back and forth on the swing. 'Back in the warmth, all dry and snug.

Just need to wait a few more minutes.' I look at my watch, stifling my frustration. 'Then the world's our oyster! You can look at a map and choose where you want us to go. Your choice, a hundred per cent. Isn't that exciting? We can have the most wonderful adventure.'

'I don't want to go anywhere!' you shout. 'I want my mum!'

'Well, darling,' I say, trying to control my temper, 'your mummy – your real mummy – isn't here right now.'

'My mummy *is* my real mummy!' you sob. 'I want her and Daddy. Please.'

You try to get off the swing, but I hold you down.

Not hard, just firm.

You flinch away from me and I can't tell you how much that hurts, Isla. I tuck a strand of your hair beneath the hood of my coat. 'I know this all feels very strange now, but you will understand one day,' I say in as soothing a voice as I can. 'I didn't even know about you, can you believe that?' I laugh, shaking my head. I know I'm crying, but that's fine, you need to see your father has feelings, that I care. 'Your mother didn't tell me about you, she just gave birth to you then gave you away.'

'Because she loved me!'

I laugh. 'That isn't love, giving your child away!'

'Mum and Dad say it is, that it's proper love.'

I think about it. 'You know, maybe they're right. That's why Emma and Dele are giving you to me, your real daddy. Because they love you!'

'No, you're lying! They wouldn't do that!'

You wriggle to get free so I hold your shoulder even harder. You yelp and it breaks my heart.

'Stay. Still,' I say. 'Then I won't have to hurt you, Isla!'

You turn your face up to mine, your brown eyes so like Jade's, full of fear.

Then you turn away from me, your face lighting up.

'Mum!' you cry out.

I turn to see your fake mother appear from the trees. She goes to run towards us, but I put out my hand.

'Stop right there, Emma, or you'll regret it!' I shout.

My other hand tightens on your shoulder and you whimper.

Just a little pain to get us through this, Isla. Then nothing but love.

Chapter Forty-Four

Saturday 21st November
11.05 p.m.

Emma came to a stop and looked at Isla, giving her a shaky smile.

'Mum's here now,' she said. 'Everything will be fine, do you understand?'

Isla nodded, her lips trembling. The sight of her daughter looking like that – wet, sobbing, terrified – made Emma want to sob herself.

But she *had* to be strong.

'Just look at me,' she continued. 'Look right at me. Dad will be here soon – and the police, too.'

Isla blinked, then nodded again.

Emma's heart went out to her. *She is such a brave girl.*

Emma looked at Lawrence. He was wearing trousers and a white shirt that was soaked through, his blond hair plastered to his head. His eyes were wild.

'It's over, Lawrence,' Emma said to him, taking one small step forwards. 'You won't be taking her from us.'

'We were just having an interesting conversation, weren't we darling?' Lawrence said, smiling down at Isla.

Isla frowned, her eyes still on Emma.

'She's very clever, my little girl,' he continued. 'She was telling me how true love means letting a child go, like Jade did. Like *you* should.'

'I will never let her go. I'm her real mother,' Emma said firmly.

Lawrence laughed bitterly. Behind him, there was the sound of creaking. He peered over his shoulder towards the tallest tree, which was swaying haphazardly. He turned back to Emma.

'Mother?' he said. 'You call yourself a mother? A *good* mother doesn't spend most of her time working. A *good* mother doesn't palm her child off on other people. A *good* mother doesn't forget important things. A *good* mother—'

'Mum's the best mum ever!' Isla shouted, her voice echoing around the clearing, so loud Emma could hear it through the rain.

Emma smiled, tears filling her eyes.

'I *am* a good mother,' she said. She took another step forward. 'No, I am a *great* mother. Everything I do, I do for Isla. Everything *Jade* did, she did for Isla. Trying to get away from you, her abusive boyfriend – something Tatjana's doing right now, too,' Emma continued, still approaching. 'All good mothers doing what they can to ensure their children are nowhere near a monster like you.'

Lawrence's mouth dropped open and Emma took the chance to dart forward. But he pulled Isla off the swing, squeezing her close to him as he backed away. He didn't seem to notice as Isla pummelled his chest with her little fists.

Then he turned on his heel and ran into the forest. Isla screamed for Emma, her hand reaching out towards her mother as Lawrence headed right in the direction of the swaying tree.

'Lawrence, no!' a voice shouted out.

He paused, turning around. Emma followed his gaze to see a familiar figure behind her. At first she thought it was Tatjana – but then she realised who it really was.

Chapter Forty-Five

Saturday 21st November
11.10 p.m.

Jade? My Jade!

She looks so beautiful. She always was, but the drugs, they diminished that beauty. Not now, though. Now her skin radiates, her black hair long and braided.

She is everything she was supposed to be. And now she is here, just as we agreed, to make the family we were always supposed to make.

I'd lost hope after she stopped replying to my text messages and answering my calls. Garratt managed to track her down to Brighton a couple of weeks ago. Jade Fisher is her new name, married to some hippy and living with him in a tiny little shack near the beach. I can't grumble too much about him. He's the one who got her off the drugs when she booked herself into a rehab centre in Thailand five years ago. Holistic healer, he calls himself on his website. A website Jade designed.

Yes, she's a web designer. She has a career, she's kicked the drugs, she's the mother you deserve, Isla!

And as I look at her now, I realise she really is my one true love. The fact she's here must mean she feels the same about me and is not happy with her husband. When I messaged her earlier about my plan to take you, I knew I was taking a risk. It helped when I added if she should go to the police or your fake parents about it, I'd take you somewhere she would never find you. She replied straight away, saying she was travelling to Forest Grove anyway after reading my message the night before (I admit, I got drunk and sent her a rather long rambling message).

And she kept her word, because she is here!

She walks past Emma and approaches me, a smile on her face.

'You came!' I said as I walk towards her with you still struggling in my arms. 'See, I told you she was on her way, Isla!'

Jade's eyes settle on you, and the pain is clear to see. It must still hurt so much to have given her daughter away and to have lied to me. But we forgive her now, don't we, Isla?

It all became suddenly clear to me recently that this is the way it was meant to be. Not with Tatjana but Jade – always Jade.

'Look, Isla, your real mother,' I say to you. But you won't look at her, you just keep looking at bloody Emma!

'Come, Jade. Come see her,' I say, beckoning Jade over. 'The three of us, together at last.'

Jade sighs. 'Just stop, Nathan.'

I frown. 'Stop what?'

'Stop trying to ruin Isla's life.'

I shake my head, confused. 'Ruin? I'm trying to make her life better! Put things back to how they should be. It was always you, me and our daughter, just like I said in my message last night.'

'Oh, Lawrence. Look at her. All she wants is her mum.'

'You're her mum!' I say.

'No! Emma is,' Jade says. 'And she's a great mum, too, from what I've seen on her Instagram feed.' She looks over her shoulder at Emma. 'You're a wonderful mother, Emma, thank you.'

I look between the two women – the two mothers – as they smile at one another. Emma and Jade.

'You've got it all wrong,' I quickly say. 'She's a terrible mother. Haven't you been reading my messages, Jade?'

Jade looks at me. 'I did read all your messages, Lawrence, and that's why I'm here, to protect Isla.' Her face softens. 'You're not right, Lawrence, this isn't right,' she says, gesturing towards you and me.

Jade turns her gaze back to me and gently walks forward, putting out her arms.

'Let me take her,' she whispers, and the look on her face reminds me of the first time I met her, the way she held me as I cried after that bad beating from my dad. 'Lawrence, please, let me take her,' Jade says. 'The police are coming, there's no way out. Don't let her see you like this, forcing her to do something, be something, like your dad did.'

I close my eyes, my arms going weak.

I let you slip from my hands.

Chapter Forty-Six

Saturday 21st November
11.15 p.m.

Emma watched as Jade took Isla from Lawrence's arms. Isla stared up at her birth mother, her eyes hungrily exploring Jade's face.

Jade smiled down at her, tears falling from her eyes.

For a moment, Emma was terrified that Jade would just turn and walk away with her daughter.

But instead, she went straight up to Emma, gave Isla a kiss on her cheek and handed her over.

Emma sobbed, holding her daughter so close.

'I love you,' she said, 'I love you.' She said it over and over again.

Lawrence was sitting down in the grass, his head in his hands. Emma watched as Jade went over and sat down beside him, wrapping her arms around him.

In the forest, people started to appear, their torches lighting up the darkness.

'Dad!' Isla shouted.

Dele ran towards Emma and Isla and hugged them.

Emma smiled.

Family, she thought.

In the distance, she saw Harriet walk away through the trees, leaving forever, finally at peace.

Epilogue

Emma ran up to the forest clearing, her picnic bag bouncing against her hip.

'Sorry we're late,' she called out. 'Isla took a million years to get ready.'

'Why do we bother making excuses any more, Mum?' Isla asked, jogging to keep up with her mother. 'We should embrace our lateness.'

Emma laughed. 'You're so right.'

She came to a stop in front of a huge picnic mat that had been laid out on leafy ground beneath a blossom-filled rowan tree. Tatjana jumped up, pulling her into a hug. 'I'm *so* going to buy you an alarm clock for your birthday, Emma.'

Emma laughed, hugging her back.

'Hey, you,' a voice said.

Emma looked down at Jade. Her newborn son was snuggled against her breast as he fed.

'Say hello to Isaiah,' Jade said.

She looked so contented – and why shouldn't she be? She'd turned her life around and was living on the coast with her lovely husband. She'd even got back in touch with her mother and they met regularly. And now she was able to see her birth child after denying herself the chance, telling herself back then that she didn't even deserve letterbox contact. Now she finally felt she *did* deserve it.

Emma had invited Jade back to the house after Lawrence was arrested and Isla was safe. Emma and Dele hadn't wanted her driving back in the storm. It should have felt strange, especially as Emma had been so scared about the possibility that Tatjana was Jade and had come to get Isla back. But instead, it felt natural, even normal. The next morning, Jade and Emma had talked while Dele took Isla to the police station to give a full statement. The police had offered to come to their home, but Isla really wanted to see inside a police station, a fact that made Emma realise her daughter might be okay after all the drama.

As Jade and Emma had talked that morning, Emma realised what an amazing woman Jade was. Like Lawrence, she had dragged herself up from a difficult start in life. But unlike Lawrence, she had done it with grace and positivity, leaving the country with a friend and getting herself clean in Thailand.

The more Jade told Emma about Lawrence's upbringing, though, the less surprised Emma was that he had turned out the way he had. At least he had a chance of getting the help he needed now. Lawrence had been jailed for two years for breaking and entering and kidnapping a minor. Tatjana had told Emma that he was seeing a therapist in prison, and when Tatjana spoke to Lawrence during the supervised calls he was allowed with the boys, he seemed better and better each time. He'd had time to reflect on his actions and seemed genuinely contrite.

Emma leaned down now, stroking Isaiah's soft head. 'He's beautiful,' she said to Jade. 'Isla, look, your new brother!'

Isla sank down by Jade, staring in awe at the baby.

'Hello, Isaiah,' Isla whispered. 'He's so tiny.'

Jade smiled. 'Just like you once were, sweetie.'

The three women looked at each other, smiling.

'Not me though!' Zeke declared, flexing his little muscles. 'I was huge.'

They all burst out laughing.

Jade handed Isaiah gently over to Isla as Tatjana's two boys joined them, crowding around to look at the new addition to their strange but beautiful family.

Tatjana smiled, squeezing Emma's hand. 'It all worked out in the end, didn't it?' she said.

Emma peered down at Isla with her three brothers. 'It did.'

Above them, a cluster of creamy white petals from the rowan tree floated down towards them, hints of a new season to come.

AUTHOR'S NOTE

Hello,

I'm so grateful you've taken the time to finish my latest novel. As I write this note, we are all in the midst of the Covid 19 crisis here in the UK and I've been working hard on edits for this book as the crisis unfolds around me. Luckily, my husband is on a sabbatical from his job as a police detective so can home-school our daughter as I work. But every day there's a chance he might be called back to the frontline, so I've been working super hard to get this novel finished for you before my time is taken up with a potential new role: teacher to my daughter!

I hope you're now reading this safe and well. One thing that's been reinforced to me lately is just how much of a solace reading can be. So many of you messaged me after reading WALL OF SILENCE, my first book set in Forest Grove, to tell me how much you enjoyed disappearing into the village and the stories woven within it.

If you've enjoyed being immersed in this new story, I would be super grateful for a review on Amazon. As I worked on this novel, trying to push through the worries circulating my head as the world battled a pandemic, reader reviews gave me the energy to plough on.

If you find yourself wanting to know more about what happens to the characters in CIRCLE OF DOUBT after the story ended, I have a little treat for you. If you sign up to my enewsletter at www.tracy-buchanan.com/mailinglist, you will receive a free epilogue!

I also absolutely love reading messages from readers, sent via my website at www.tracy-buchanan.com, via my author page at www.facebookcom/TracyBuchananAuthor or on The Reading Snug group I run, which I welcome you to join if you haven't already – just do a search for it on Facebook.

Thank you again for taking the time to read my latest novel.

Take care,

Tracy.

ACKNOWLEDGMENTS

I'd like to start by thanking my friends, Suzanne and Gareth. It really helped to sit down with Suzanne and go through the adoption process with her from a mother's point of view. Not just the admin side, but also the emotional side. Not only did the information she so generously shared help me to get the facts right but they also helped enrich the novel, bringing my attention to thoughts and feelings I may not have first considered.

More than ever before, I want to thank my husband, Rob, who has allowed me to hide away in my office and finish this novel during the most uncertain times we've ever experienced. An amazing home teacher to our daughter and fabulous emotional support for me, he really is like one of the solid oak trees from Forest Grove: a strong and loving support to lean against when times get tough.

My acknowledgements must always include a huge thanks to my amazing mum. She gifted me with my love of words. Watching her read as much as she did when I was a child taught me to be fascinated with stories too. In 2020 in particular, she's had her own battles to fight and I have never been prouder of her. A million thanks for being the best example of strength and smiles to me. I love you, Mum, and my wonderful stepdad, Vic, for his support and love for you.

To my family and friends as a whole, too, who are all so supportive of my books. You all rock!

Speaking of rocks, my readers are total rocks, motivating me to write no matter what's going on around me, your messages and reviews driving me on. In fact, one of my readers suggested the very title of this book. Thank you to Jody Bennett, who came up with *Circle of Doubt* after I put a call out for help in The Reading Snug.

Finally, a massive thanks to the publishing people who make it possible to get this book into the world, from my agent Caroline Hardman and also Therese Coen who helps brings my books to an international audience. Plus the brilliant staff at Lake Union, in particular my editors Sammia Hamer and Ian Pindar, and the copy-editors, proofreaders, publicity team and more who continue to work hard during tough times to make my books the best they can be. A big THANKS!

ABOUT THE AUTHOR

Photo © 2018 Nic Robertson-Smith

Tracy Buchanan is a bestselling author whose books have been published around the world, including chart-toppers *My Sister's Secret*, *No Turning Back* and *Wall of Silence*. She lives in the UK with her husband, their daughter and a very spoilt Cavalier King Charles Spaniel called Bronte.

Before becoming a full-time author, Tracy worked as a travel journalist, visiting and writing about countries around the world. She has also produced content for the BBC and the Open University, and rubbed shoulders with celebrities while working for a London PR firm.

When she isn't spending time with her family and friends, Tracy now spends her days writing with her dog on her lap or taking walks in forests.

For more information about Tracy, please visit www.facebook.com/TracyBuchananAuthor and www.tracy-buchanan.com.